PRAISE FOR KIM SAKW
THE PROPHECY

"Gwen and Greylen are truly the power couple from the 15th century. Best book I have read all year."

—L.A. MOORE, GOODREADS USER

"A wonderful and enchanting love story with strong likable characters."

—AMAZON REVIEWER

"The story not only contains humor, but romance, action, and unconditional love…It completely pulled me in."

—AMAZON REVIEWER

"Unique, powerful storytelling carries the reader seamlessly from century to century, character to character, longing to longing, until fate unites the lovers."

—LYN, AMAZON REVIEWER

"I love time travel romances with huge hunky highlanders and this one did not disappoint."

—AMAZON REVIEWER

"Gwen's fiery and personable character charmed me."

—KAURIE, AMAZON REVIEWER

"Excellently written and absolutely enjoyable... At least for a few days, I lived in 15th century Scotland... I highly recommend this book."

"This is a fabulous read, one that I really enjoyed. I found myself laughing throughout the book."

"*The Prophecy* will take you away from the stresses of today, and into a completely different world."

NEVER SAY GOODBYE

NEVER SAY GOODBYE

<< A BROTHERS MONTGOMERY BOOK >>

KIM SAKWA

Taggart
Press

Never Say Goodbye is a work of fiction. The names, characters, businesses, places, events, locales, and incidents are either products of my imagination or used in a fictitious manner. Any resemblance to actual persons, living or dead, or actual events are coincidental.

ISBN 978-1-7336172-3-9

Library of Congress Control Number: 2020906019

Published in Clarkston, Michigan.

CHAPTER
ONE

Six-year-old Callesandra Eleanor Montgomery arranged her favorite dolls and stuffed animals, then sat to pour them some imaginary tea and tell them a story. Her little legs crossed beneath her blanket as she got comfortable, and her fingers brushed back the soft auburn curls that had come loose from her bow. At this time of day, she was supposed to be resting, but Callesandra was a precocious child with lots of energy. And perhaps by choice or need, this story was one she repeated every day without fail.

It started with a stormy night, like all good stories should. Her papa, Admiral Alexander Montgomery, had thrown a party that night. Callie loved when her papa had parties. The men dressed in blue uniforms with big gold braids and the ladies wore pretty ball gowns with lots of lace. Music played all throughout the house and the tables were always filled with her favorite foods, like white soup, meat pies, jellies, and dry cake.

But that night, the night in question, Callie didn't care much about the party. She wasn't feeling well. Janey, one of her nannies, kept trying to give her awful-tasting medicine, so to escape, Callie grabbed her three favorite dolls and snuck into her papa's study. Her papa was busy at his desk, but when Callie came up next to him, he lifted her to his lap and hugged her tight. Her papa always hugged her. Then they heard Janey calling after her, and Papa put his finger to his lips, then moved his legs so she could hide beneath his desk. Callie loved it under Papa's desk. She had a blanket and toys and, of course, her papa's legs, so it was warm and cozy. She had just finished arranging her dolls when her papa's best friend, Gregor, came in. Gregor was her favorite because he always picked her up and spun her around until she was twirling high in the air. But tonight, he sounded very serious.

"There's trouble, Alexander," he'd said, and Callie stilled immediately.

Her papa swore, something Callie had never heard before, and it scared her. His chair scraped the floor so loud she had to cover her ears from the sound.

That was the night Callesandra met her new mama.

After her papa and Gregor had left the study, Callie went back to her room. Janey made her take the yucky-tasting medicine after all, then helped Callie change into a nightgown. It was a short while later that she saw her new mama for the first time. She and Janey were in the hallway outside her mama's room on the way back to bed when her mama called out, "Wait."

Callie was scared at first, because her mama was mean and pinched her a lot. Callie figured that's just how mamas were, but when she stood before her, *this* mama spoke softly and was nice. Her new mama looked just like her old mama, but she wasn't mean and didn't hurt her. She had prettier eyes too. They sparkled blue, whereas her old mama's eyes had been brown.

The whole house had changed now that her mama was different. Now, Mama made her papa smile and laugh. And her mama taught Callie to play the piano and dance. She taught Papa how to dance too. Not that Papa didn't know how to dance. It was just that Mama danced different. Callie loved this new mama so much and knew her papa did too.

Callie still had her hiding spots, though, so she sometimes heard her mama and papa whisper about things. Things like her papa insisting that her mama was never to go near the cliffs again. *Ever.* Her papa was really fierce when he told her mama that. He was fierce anyway, even though he was always kind to Callie. He was an admiral in the Royal Navy. Callie thought it was funny to sometimes call him Admiral, just like Goodly, their butler.

The second night that changed their lives forever came three months later, when her papa said that they were sailing for America. He was in his study barking orders. Her papa was really good at barking orders. Her mama said, "If you have a crisis, Papa is the only person you need with you." Callie was hiding under his desk again; it really was the best hiding place. Her uncle Stephen, Gregor, and the rest of Papa's men were carrying big, heavy chests down to the shore. Callie knew they were filled with gold and silver because she had peeked when she saw them piled up in the front hall. She had also seen the things that were really important to her papa in the trunks, like the instruments he used to make maps and to measure the stars. Janey and Beatrice were upstairs packing like the dickens so they could take their things with them. And her mama, well, she was looking for *her*!

Her mama had come in earlier to tell Papa she had a bad feeling, but that wasn't anything special. Callie's new mama always had bad feelings, and Callie had to cover her mouth because she almost laughed when Papa said, "Really? *You?* A bad feeling?" Mama didn't say anything, but Callie knew she was rolling her eyes. She knew everything about Mama now. Ever since that night with the yucky medicine and new mama arriving, they had spent so much time together that Callie almost forgot there had ever been a time when she *wasn't* there.

"Twenty minutes, Amanda," Papa said. "That ship— we're on it. If there's anything you can't live without, you'd better fetch it now." Callie figured the one thing that her mama was trying to fetch was her. She'd seen the ship her papa was talking about too. It had been anchored offshore all day. When her mama came back a few minutes later, she told her papa that she needed to talk to him, but Papa said it had to wait. Callie was starting to get a bad feeling all of her own because her mama had sounded so worried. So, while they rolled up maps and started tossing big leather books in another wooden chest, she snuck out of her papa's study.

Callie hid in the hall behind the tall clock until she saw her mama come out. She called Callie's name, looking up and down the hallway before she started walking outside toward the stables. Callie ran to catch up with her. She had just come through the gates when someone grabbed her from behind and covered her mouth so she couldn't scream. That was when she saw her mama up ahead, slung over another man's shoulder. Her papa was going to be furious. Especially when he realized they were being taken to the cliffs. He was going to roar.

Rain and lightning started just as the two men carrying Callie and her mama set them down and made them walk backward toward the opening of the tunnel that led right out to nothing. Callie knew it was a three-hundred-foot drop to the sea because her papa had told her so. She didn't know how far three hundred feet was, but she knew it was too far. Callie hoped he was fibbing, but she knew better. Her papa never lied.

The big, ugly man had a gun and the shorter one, the one who'd grabbed Callie, had a saber. Mama started crying, pleading with the men to let them go, or at least just Callie. She offered them anything they wanted, just so long as they let her daughter go. Callie started crying then too. She was so scared, but she knew her mama would do anything for her. The bad men didn't care, though; they just laughed. That was when her mama took her chance. While they were laughing and not paying attention, her mama grabbed Callie's hand and whispered that there was a ledge just beneath the opening and to hold on to her tight. Callie didn't have time to wonder how her mama knew about the ledge, she just did as she was told. Her mama stepped over the cliff's edge, and Callie went with her as they dropped down to the ledge that really was there, and not even that far down.

Callie had no idea how strong her mama was until that night. She kept Callie safe and secure, pressed super tight between her body and the wall of the cliff while she held on to the rock above her head. Hidden now by the rock face, Callie heard the bad men start yelling at each other that they'd lost them. After a while, Mama said she thought the bad men were gone and she was going to try to lift Callie up so she could climb back inside the tunnel.

Callie nodded, but before Mama could get a grip on her, lightning struck so close that Callie startled and slipped from the ledge. Her mama cried out and grabbed her with one hand, just in the nick of time. Her wrist hurt badly where Mama was gripping it, and her shins were scraped from her fall, but as Callie peeked down at the swirling water and sharp rocks below, she knew this was better. That was when Callie heard her papa roar from above. She couldn't see his face, but Callie had never heard him roar like that before. She twisted around to see his hand clutched around her mama's wrist and her hand clutched around his. Over the whipping wind, Callie heard him tell Mama he was going to lift them out. Callie could hear Uncle Stephen, too, and when she craned her neck, she saw he was lying on top of her papa's legs so Papa wouldn't fall.

Callie panicked and cried out when her wrist started to slip through Mama's hand because of the rain. Her mama told her papa and Callie heard something in her mama's voice she'd never heard before—fear. Papa yelled at Uncle Stephen to let him go so he could jump down and get them. But Uncle Stephen wouldn't get off Papa's legs and her papa roared at her mama, "Don't let go!"

But Mama said, "She's going to fall, Alexander!"

That was the first time Callie ever heard her papa beg. She would never forget it. More than how it felt to be dangling there, soaking wet and afraid, she'd remember her papa's voice.

"Don't let go, Amanda! Promise me! Don't! Let! Go!"

Then her mama made the saddest sound she'd ever heard. Callie remembered thinking that the last roar she'd heard from her papa sounded like he was being eaten by a pack of wild animals as her mama wrapped her body around her, and they fell.

They kept falling and falling and Callie was sure they would crash soon, but they didn't. They landed in the water, and her mama swam them both to shore. Callie remembered then what Grandpapa Montgomery used to tell her about stormy nights, the cliffs, and the tunnels: "Every once in a while, something fantastical happens on a stormy night and a horrible wrong is righted." Callie figured that's what happened to her papa and her new mama, that something fantastical had taken place on that first stormy night.

Callie didn't know what made the cliffs and tunnels special, but her papa had once told her that whenever he was out on one of his ships, he could see a special pattern that ran down that whole side of the rock wall. Callie told her mama about it when they were resting on the shore, what her pappy had said about fantastical things, and that must be why they were okay. And maybe also why it wasn't storming anymore.

But then Callie saw her mama's hand and wrist. It didn't look so good. Papa had been holding her tight. Callie looked at her own hand and wrist then—it was reddish and hurt, but not like her mama's. Her mama's wrist was kind of purple and the top of her hand and one of her fingers was bleeding really bad.

When they got back to the house, her papa wasn't there. The house wasn't Papa's anymore, Mama explained. It was just Mama's. Her mama got really fierce then, just like Papa would when he wanted Callie to remember something very important. She'd said, "Callesandra, no matter what happens, you are *my* daughter." She made Callie repeat it. Then she said, "No one will ever, *ever*, take you away from me. Do you understand me?" Callie didn't. This was her mama, of course that was true, but she didn't tell her that, wondering instead when her papa would come, and everything would be okay. Her papa could fix her mama's hand like he had before when it had to be stitched. He could fix everything.

But Papa didn't fix her mama's hand this time. Instead Mama called someone named Aunt Sam. Callie had never met her before, but her mama had talked about her all the time. When her mama brushed her hair at night, she would tell stories about how she and Aunt Sam became friends—

best friends. Now, as Callie looked around the house, she realized just how very, very different it looked than before. All the furniture was new and funny-looking, nowhere near as lovely as the furniture she was used to. The pictures on the walls were different, too, and the kitchen was filled with odd gadgets and shiny objects that looked like nothing she had ever seen before. Callie was about to ask her mama where they were, how they had gotten to this strange place, when Mama grabbed something off of the kitchen counter and held it up to Callie. It didn't look like too much to her, but Mama explained to her that it was called a "phone" and that if she pressed in just the right spot, it would connect her to Aunt Sam, who had one too.

Callie was skeptical at first about her mama's phone, which was just a little smooth and shiny rectangle that she had to be very careful with, but then she realized she really liked it. A lot. Mama cried when she heard Aunt Sam's voice; she was on the speaker, so Callie heard her too. At first, hearing Aunt Sam's voice magically blare into the room scared her, but then she realized it was okay because her mama was so happy about it.

"Jesus, Ammy—are you okay? Where have you been? Amanda—" Aunt Sam started crying then too.

"Sam," Mama choked out. "I need help."

That night, Callie met a man called Mr. Finch, who, according to her aunt Sam, was the person who would take care of everything. But her mama told her that Mr. Finch was a bodyguard, someone who protected people. And since Papa wasn't here to protect them, Mr. Finch would. Callie was okay with him either way because when he first came to the house, he knelt down right in front of her and smiled really big. He spoke softly and told her, "It's going to be okay, Cal." No one had ever called her Cal before, but she didn't mind, she liked the way he said it. And there was something about Mr. Finch that made her feel safe.

They rode together in a big truck. Callie was scared at first because she had never seen one before. But her mama explained that it was quicker than a horse and it was how they traveled places. Mr. Finch lifted her inside right onto her mama's lap, then put what he called a "seat belt" over them both. Her mama rubbed Callie's back and hummed pretty music while Callie looked out the windows. They went super fast, reminding her of what it felt like when Gregor would spin her around. And even though the house and the land they drove by looked kind of the same, everything was so very different.

It was dark by the time Mr. Finch stopped behind a building. A man was waiting outside, and he told Mr. Finch that it was "clear" to go in. That was when her mama told her that she had to have surgery. Callie didn't really know what that was until the man who was waiting for them told her that he was a doctor. He said that her mama probably needed to have part of her bone replaced because it had been crushed. Callie felt her own wrist then, imagining it crushed instead of nice and whole. The doctor told her mama he would fix her finger and the back of her hand, too, so there wouldn't be scars, but Mama shook her head. "They don't have to be ugly," she said, her voice firm, "but I want to be able to look at these scars forever."

Right before they took her mama to the operating room, she turned to Callie and gave her a long, hard look. "We're going to be okay, baby. I promise," she said. "Mr. Finch is going to take care of you and Aunt Sam will be here tomorrow." Callie cried because she hadn't been away from her mama for so long before. But then Mr. Finch picked her up and hugged her tight, just like one of Papa's hugs. And it wasn't too much later before she and Mr. Finch were able to sit in the same room as her mama until she woke up.

As the days turned into weeks, Callie kept waiting for Papa to come, and she knew her mama did, too, even though this was her house now. It took some time, but between her mama, Aunt Sam, and Mr. Finch, Callie got used to her new life. She had pretty new clothes that she loved, like sundresses and blue jeans, shorts and T-shirts and lots of shoes. Her mama got her a new tea set similar to the one she'd had in her old room, and new dolls and stuffed animals too. Callie learned about TVs and cell phones and computers, but she wasn't allowed to spend a lot of time using them. Her mama liked to do puzzles and play games with her instead. And of course, her mama continued with her piano and dance lessons.

They stayed in their home in Great Britain through Callie's birthday. She turned six on May 20, that year. Her mama made her repeat the date over and over again. Not the May 20 part, the year part, which at first seemed very silly to Callie since it wasn't even a real year. She also made her memorize what Mama called her "birthdate"—the day, month, and year. Mama and Aunt Sam and even Mr. Finch would ask her at odd times, "What's your birthdate?" She didn't even have to think about it anymore.

After a while they left Great Britain and moved to a place called New York. Aunt Sam and Mr. Finch came with them and they flew on a plane they had all to themselves. Her mama told Callie not to be scared, that the man who flew the plane in the sky—their pilot, Captain Morgan— would keep them safe. "Just wait, baby," she'd said. "That feeling you love, that you get right here"—her mama patted Callie's stomach then—"this time will be even better." Her mama was right too. Callie remembered looking at her as they took off and she laughed out loud when that feeling came. She couldn't help but think of Gregor then, and how much he would have loved it too.

Callie liked their house in New York; it was big like their other house and also on the water. The first night they got there, her mama lit a candle and put it on a table by the big picture window. Callie asked her what it was for and her mama picked her up and stood so they were both looking out at the ocean. "Your papa was taking us to America, Callie. That night we were separated." Mama rarely cried in front of her, and if she did, it was really quiet. Tears would run down her face but she'd pretend they weren't there. When she was able to speak again, her mama said, "I lit it for your papa, Callie." Then she placed her hand to the glass. "We made it, Alexander. We're here." Mama's voice caught on a sob then and Aunt Sam took her from her mama's arms.

They stayed in New York only for the summer before moving to a place called California where Mama had lived when she was a little girl. Aunt Sam and Mr. Finch came with them again. In California, Mama's belly grew big, and she told Callie she was going to have a brother. Her mama used to cry before, a lot, but now she cried even more. Not during the day, but at night when she thought Callie was asleep. Callie didn't like hearing her mama cry, but she knew it was because she loved her papa so much. Her mama didn't think they were ever going to see him again. But Callie had been watching a lot of movies and she knew her papa was better than all those superheroes put together. He would be able to find them no matter what.

It was when they moved to California that Callie learned her mama was a famous songwriter and that people all over knew who she was. Callie went to a fancy school where she had to work really hard. One day at school, the fourth graders put on a performance about something called the American Revolution. Callie would never forget sitting there looking at the stage and all the scenery and decorations. She hadn't thought about her old life for a long time. But she did now. There were pictures and posters of ships like her papa used to command. A ship just like the one he'd been trying to get them on that night she and her mama were taken by those bad men. And when the students came on the stage, she gasped at their costumes. The girls were in dresses like the ones she and her mama used to wear, and the boys were in uniforms. One boy in particular was wearing a uniform that looked just like her papa's. Callie sat there stunned, hanging on every word.

As she watched the play, Callie wondered if her papa worked with the man named George Washington. Maybe that was why he had been packing them up that night and taking them to America. Callie thought about that book then. The one that had made her mama cry. They were still in their home in New York when she found it. Callie had opened it to the very same page later and gasped when she saw her papa's name written there: "Alexander Montgomery." It said her papa had been found guilty of reason and had to write a sentence about death. It had taken her a long time to sound out all those words and she didn't understand what they meant, but shortly after that Mama decided they should move. She told Callie that Papa wouldn't be able to find them after all. Callie didn't believe her mama. She didn't tell her that, of course. But Callie would never believe her papa couldn't find them. Never.

CHAPTER
TWO

JANUARY 31

2:00 A.M.: NORTHERN CALIFORNIA

ST. ANNA PRIVATE HOSPITAL

The security guard didn't stand a chance. Alexander Montgomery watched as three of his men disarmed him, *then* showed their credentials.

At the present hour, the hospital corridors were all but deserted. A nurse pulled out her cell phone to record Alexander's fifteen-man entourage as they passed. Her phone was taken and destroyed as she was ushered away. They separated at the bank of elevators. Alexander's group was made up of his brother Stephen, Dr. Evan Childress, tech specialist Michael Bowers, and his attorney Christopher Bennett.

The nurse stationed behind the desk reached for the phone as they commandeered the west wing of the eighth floor. Alexander couldn't be sure what shocked her more. Him and his men, or the two hospital board members accompanied by head psychiatrist Dr. Jay Meyers approaching from another corridor. She dropped the phone and sat in silence. Smart woman.

"I'm not happy about this," Dr. Meyers said as he reached Alexander.

"Dr. Meyers," Alexander began, "I can unequivocally assure you no one is unhappier than I." He looked to his attorney, Chris, who withdrew the necessary paperwork. After a careful inspection, the documents were signed. Under almost any other circumstances Alexander would have felt victorious. This was none of those. "Where is she?"

He followed Amanda's doctor down the hallway. Considering the press she'd had over the past nine months and that she was a celebrity in this century in her own right, Amanda's room was the only one occupied on this hall. Three men stood at the end. At first glance they seemed harmless. Perhaps visitors loitering outside a patient's room. But they weren't harmless. Or visitors. Until twelve hours ago, they'd been Amanda's private security detail. Now they worked for Alexander.

"Finch." Alexander shook Stan's hand, a wave of relief washing over him to finally meet the man who for all intents and purposes held his family's charge. He owed the man more than he could ever repay. Finch had kept his family safe when he could not. He'd kept them hidden too. Bloody hell, he'd kept them so hidden Alexander had had to purchase the company to find them. It was the sixth of such businesses he'd acquired in his effort. Amanda had been signed into the hospital under an assumed name. Alexander hadn't even known she was pregnant until the papers were signed and JDL Security had become his.

Since landing in the twenty-first century seven months ago, he'd done nothing but try to find his wife and daughter. Why he'd thought it would be as simple as walking through the front doors of his estate escaped him. Amanda and Callie weren't even there. Nor was anyone for that matter. He'd learned later they had left only the week before, closing the house for the time being. He didn't realize how lucky they in fact were to be alone while gathering themselves in their new current circumstances.

He, Stephen, and Gregor had spent days searching for, finding, and digging out the chests of gold and silver bullion, jewels, and other personal items they'd buried in the tunnels. Then there had been the three goats they'd experimented with while trying to determine the best place to actually "jump" from. Since he and Amanda could never be sure of the portal opening that she had originally come through, he decided it was best to go with the one from which she left. It wasn't hard to locate the exact spot where Amanda and Callie had fallen—a moment Alexander would never forget, one forever imprinted in his brain—but with Stephen halfway down the cliff wall and Gregor waiting upon the rocky shore as Alexander pushed the goats into the sea, they'd determined that the portal opened no more than twelve feet below from where Stephen stood. They tested again and again with various small game until they were sure of the exact location of the portal before making the leap themselves.

Shaky and amazed that they'd actually made it, the trio quickly realized that the twenty-first century was even more different than the eighteenth than they'd ever imagined. They hadn't calculated it would take so much time to acclimate to their new surroundings and the advancement of science. All sciences. Thankfully, the Abersoch property had been updated by its previous owners over the centuries, which gave them a softer introduction into what he now knew of modern technology in its truest form. "Disturbing" would be putting his reaction to the new order of things mildly. It was one thing to listen to Amanda speak of how things were in her time, in *the great fantastical future* as they'd jokingly called it while they were together. It was something else entirely, though, to experience them firsthand. Stephen managed with the changes quite well, and Gregor, bloody hell, Gregor's eyes lit with each new gadget large or small they happened across. Be it light switch or automobile, electric knife or jet.

Having been a spy during simpler times had its advantages. They'd cracked Amanda's safe, which was, thankfully, exactly where she had told him it would be back in his own time. On a lark one evening, Amanda had taken him on a "tour" of his own home, gleefully pointing out how things were different in her time. It took only a small amount of the explosives Alexander had packed in one the chests to open the safe. Inside, they found she'd left behind multiple passports all with varying aliases and addresses, both for her and for Callie. All of the information was bogus. He did however find the remnants of a receipt in Amanda's nightstand drawer that brought him to the bowels of London, to the establishment where Stan had taken her to purchase their illicit traveling papers. Stan, he later learned, was a longtime friend of Samantha's and had a reputation for being what people in today's world called a "cleaner"—someone who could, and would, take care of anything and everything for his employer.

The seedy back-alley storefront was just that, a *front* for anyone plying in the trade of secrets. Its patrons ran the gamut from legitimate blokes working for various intelligence agencies to the dregs of society using it for things like black market trades and human trafficking. As such, it was a hive of activity and under constant surveillance. Alexander had thought he, Stephen, and Gregor had done pretty well with their futuristic "present day" disguises, but looking back now, he realized how off they'd been. They must have stuck out like sore thumbs. As a result, they'd been tailed back to the estate by Michael and Trevor, who at the time worked with and sometimes for what the Crown now call the Secret Intelligence Service, or MI6. Alexander and the boys had had their obligatory pissing match, then threw their cards on the table. Alexander won them over, so Michael and Trevor helped him obtain all the necessary identification and travel documentation for himself, Stephen, and Gregor. More than that, the boys taught Alexander and his cohorts what they needed to know about current weaponry, wireless gadgetry, and military issue surveillance equipment. In turn, Alexander taught them how he'd trained in hand-to-hand combat and the fine art of mind bending without all the textbook bullshit. He'd tried to pay them in cash, even gold, but they'd refused. Instead, they'd been impossible to shake and joined what he now considered to be his merry band of brothers in the new order of things. Michael and Trevor themselves were *actual* brothers and essentially orphaned. Having only each other, they'd somehow gotten it into their heads that they'd join forces with Alexander, Stephen, and Gregor. He referred to them as the "boys" and in all honesty was rather fond of them. It was Michael who'd introduced him to most of the men who worked for him now. All retired military, British and American alike, not to mention a random spray from other countries. The more they brought within their circle, the more that stayed.

They'd followed Amanda's trail and found she'd paid cash for everything. But as that was the only trail he'd been trained to follow it had been simple for him. Not easy, only simple. They found the doctor who'd repaired her hand, the stores where she'd purchased clothes for Callie. The skeleton staff she'd hired for the estate. The document lab and Captain Morgan, who'd flown them to the States. Lastly, the New York estate where they'd spent the summer. Then they'd vanished. Literally. Stan was that good.

Alexander had used the resources at his disposal, his new band of brothers, and an exorbitant amount of money to buy JDL. The purchase included a training facility and compound in northern California. It was constantly bristling with activity, combat training, weaponry, explosives, surveillance. Providence that it's where he'd ultimately found his family. It was because of Amanda he'd decided to make the business of security his actual business.

One, he needed to find her, and two, it was lucrative. Half of his current employees worked private security like Stan, the other half, bloody hell, they were hired mercenaries.

He shared a look with Stan now as the guard changed, never more grateful to resume such an awesome duty and responsibility. The care of his family, Amanda, Callesandra, and their newborn son.

He'd just pushed the door open when Dr. Meyers stayed him with a hand. "Mr. Montgomery. You've taken steps to provide medical and psychological supervision? As you're now aware, *our patient* suffered a traumatic nervous collapse. She needs time, not just to recuperate physically from the delivery, but she'll require specialized care to address her memory loss as we—"

"Dr. Meyers," Alexander said, cutting him off. He wasn't an idiot. He motioned Evan forward. "May I introduce Dr. Evan Childress." No other explanation was necessary.

Dr. Evan Childress was a world-renowned psychiatrist. He'd consulted for Art Fisher and JDL over the years. Once Amanda's records were digitally transferred, Evan studied them while on the plane ride over from New York. Alexander sat white-knuckled on the G5, his new company's private jet. He *hated* flying but it was an unfortunate necessity considering this life they'd found themselves living. After what seemed an inordinately long time, Evan looked up and informed Alexander of her condition, equating Amanda's diagnosis to what he called *psychogenic amnesia*. "When you just can't deal with pain, Alex, the psyche effectively does it for you." It was only one of many times throughout the past nine months Alexander had felt a tightening in his chest, which he assumed was a very real reaction to his failure in protecting his family and keeping them safe. He'd winced, flexing his hand as the pain abated.

Evan had prepared him for one of three reactions Amanda could have. The first that she would recognize him instantly and her memory would return. The second, she would instinctively recognize him, but her memory wouldn't come back right away. She might intuitively trust him, for example, but not know why. The last possibility Evan suggested was that Amanda wouldn't recognize him on any level, and she would never remember their lives together.

Not wanting to waste another moment, Alexander nodded, pushed past Dr. Meyers, and walked into Amanda's room. Four days ago, she'd endured what he'd been told was a terribly difficult delivery. Followed by a breakdown of epic proportion. She'd had to be sedated hours after the fact. Alexander glanced at the dial of his Breitling Navitimer. He'd missed her by three days. His breath caught as he laid eyes on her for the first time in what *felt* like the quarter millennium of time that had separated them. The relief he felt was almost overwhelming, surpassed only by regret. He flexed his hand as that familiar sharp pain presented. It lasted at most a second, but long enough to divert him from losing control of his emotions.

Helen, the private nurse Stan had hired, sat at Amanda's bedside. While Evan spoke with her, Alexander started unbuckling the restraints around his wife's wrists. The first fell against the rail, revealing deep purple and yellow bruising. His fingers gently brushed her skin, then gripped—Jesus, he had to force himself to let go—so affected by being able to touch her. She made a sound and tried to roll over as he started on the second of her manacles. Then her eyes shot open. "Who...where..." Bloody hell, she sounded worse than she looked. And she looked like a disaster.

"Shh." His hand cupped the side of her precious, beautiful face as he tried to soothe her. "You've been discharged, Amanda. I'm taking you home." Her free hand started frantically scratching the leather around her other wrist. He knew what it felt like to be trapped and let her help.

"My son," she said as she tried to sit up.

"He'll be here in a minute," Alexander told her as he helped her.

She grabbed his hand, big cornflower-blue eyes wincing in pain as she begged, "Take them off—*please.*" She covered her face as fat tears fell, but he didn't know what she was talking about. He looked around the room, and then down at the end of the bed. *Jesus Christ.* They had her ankles locked down. He was so angry he almost ripped the bindings holding them to the bedrail. Then he lifted her out of her prison, giving her a reassuring squeeze once she was safely cradled in his arms.

"Bloody hell, sweetheart," he whispered as he started for the door. "I'm sorry."

"My daughter's British," Amanda told him drowsily.

"I know," he said grimly, realizing his wife didn't remember him. *Jesus, was it option three?*

Alexander stopped at the desk again. His son had been brought up from the nursery. They checked his bracelet against Amanda's. Satisfied they had a match, the nurse placed him in Stephen's outstretched arms.

Amanda stiffened suddenly. "Where are we going?"

"I'm taking you home, Amanda," he reminded her.

"Zander! My baby! I have to get my baby!"

"He's right here." Alexander turned her so she could see him. "See?"

Her eyes filled with tears again. "Thank you."

Bloody hell, he wanted to cry with her. He didn't and considering how grievous the past 278 days—not that he was counting—had been made it terribly difficult. She sighed and put her head back down.

It was close to four in the morning by the time they arrived at Amanda's. She'd slept in his arms the entire ride over. Burrowed herself into the crook of his neck, just as she'd always had before. It buoyed his hopes that perhaps she did at least instinctively remember him. And it felt amazing. He couldn't hold her tight enough and rocked her—*bloody hell*—just because he could.

Sam, Amanda's best friend, was waiting outside the front doors. They'd never met, but Amanda had talked about her frequently. Amanda had known that he and Stephen believed her when she'd finally revealed she was from the twenty-first century; she knew, too, that they would protect her with their lives. Stephen had also been present for a lot of Amanda's stories about "the future," most of which included Sam. In fact, Alexander had been furious at first that his wife spoke so often of another man.

When he finally voiced his anger, Amanda had used one of her favorite phrases, "Really, Alexander?" She'd rolled her eyes too. He smiled thinking of it. Then she'd told him that Sam was short for Samantha. Now, Sam only nodded upon seeing them arrive, rubbed Amanda's cheek, and said, "Follow me."

Putting Amanda in her own bed was difficult but necessary. After speaking with Evan and Helen, he reluctantly left Amanda in their care. Time to find his daughter. Sam cornered him in the hall as the door snicked shut behind him.

Samantha Gilchrist was as beautiful as his wife. And from what he'd gathered, and he'd gathered a bloody lot, she was equally smart and talented in her own right. Sam and Amanda had met at a private girls' boarding school and later attended college together. Amanda followed the fine arts of dance and music while Sam studied law and journalism.

"She thinks you're dead," Sam said expressionlessly.

"I'm not." Alexander wasn't surprised by her tone or lack of emotion. Amanda had often said Sam warmed up slowly, if at all. But if you were lucky enough to gain her trust, her friendship and love was gift like none other.

"*Duh.* You missed her by—"

"Three days, Samantha. Story of our lives. Always just this side of too late."

"Don't be pathetic," she shot back. "You're here. I'm not sure how and I'm not sure I want to know. Hearing Amanda's side of the story was absurd enough." A look crossed her face. "If anyone finds out—"

"We've covered our tracks. Destroyed everything we can. Dr. Childress has already convinced me that it's in Amanda's best interest to let her draw her own conclusions."

"He knows?" Her expression was incredulous.

"Yes." Alexander didn't find it necessary to expound at the moment. If ever. To her point, however, there *were* a handful of people who were indeed aware of how he and Amanda had met, and also how he had lost her and his daughter. He couldn't be expected to keep something like that to himself—Amanda clearly hadn't.

"So, until she remembers? If she remembers?"

"*Until* she remembers," Alexander said pointedly, "I'm the new owner of JDL Security." On the ride home from the hospital, he'd decided to change the name to Calder Defense, the first three letters of Callie's name and the last three of Zander's. "Amanda's a client and my brother's her new detail." Which granted Alexander access to her and his children's lives, he'd decided, even if the cover was a bit of a stretch. He was relying on his wife's love of family, immediate and extended, so this was right up her alley.

"Wait," Samantha said, putting up her hand. "You bought JDL?"

"Yes. And all their subsidiaries."

"Your fortune traveled with you?" Sam asked, lowering her voice to a whisper.

If she only knew how long his men had worked to bury everything deep within the cliffs.

"It multiplied, actually." He'd been shocked to find his gold and possessions were worth over a billion dollars in today's market. He'd gladly give it all away for his wife and children. "Where's Callesandra's room?"

"You're going to wake her up?"

"Damn right I am," he said, a little louder than he'd intended. Samantha's initial surprise was quickly followed with a nod of understanding, and she led him to the room down the hallway on the right.

His hand splayed the solid wood panel a moment before covering the large pewter lever that opened her door. Alexander stood in the threshold as his eyes adjusted. Soft light illuminated her entire room. It was a little girl's dream; an immense four-poster bed sat against the wall facing the doorway where he stood. To his left were bookshelves and a desk. To his right, large picture windows overlooked the sea. One corner was filled with a dress-up and play area, the other held a small table and chairs. The table was set for tea, and dolls and stuffed animals filled the chairs. It brought tears to his eyes. Amanda had done a remarkable job under the circumstances. That Amanda held on to her sanity as long as she had was astounding. He'd come close to losing his mind himself.

He sat on the bed next to his daughter. She was facing the other way. His hand covered her little back. "Callesandra."

His heart nearly turned over in his chest at her whispered response. "Papa." Then she rolled over, rubbed her eyes, and her sweet little face fell in shock. He grabbed her with both hands and pulled her in, rocking her as he buried his face in her neck.

"I knew you'd find us, Papa."

He was so overcome with emotion he couldn't speak. It took him a solid minute to choke out, "I'm sorry it took so long, angel."

"Are you crying, too, Papa?" Callie's little hands framed his face.

"I am," he confirmed, nodding his head.

"You never cry, Papa."

"I've done a lot of things I never thought I'd do, Callesandra." Things he couldn't speak of. Things that most likely added to Amanda's breakdown.

"Did you see Mama?"

"I brought her home," he told her. "She's very tired, angel. Having a baby…she got really sad in the hospital. Her memory is taking a little break right now."

"Aunt Sam said she has anemia," Callie said, her voice very serious now.

He smiled at her attempt to set the record straight. "Mama has a form of amnesia, angel. She can't remember—"

"She remembers *me*, Papa. She called me. She was really sleepy, but she called." Her eyes got really wide. "At three in the morning." She grinned and held up her fingers to show him. "Mama said I had a baby brother and he was going to love me so much. And then she said she loved me so much too."

Alexander smiled again at her summary of events. "We both love you so much," he assured her.

"Are you gonna stay with Mama?"

"No, angel. Mama can't remember me right now." He kissed her face again about a hundred times. "I'll be here, though. A lot." He noticed Stephen had cracked open the door while he waited in the hall. He knew Callie would be thrilled to see her uncle again. "I won't be staying for now, but Uncle Stephen will."

Stephen came in then, and Alexander chuckled as Callie's mouth fell open, then she scrambled off the bed and into his arms. Alexander checked on Amanda once more and found her sleeping while Helen rested in a chair beside the bed. Zander lay in a bassinet between them.

Helen gave them a few moments alone and Alexander knelt at the bedside. Amanda had pushed the pillows to the floor and her head lay pressed to the mattress. He brushed the hair off her face, so overcome at being able to touch her again. *Bloody hell—she was alive!* He remembered that first time he'd seen Amanda, a dead ringer for his wife, Rebecca, and the difficulty he'd had reconciling his reaction to her. Why the instant he stood next to her, he was drawn to her and not repelled. It was only when she'd looked up at him and he saw her bright blue eyes that he knew she wasn't the evil woman he had been married to.

His head fell to the bed. Just being able to inhale her scent brought a sense of peace he hadn't experienced in far too long. Even in the darkness he could see the dark circles beneath her eyes, the bruises on her wrists... She'd fought like hell. He reached for her hand and rubbed the scar that ran diagonally across her palm, then he kissed it. Evidence of their time together when she first came to him in his century. The other hand showed the evidence of the night he'd lost her and Callesandra back to hers. He thanked God again that he'd found them, that he, Stephen, and Gregor were allowed through the portal, not the portal in the tunnels that brought Amanda to him in the first place, but the one that ultimately took her back out—with his daughter. That they'd created a life together as well, *that* was bloody amazing.

He took Zander from the bassinet, sat in the chair Helen had vacated, and marveled at what a miracle he was. Eleven pounds four ounces, *bloody hell*. "You gave your mama a difficult time, didn't you?"

"Stan said you're the new owner of JDL. That you bought the hospital to get me out."

Amanda hadn't moved; the side of her head was still pressed to the bed, but her eyes were open now, her voice painfully hoarse. He thought for a moment of what she'd said. "I only gave an endowment that should pay for a new hospital," he chuckled.

"Why?"

"Besides the fact that Art Fisher considers you the daughter he never had and would have my hide if I wasn't inordinately overprotective of you, you're one of our most influential clients, Ms. Marceau. I take my responsibilities very seriously. So seriously, I've put my brother in charge of your keeping. And my brother and I are very close, family means everything to me, so I'll apologize now for many upcoming intrusions."

Her eyes teared and she smiled just a bit. "I like family." Then she said, "Thank you for taking me out of there."

"You already thanked me at the hospital," he reminded her, shaking his head. He stared at her for moment, wanting nothing more than to crawl into bed next to her and take her into his arms. "How do you feel?" he asked instead.

"As good as I look."

She patted the bed and reached out her hand, motioning for Zander. Alexander brought him over and laid him next to her. He knelt again, watching as she examined him. "Helen will be back in just a few minutes," he told her. She was trying to remove the blanket he was swaddled in but didn't have the strength. He could feel her frustration. "Shh…" Alexander said, unwrapping the baby. He placed her hand on Zander once he had him down to his nappy. She smiled, eyes sparkling with unshed tears. "Can you see his little fingers?" he asked her. She shook her head, so he held up one hand at a time and counted off each finger for her, then he did the same with his feet and toes.

"What color are his eyes?"

Alexander smiled at her and shook his head. "I don't know," he told her. "They've been closed each time I've held him." She tried to smile but sighed instead and closed her eyes. She was asleep seconds later, her hand firmly on top of their son. He laid his hand on top of hers, where it remained until Helen returned.

"I'll be back later today," Alexander said once he'd stepped out into the hall with Stephen. He touched his brother's shoulder as he passed him, squeezing once for good measure. Then he walked out of Amanda's house, down the marble stairs, and stopped on the circular stone drive. Five Navigators, two Escalades, one Range Rover, and a 911 Turbo S Cabriolet lined the road that led to the gates far below the estate. The Navigators' engines started in unison, headlights on as they circled. He climbed in the back of the third, the one Gregor was driving. Alexander only wished now Amanda remembered so she could "see" it. She'd always said if they could figure out how to safely use the portal, Gregor would take to the *great fantastical future* the best.

His chest tightened as he thought, *We figured it out, sweetheart.*

His men remained quiet as he flexed his hand and got his bearings. Then he punched the seat in front of him. "*Bloody hell!*" he yelled, as Trevor pitched forward.

"God damn it, Alex!" Trevor, Alex's technical boy-genius, sounded none too happy.

"Chris secured the house next door," Gregor said, clearly trying to calm Alexander down. "He'll have the paperwork ready today. We'll be in tomorrow."

"For now?" Alexander asked.

"We're forty minutes from our accommodations."

Alexander leaned back as Siri instructed Gregor how to get to wherever it was they were going. His hands pressed the sides of his head. Bloody hell. He was in America. His family was as well.

Cosmic fucking joke.

It was two hundred and forty-five years later.

CHAPTER
THREE

It was late afternoon by the time Alexander and his men returned to Amanda's. When they arrived, Alexander went straight toward the large living room with floor-to-ceiling windows that overlooked the sea. Samantha was seated on a white ultra-suede stool, her hands atop a glistening marble countertop. A nightclub-sized bar filled the area to his right.

Amanda had impeccable taste. Her home reflected that.

"How is she?" Alexander asked Samantha, who turned, her eyes narrowed slightly.

"*She* is resting comfortably right now. *I*, however, am becoming irritated with your brother."

Alexander turned to look at Stephen sitting on another stool, positioned so he could see the entirety of the room and the estate's front doors. Files and paperwork were spread before him, as well as his iPhone, two-way radio, and Sig. Bloody hell, how their lives had come to this was...well, it just *was*.

"I only asked you a question, Samantha," Stephen said bitingly as he gestured to Stan, who had appeared just inside the room. Stan nodded and did a quick pivot. Stephen was great under pressure.

God bless his brother.

"A *personal* question," Sam said coolly. "Why it's your business, Stephen, I'm not sure. But no, I'm not seeing anyone."

Ah, now Alexander understood. Amanda had always said Stephen and Samantha would suit. This must be the result of his brother's two-hundred-plus-year fascination with Ms. Gilchrist. Stephen gave a curt nod, but Alexander detected a slight smile too. Then his brother checked the time on his Breitling Avenger and asked, "Drink, Alex?"

"See if there's any Macallan."

Samantha laughed knowingly, and when Alexander walked behind the bar, he saw it. The bottle was right there, already opened. A beautiful, yet utterly masculine, cut crystal rocks glass sat beside it. *Bloody hell, sweetheart.*

"There's four cases in the bottom left cabinet behind you," she told him. "And if you'll look up, you'll see the rest."

He did; at least twenty empty bottles lined one of the open shelves.

Samantha sighed, a clear indication of a chink in her armor. "She poured you a glass every night. Placed it on the piano." She pointed at the gorgeous grand piano in the corner of the room on display before the windows. "And then she played for you." Sam got up and shook her head, and tears laced the words that followed. "It was fucking *heartbreaking*."

She walked behind the bar, grabbed another glass, poured some Macallan for herself and knocked it back. *Impressive*. Their eyes locked and as the proverbial ice melted, her shoulders sagged in resignation. "I can't believe you're here. Or you," she said, looking at Stephen. "And Amanda told me about Gregor, so him too—*Jesus*." It must have just hit her. "He *drives* one of your Navigators!"

Alexander actually chuckled. If anyone was born to live in the twenty-first century, it was his best friend. "Gregor loves to drive." He shook his head. "There's not a vehicle he's come across that he hasn't mastered in a day." Alexander remembered the first time Gregor had driven an automobile, an Aston Martin on the estate in Great Britain. He'd been so exhilarated, he finished with a doughnut, then jumped out of the car and chest bumped Michael.

"Great." She rolled her eyes. "I'll alert the creators of the Transporter franchise. Now back to the important stuff—how did you escape?"

"Stephen and my men freed me from prison ten hours before my scheduled execution." He had to admit, it was a good line, and somewhat relished the look of shock on Sam's face.

"How did you get caught? Amanda said you were sailing for America that night. She and Callie were convinced you'd killed the men who abducted them."

Alexander looked at Samantha. The woman didn't mince words. He took a long pull of whiskey before he answered. "I did kill them, Samantha. With my bare hands." He grew angry just thinking about the men who'd kidnapped his wife and daughter and left them for dead. "After Amanda *let go*—"

"She said you would blame her for that," Samantha snapped on her best friend's behalf.

"Back off, counselor," Stephen warned. It was a terribly touchy subject. For all of them.

"She said that you'd blame yourself too," Sam conceded to Stephen.

"Which is it?" Stephen asked. "Her fault? Or mi—"

"Bloody hell, stop with the blame! *I* was a spy, they sought to hurt *me*. And they did." Alexander knocked back his own drink, then turned away for a moment. That evening was a living, recurring nightmare in his head. "When she looked at me and said Callie was slipping, I knew she was going to let go. I just *knew*." He rubbed his left hand where faint scars remained from that night. The scratch marks Amanda had made in her desperation to take hold once he'd found them dangling from the cliff's edge. And crescent-shaped nail marks on the underside of his wrist from when she'd dug in once he'd grasped her.

"Amanda was terrified you had jumped in after them," Sam said. "She wasn't even sure she and Callie would be okay."

In fact, Alexander *had* tried to jump after them and he was about to open his mouth to say as much, but Stephen swore and got up to pour his own drink. "I wouldn't let him."

"Amanda and I never had time to test our theories on where, when, and how the portal would open." He took another pull of scotch. "We had only four months together before I lost her." His words were laced with regret.

"Alexander." Samantha waited until he gave her his full attention. "Amanda was devastated she'd been torn away from you. She was so worried that you would try to go through, too, and something awful would happen. Until we found the ledger last summer." She shook her head before saying, "When we were still in New York, she would stand in front of that big picture window and stare at the Atlantic as if willing you to sail home to her. It was the saddest thing I've ever seen."

"That bloody ledger. We almost had our hands on it." Alexander and his men had been searching for it since they arrived. "Stan's men beat us to it by a day, if not hours." It was the last piece of hard evidence of who he really was, and from where he really came.

"If you wanted it to be expunged, then it was," Samantha told him. "It's gone."

"Gone?" Alexander repeated.

"Destroyed. The night Zander was born. Once they'd sedated and restrained Amanda, Stan came back to the estate. I didn't wonder why he was here. Your wife was on a seventy-two-hour psych hold. We didn't want anything adding to or setting back her fragile state of mind. We met at the front doors. I'd already taken the ledger from the safe. We walked to the beach together and lit that fucker up. Then we collected the ashes and drove the boat ten miles off the coast before we dropped them into the ocean."

While he appreciated their thoroughness, he'd give his right arm for Amanda to have not gone through the torment she had in thinking he'd been executed. It felt like each time she or Callie had encountered tragedy or misfortune over the past year, he'd been so close! Alexander swore under his breath; blast his bloody timing.

"Wait, let's go back. How did you get caught?" Samantha asked. "You should have at least made it to America, based on what Amanda told me about those men, that night."

"After searching the water beneath the cliffs," Stephen jumped in, "he stood on the rocks beneath the ledge and waited." Stephen didn't say *for their bodies to wash ashore.* "He didn't want Amanda and Callie to be alone. Twelve days and twelve nights he stood sentinel. The only reason he left was because they'd dragged him away in chains. He begged me not to leave."

"My brother kept vigil for six more days," Alexander said. "Then he and our men came to the same conclusion I already had. Amanda and Callesandra had somehow made it through the portal. Together."

"Amanda said you knew there was something about that cliff that made it different."

"When I was just a boy, my father showed me the odd pattern that ran up the entirety of the rock wall," Alexander said, remembering. "He often told me tales, but they weren't tales after all." He shook his head. "Bloody hell, they were real."

"What kind of tales?" Sam asked, her glass empty, but still in her hand.

"He'd say that sometimes one of our ancestors would, by a twist of fate, have a terrible wrong righted."

"So, Rebecca was your wrong—and Amanda righted it."

"Simply put, I suppose so."

"You know, Amanda had a fascination with you before she even met you. Did she tell you?"

He tilted his head. Very little surprised him anymore, this however did. Warmed his heart too. "No," he told Samantha, "I had no idea."

"Without jumping too far ahead and leaving off much of the story," Sam said, "she found an accounting of your ancestral history, your military rank, your marriage to Rebecca, the birth of Callesandra, the death of your son...that all mysteriously ended in 1774. When Amanda returned to the British Isles with Callie, she eventually told me everything. It wasn't easy getting the story out of her, and there was the matter of her wrist."

Alexander's hand flexed at the mention. He'd tried to hold on to her, even after she'd let go. He'd crushed her wrist in the process. It was now healed, post-surgery, and worked just fine thanks to titanium and the wonders of modern medicine.

He walked out from behind the bar and to the large picture windows facing the sea. He turned back to Samantha and shook his head. "Losing Amanda and Callesandra changed everything." He circled the piano, then fingered the coaster before setting his drink on it. When he looked at Samantha, she nodded, confirming it was where his wife had placed his drink each evening.

"She played the most wonderful music I have ever heard." He could picture them at home, their home in eighteenth-century Great Britain. He smiled as he recalled one of many evenings he and Amanda would sit upon the piano bench after Callesandra had been put to bed and his wife would play and sing to him. She was amazing. "God, I've missed her. She made me laugh more than I ever had before." He brushed his fingers across the keys. "Amanda changed our lives, *my life*, in a way—"

"Are you talking about me?"

Amanda was standing in the doorway. They all turned to look at her.

She stood within the massive entrance to the room as if she belonged there. Star that she was, a presence of her own. Tall with auburn hair and breathtaking cornflower-blue eyes. She was gorgeous, even five days after giving birth. Fresh faced, hair straightened and pulled back, wearing a soft gray cashmere lounge set. She had Zander tucked up tight to her chest, and Helen stood less than a pace behind her, lips pursed.

Amanda was obviously in charge and Helen none too happy about it. Stan appeared next.

Sam spoke first. "You look pretty, sweetie."

"For a mug shot," Amanda replied dryly.

"Mama!" Callie hollered, coming running across the foyer from God knows where with Rosa, Amanda's house manager, hot on her heels. Callie came to an abrupt stop at the sight of everyone and wrapped her arm around Amanda's leg before pressing her face to the side of her long, lean thigh.

Amanda looked down at Callie and smiled. "Hi, baby," she said, rubbing her head affectionately, which caused the cuff of her sleeve to move, revealing still-dark purple bruising. When Amanda brought her arm back up, she readjusted her sleeve to cover her wrist.

"Hi, Admiral," Callie said before sticking two fingers in her mouth. A rank Alexander in fact carried, and one she had often called him, as had been his man Goodly's practice. Callesandra had loved Goodly and had mimicked most all of his salutations. "Hi, Aunt Sam," she giggled softly, her shoulders scrunching, before she looked at Stephen and said, "Avun." Callie called her Uncle Stephen "Avun," short for *avunculus*, the Latin word for *uncle*. Though her pronunciation made it sound like "aboon" instead. It was adorable.

"I'm going to New York," Amanda announced.

Evan walked into the room at the tail end of Amanda's declaration.

Bloody hell, welcome to the circus.

"Amanda, we spoke of this just moments ago," said Dr. Childress.

"Why do you want to go to New York, sweetie?" Sam asked.

Amanda looked at Sam for a long moment, a very long moment, then said, "I don't know."

Alexander knew Amanda had stayed in New York upon her return from Great Britain. She had an estate she'd inherited from her father overlooking the Atlantic. According to Stan, in the terribly short time he'd been able to speak with him, Amanda had never wanted to leave that New York estate. She'd only done so because she felt it was in Callesandra's best interest to settle in her home state of

California. Frustrating, but under the circumstances that was as far as they had gotten.

Dr. Evan Childress guided Amanda toward the deep oversized sectional. Helen helped her sit and then pushed two pillows behind her back. Evan continued, "Amanda, you were heavily sedated for forty-eight hours. We need to give your mind time to clear itself of the effects of the drugs you were given. I'm sure your body would like some time as well."

Callie crawled onto the cushion and tucked herself against her mother's side. Helen reached out her hands, but Amanda shook her head and stroked Zander lovingly. Helen looked to Alexander pleadingly. He understood her frustration and told her in French he'd give the baby back to her charge shortly. He also thanked her for taking such good care of Amanda. There was no way she'd been able to shower and dress so impeccably without assistance. Of course, Stephen had to add his two cents of gratitude, and not a moment later Callie's head popped up from where she lay and asked, in French, if he and Stephen were staying for dinner.

Amanda did a slight double take and sat up a little straighter. She looked at her daughter. "Callesandra Eleanor—you speak French?"

"Oui, Mama." Callie grinned.

Amanda looked at Sam, and then back to Callie. "Do I?" Amanda seemed to consider it, then shook her head. "No. I don't. Jeez."

And so ended the length of her mental and physical rally. She tried not to let it show, but Alexander easily saw through it. Her eyes stayed closed longer than her usual blink, and she began to inhale deeply through her nose. He was fondly aware of his wife's *tells*, so to speak. Coping mechanisms she'd learned over the years, useful especially when she was in large crowds or had to give a performance. Seconds later, he was at her side to take Zander into his arms without drawing undue attention. She hesitated a moment, in which he assured her it was okay. It seemed to be all she needed.

"Option two," he whispered fervently into Zander's tiny ear. "Option two."

Alexander transferred his son to Helen's eager, capable hands, then reached back down, intent on taking Amanda back upstairs, relying on her instinct to trust him as her lifeline.

◁◁ ▷▷

Amanda shook her head; she didn't want to leave the room. She just needed a few moments to adjust. She couldn't remember her home being so full before. Seriously, she couldn't remember a lot. Which reminded her. "Were you speaking about me?" she asked Mr. Montgomery. She'd grilled Stan as much as she'd been able to. Aside from being told Mr. Montgomery may be richer than God and required a large retinue as well as the fact that she felt she owed him more than gratitude for freeing her from her restraints *and* the hospital, she still knew only two things. No, three.

One—there had been a changing of the guard.

Two—the brothers Montgomery were now in charge.

Three—she should feel way more apprehensive than she did, but for some reason she didn't.

"We were. I had just remarked on what a talented pianist and vocalist you are."

Good lord the man had an incredible voice and accent. She remembered now how it made her feel safe and grounded last night. Talking to Art Fisher about the Montgomerys helped a lot too. He really was like a father to her. Mr. Montgomery looked at the face of his watch, then signaled Stan and his brother on the other side of the room. Seriously, the man *signaled*, like made a motion with his hand to tell them something. She almost laughed when she saw it. Stephen walked out of the room and Stan said something to Rosa. Then Amanda remembered. Stan and his cohorts often used hand signals when she was in need of more than just his assistance.

Light flashes came to mind as she remembered a morning news program and the subsequent award show. *Gosh, when was that?* She'd had a detail of three then. Sam had been holding Callie just off set. It had to have been months ago, September maybe? She could picture what she was wearing—jeans and heels, blouse and cardigan, her favorite belt. She hadn't been showing, pregnancy wise. Jesus, how could she not remember who the father of her children was? Or giving birth to not one, but two babies?

Tally off the memory column: Amanda Marceau, singer and songwriter. Check. She loved to dance too.

Check. Wait, she'd been teaching Callie ballet. And piano. Check. Check. Heir to the Marceau fortune. Check. She fought off a wave of sadness thinking of her father, who'd died in a plane crash with her stepmother a few years ago. She looked around the room—where was Robert? Her stepbrother was usually around to mark important occasions. You'd think the birth of a child would be one. Not that she missed him; she always had a bad feeling when he was around. Sam, best friend, boarding school and college roommate. Check. Stan, guy who takes care of everything. That was a weird thought. Bodyguard, check. Rosa, best house manager and cook ever. Check. Done with her mental housekeeping, she looked back at Mr. Montgomery.

"What did you tell them?" she asked.

Mr. Montgomery smiled, and the corners of his eyes crinkled. *Handsome* did not do this man justice. At well over six feet tall, with dark eyes, dark hair, and a ridiculously impressive physique, he was nothing short of extraordinary. There was something so very familiar about him, yet she would swear she'd never met him before in her life. Maybe it was just that he'd taken her from the hospital, and she was still under the influence from the medication they'd given her.

"I told them I needed to speak with them privately. And the count for dinner tonight."

"I like big family dinners," she told him, not knowing if was true, but the second she said it, she wanted it to be. "The bigger, the better."

He took her hand, embracing it within both of his. "Then you'll be ridiculously pleased as our current head count is twenty-two. However, only fourteen of us will actually dine together, and that number includes Zander." He looked at the scars that marred the back of her hand. "Your house is entirely wired, Amanda, as I'm sure you're aware. As am I, and all of our men," he told her, pointing to his left ear. "We're all just a call away."

He walked from the room and Evan followed him. Which left only the girls and Zander. She hugged Callie closer as Sam joined them on the sectional, then she reached back out for her baby. Helen deposited him back in her arms.

Sam stroked Amanda's forehead. "How are you, Ammy? Really?"

Samantha was the *best* best friend. Ever. Memory loss aside, *that* she knew. And that Sam only used "Ammy" when it was really important.

"Sore. Tired. And missing some things." She rolled her eyes toward her forehead. "Like upstairs."

Sam laughed. "It'll come back and you'll be feeling better in no time. You just need some rest."

Amanda woke up later, with neither Zander nor Callie anywhere to be seen, but Sam was reading next to her and she could hear male voices coming from the bar. The sun was making a beautiful, picture-perfect descent outside. *Jeez*, she must have slept for a good few hours.

"She's up," Sam said.

"Good, let's eat." Mr. Montgomery's reply carried from across the room. He was at her side a moment later and reached down to assist her. He wrapped an arm around her shoulders and helped her from the sofa. "Can you manage?" he said quietly in her ear.

She turned her head and told him just as softly, "I'm going to try."

"Then let's do this, sweetheart."

That startled her. *Sweetheart?* She remembered he'd called her sweetheart in the hospital. There was nothing placating or sexist in the way he said it. It was as if he'd dubbed her that nickname and it fit perfectly. Which was a really weird thought. Maybe she *was* still under the influence of what they'd given her in the hospital. She'd been home only a day now. She did feel oddly comfortable with him, though. She couldn't say why, she just did.

Mr. Montgomery stayed by her side as their large procession slowly made its way to the kitchen.

"Why did Callie call you Admiral?" Amanda asked as they continued down the hallway.

"It's my rank," he said, not looking at her.

"You're really an admiral?" she asked, not knowing quite what being an admiral meant, but just that it was impressive.

"I was."

"Wow. Here in the States?"

He looked at Evan before he answered. "British Royal Navy."

"Admiral of the White," she added without thought. *Where did that come from?* "Wait. How do I know that?" she asked.

"You're terribly smart, Amanda," he said, suppressing a smile.

She put a hand on his chest when he would have ushered them forward. *Was her memory wrong?* "No, I mean *you* are an Admiral of the White."

"Admirals of the White don't exist any longer."

Amanda shook her head. "Maybe I'm getting confused. My father bought an estate in Abersoch years ago. As a young girl, I loved to travel there. Honestly, it was one of my most favorite places on Earth." Her eyes widened with realization. "You share a name with one of its ancestors. I wonder if you're related."

Mr. Montgomery only stared. The man was utterly still. Then she realized how quiet it had become. She looked at Sam for a cue. "What? Don't you remember?" Amanda had definitely talked about it with her best friend before. She'd been fascinated with the Montgomerys as a teenager. "Come on, Sam. I researched everything I *could* on that castle—oh! And I remember now. That story I found, so intriguing, but so sad." Amanda was on a roll now, her memories of being a girl poring over books in the estate coming back to her. "It was about one of the original descendants' great-great-great-grandsons, Alexander Montgomery." She jabbed Mr. Montgomery's chest playfully. "Isn't that incredible?"

"Yes, incredible, Amanda," Mr. Montgomery said, nodding.

Amanda was so excited to have remembered something like that, she didn't mind being pulled along once again as they made their way to dinner. Instead of stopping in the kitchen, however, they continued through the French doors to the terrace. The long, glass-topped wrought-iron table was impeccably set. It looked beautiful; linen placemats with china plates, silver cutlery, crystal glasses, and cloth napkins displayed perfect settings. Rosa and a couple of young men began to bring platters outside and placed them on the runner that ran the length of the center.

Mr. Montgomery pulled out a chair for her as everyone took their seats. "Good?"

"Very," Amanda said, sinking down into the chair.

Helen came in with Zander. Stan, too, with Callie on his hip. Her previous entourage of four had become an entire troupe. Mr. Montgomery and his men had seemingly taken over, but if Stan and Sam were okay with them, then she knew she had nothing to worry about. Jeez, even overprotective Rosa seemed okay.

Mr. Montgomery took the seat next to her at the head of the table, looking like he belonged there. His brother sat to his left, Sam next to him, and Evan took the other seat next to her. Callie was at the other end where Stan, Rosa, and Helen were talking with four men she hadn't yet met, but one looked vaguely familiar, though she couldn't figure out why.

"Amanda," Mr. Montgomery said, "may I introduce Gregor, Chris, Trevor, and Michael." Each bowed their head in greeting. "Gregor holds the keys after my brother and me. Chris is my attorney and head counsel for Calder Defense. Tre—"

"Wait." Amanda put her hand on his forearm. "I thought you bought JDL from Art Fisher?" Something seemed off and she felt a moment of panic for the first time.

"You're correct, Amanda," Montgomery said, assuring her. "I did purchase JDL. I also changed the name."

She looked to Stan, who nodded, and smiled in relief. "Carry on then, Admiral."

He grinned and gestured to the two men he'd yet to introduce. "Trevor, tech genius from London. And Michael, weaponry expert, also from London. Brothers, and both of whom I stumbled upon and have yet to shake since."

She leaned in. "Stumbled upon?"

"Seedy back alley storefront outside of London."

"What on earth brought you there?" she asked, intrigued.

"I…" He paused as if searching for the right words. "I was tracking someone."

"And just what did you come across at this seedy back alley storefront?" Amanda asked.

She watched as Montgomery looked to Evan, who gave a curt nod. Strange.

"The storefront was just that, a front. It hid a high-tech document lab," he said.

Her eyes narrowed for a moment. She felt like something was there and she just couldn't grasp it. She looked at Sam. "What is it, sweetie?" Sam asked. "Remember something?"

Amanda shrugged and shook her head as nothing pressing came to mind, then gave her attention back to Mr. Montgomery. He wouldn't get off so easily. "So, tell me, Admiral, what kind of documents might one procure from such an establishment?"

"The person—persons," he corrected, "I was searching for had purchased birth certificates, passports, and adoption papers. So, those. As well as any and all corresponding and essential background files that would be necessary to accompany such documents."

"Ooh, that sounds intriguing. Did you find them?"

"I have."

"So, what's the story?"

"Still unfolding."

"Well, it sounds fascinating. Will you keep me posted?"

"I will."

She sensed she'd reached the limit of his disclosure and moved on to another of her curiosities. "By the by, Admiral," she said, injecting a bit of Brit as she raised her brows and motioned with her head toward Trevor and Michael at the other end of the table. "They're terribly young, aren't they?"

He grinned. "Yes, they are. Trevor's only twenty-two. But when you add genius, and mean it, to any title, it's usually a gift and comes with such implications. He's particularly mouthy, however."

She laughed. "And Michael?"

"Michael is almost twenty-seven. He just looks like a boy. Mouthy, too, in a different way."

Platters started being passed at will. Rosa had made an exceptionally special meal. Lamb chops and bronzini, potatoes and rice, vegetables, salad, and baguettes all but spilled from their serving pieces. Conversations began, were interrupted, and restarted too many times to count. It was table pandemonium of the best kind. It felt like they'd had dinners like this forever.

There was something about the cadence of Mr. Montgomery's voice that Amanda found comforting. She racked her frustratingly foggy brain, trying to reach something oddly familiar that lay just beyond her grasp. She was aware that Mr. Montgomery was watching her intently, remaining quiet as if knowing he might stop a memory from returning, but she didn't look up or shift her gaze. The moment passed and she shook her head at him to let him know, before turning her attention back to Sam and Stephen, who were arguing about veal of all things. Apparently, Stephen ate it and Sam had very strong opinions about it.

As they began to slow down a bit, eating that is, Evan asked, "So, Amanda...what else do you remember about the descendants of your British estate?"

"Oh!" she said, startled, but glad to have the opportunity to explore her memory some more. "I remember I was so excited when my father bought that rocky coastal estate. And finding the story of Alexander, Rebecca, and Callesandra, well..." She trailed off, suddenly thinking of something else. She noticed everyone looking at her and continued. "It's just odd recalling something like this so readily, yet missing such larger, more important facts. Of me. My children."

"It will come, let's give it some more time," Evan said, patting her hand. "Sometimes just carrying on is the best way to let nature take its course. Tell us more."

"Alexander Montgomery"—she looked at the man to her left—"of *old*." She smiled. "He was an admiral born in the eighteenth century, titled and uber wealthy, who had this awful arranged marriage. Like I mean *really* bad. From what I can remember, his wife was a true bitch. But

they still had a kid together—a girl named Callesandra."
Amanda laughed. "I really must have been obsessed," she
said, motioning toward the other end of the table where
Callie was sitting. "Anyway, they had a second child,
because I guess that's what was expected in those days,
even if you hated one another. That one was a boy, but he
died in childbirth. And then I *think* I read somewhere that
the wife killed the baby just to spite her husband. Can
you believe that? She was like a sociopath or something.
And then, I couldn't find any mention of the family
beyond 1774. It was as if they'd vanished. And I looked—
hard. Alexander, his wife, and their only living daughter
mysteriously had never been written of again."

The brothers Montgomery both stood at the same
time.

"I'm sorry, it's just a story," Amanda said apologetically.

"It's not you, Amanda," Mr. Montgomery said as
everyone started to clear the table.

She looked at Evan, who patted her hand again.
"You're okay," he assured her. "You'll be okay." That was
just what she needed to hear. She leaned back in her chair
and closed her eyes.

It wasn't long before coffee, dessert, and after-dinner
drinks were brought out. The mood was light again and
Stephen was laughing at something his brother said as he
filled sherry glasses with Cockburn's or Grand Mariner.
When he placed a hand on her shoulder, she looked up and
shook her head. He smiled and gave her an affectionate
squeeze. It struck her then that she and these two brothers
were connected in some way. If not before, then surely now

and moving forward. Maybe that's what she was feeling; one of those karmic relationships in life, where you meet someone and know you're somehow connected and meant to be together.

Callie climbed into her lap as large pieces of coconut cake and fresh fruit made their way around the table. Mr. Montgomery walked to the far end and took Zander and his bottle from Helen's arms. Amanda couldn't nurse him since they'd given her a heavy concoction of drugs at the hospital. She thought he would bring him to her, but he simply sat back in the seat next to her and began feeding the baby himself.

Amanda couldn't remember a better night. Ever. She kissed Callie's forehead and shared a smile with Sam.

Then everyone's phones went off at the same time.

All eyes save hers looked to Mr. Montgomery. "Bloody hell!" He slammed his hand down on top of her phone and then picked up his.

"I'm on it." Trevor ran from the room, then everyone began speaking at once.

"Inside!" the admiral barked. Stephen was at Amanda's side not a second later, and before she knew it, he'd escorted her upstairs to her room. Helen helped her get situated on her bed, ignoring all of her questions, then placed Zander and his bottle into her lap. It wasn't lost on her that they were trying to distract her. Which mostly worked because Zander was not happy that his feeding had been interrupted, and she was still a bit addled from the post-op drugs. She rolled onto her side and tucked him in closer. "Shh, shh, baby. It's okay, Mama's got you," she whispered, trying to calm her own racing thoughts.

◀◀   ▶▶

"You have to show her," Samantha spat out as she and Stephen stood in the threshold of Amanda's room. They'd had time to watch the video in its entirety. Sam wanted to kill someone. That Amanda couldn't catch a break was killing her. She could sympathize with Alex and Stephen, of course, and what they had gone through themselves, but they weren't here when Amanda came back. Not only terribly hurt physically, but so very heartbroken too.

Stephen held a finger to his lips, and quietly closed the double doors of Amanda's master suite. There was no mistaking the uncanny resemblance between the two brothers. Both were ridiculously good-looking. Stephen, however, was lankier, his features more severe. He pulled her farther into the hallway. "No" was all he said, leaving no room for argument.

What Stephen Montgomery failed to realize was that she had a degree—and a prestigious one at that— in anything litigious. She was about to tell him just that, when he spoke again.

"I know you excel in argument," he said, looking at her straight on. "However, I beg of you, not now." He wasn't just giving orders. The man was in pain. She could see that.

"I can see how much you and your brother care for Amanda—"

"Care for her?" Stephen sounded insulted. "My brother and I love that woman. Our family and the soundness of its members are of paramount importance. In fact, it's the only thing that matters to us."

"Your presence here obviously confirms that, Stephen. What I'm trying to tell you is that it's better that she learns of that video from us."

Alexander came up the stairs, his mouth a grim line. "Trevor's working to find the IP address and obliterate wherever it came from."

The video had already gone viral. Its creator had titled it, "Amanda Marceau—Talented, Beautiful, Wealthy—Crumbles." It showed the entirety of Amanda's breakdown. Holding Zander for the first time. Her joy and sorrow combined as she looked down at the baby. Her softly whispered, "I'm so sorry. I wish you could see our son." Since she'd been back in the twenty-first century, Amanda had been overcome with guilt that she'd taken Callie from Alexander, and she'd told Sam about it again and again. It consumed her. No matter how many times Sam tried to tell her that she hadn't been given a choice, that there was nothing else Amanda could have done. Just knowing that Callie was the light of Alexander's life and that they'd ultimately left him alone was a devastation she'd lived with every day. And now to have a new baby, a son, fully aware that Alex had lost his first with Rebecca, it must have been too much for her friend. In the video, Amanda snapped, screaming again and again, the culmination of a series of misfortunate, dreadful events. Sam watched herself on screen trying to console her, but Amanda only became more agitated. Then the video showed Stan muscling into the room, yelling at the doctors and nurses to treat Amanda with care. Not that they weren't doing so; he was only trying to protect her, and his helplessness showed. Sam watched as little Zander was forcefully taken from Amanda, and the video ended with her restraint and sedation.

Sam remembered the call she'd gotten from Stan when Amanda had awoken much later. He'd said she was in a semi-catatonic state, that something was very wrong. It was then that Dr. Meyers had briefed him on Amanda's memory loss and its compartmental nature. She swallowed a breath and looked to Alexander now, who rubbed his forehead, clearly stressed.

"Chris said getting anything off the internet is a beast, but everyone has a price. He's drawing up paperwork now. Has she seen it?"

"No," Sam and Stephen answered at the same time.

Then Sam said, "You—no, we—have to tell her, Alex. This won't keep. Trust me."

Alexander scrubbed his hands over his face. "Bloody hell! Can not one thing go our way?"

"Grow up," Sam snapped. "No one said life was fair, Al—"

Stephen covered her mouth and pulled her back against him. "That wasn't necessary," he told her quietly before dropping his hand.

There was nothing rough about the way he handled her. In fact, he was terribly gentle and the manner in which he held her and spoke to her was oddly intimate. "You're right," she conceded. "I'm sorry, Alex. But she really needs to know."

Alex remained quiet. Stephen, who had yet to let go of her, said, "Don't do this to her, Samantha. Not yet."

"Don't take this the wrong way, but it would be much easier if you two weren't here."

Stephen squeezed her shoulders. "Please."

They all turned as the doors opened. Amanda stood in the threshold. She didn't have to say the words that followed: "I've watched it."

Alexander moved toward her, but she stuck out her hand. "Stop." Her eyes looked vacant.

Then she turned around and closed the doors behind her.

CHAPTER
FOUR

1774
ABERSOCH, BRITAIN

"Give me your hand, Becca!" the man shouted, his tone demanding as he stepped farther upon the ledge. Amanda watched, frightened as he gripped the rock wall inside the tunnel, bracing his weight as he reached out. Every few seconds lightning illuminated his tanned, scowling face and the fine lines at the corners of his eyes. His dark hair lay in sharp contrast to the white shirt plastered to broad shoulders and torso. Even as she shrunk from him, this stranger whose eyes flashed with anger, she couldn't help but notice how very...handsome he was. Craning her neck, stepping as far back onto the ledge as she dared, Amanda just stood there, stunned and speechless.

"Becca," he demanded again. "We've no time for games. Give me your hand!"

Amanda kept her eyes on the man; his voice was filled with contempt, yet he continued to come closer. Who was he? Why did he keep calling her "Becca"? Her hands grasped the rock behind her, her body shaking so badly she knew she would fall if she didn't accept his help.

The sea below taunted her with its white-capped waves crashing against the shore. Her arms were cut and bruised, her stomach and back as well. Fear had taken her adrenaline level to an all-time high. A survival instinct kicking in that she didn't know she had. How had she gotten here? The last thing she remembered was wrenching herself away from her stepbrother as he— *my God*, Robert had tried to kill her! How had she not seen it?

She'd only wanted some time alone and had impulsively booked the trip from New York to the British Isles. She loved the British estate that belonged to her family and had gone for an extended vacation. Actually, of all the properties she owned, this estate, built mid-sixteenth century, was her favorite. She'd visited at least four times a year since her father had made the original purchase some ten years ago. And, on each occasion, at least since she'd graduated college, she allowed select charities to use it, and her, for their benefits. This time, though, it was meant to be empty, meant to be just her.

She'd been shocked when Robert had shown up three days after she'd arrived, a large group of business associates and their families in tow. He'd made excuses about some kind of function, a party for her to perform at, to wow the guests with her presence. She'd obliged, of course, though wondered why Robert hadn't told her about it beforehand. Now she knew why.

The perfect crime.

The perfect alibi.

He'd goaded her into playing one of her pieces tonight knowing that she'd seek some privacy before performing. She always needed time alone before she played. She damned herself now for having such an obvious habit. Damned herself for being such a complete and utter fool.

When she'd left the party to collect herself and to take a walk along the cliffs, the property had been teeming with guests and servants, all in fanciful "historical" costumes. She'd walked into the mouth of the cave, heading for her favorite place, where she'd often come to think over the years.

Tonight, it seemed to beckon her as never before. Just as *he* now beckoned her. This man who called her by a different name, this man who'd pulled Robert off of her with alarming strength and thrown him against the wall of the cave. This man who'd saved her life.

She could only see his profile now; his face was concealed in the shadows. But the harshness of his features remained in her mind. The way he'd looked at her when he'd come upon them in the cave. He'd seemed angry, furious even. At her. She shivered, both from the cold and from his glare. The farther she stepped away, the closer he came. His arms were long and powerful, his white shirt rolled to his forearms, a wide silver band circled his wrist. His black cape billowed in the wind as he moved to reach her. His tall black riding boots were polished to a high shine reflecting each flash of lightning that tore through the sky. Despite the direness of her situation, she thought his costume *was* remarkable.

He had to be at least six and half feet tall, and at five-eight herself, he'd still tower over her once he got close, *if* he got close. And *why*, she puzzled again as she repositioned her feet on the slippery rock beneath her, did he keep calling her Rebecca? And who had those other large men on horses been? The ones who'd scared her so much, she'd actually felt safer feeling her way along the cliff outside the cave than accepting their offers of help while this stranger had gone after Robert.

It had been light when she'd entered the tunnels from the gardens in back of the castle, wending through the elegantly set chairs and tables awaiting their guests. Everything had been placed carefully, so the natural beauty the estate had to offer was paramount. Unable to resist the view, Amanda had sat for a while before heading to find her favorite alcove within the maze of tunnels in the torchlit caverns by the sea.

Somehow, she'd become lost—something that had never happened before—winding around for what seemed like hours. She'd worried that someone would notice her missing, that the guests would be eager for their performance, but no matter what turn she took, Amanda remained lost. The ground beneath her feet had become damp. The beautiful furnishings that her father had had set within the secluded alcoves years ago were mysteriously gone. The only things that remained were the torches affixed to the rock wall lighting her way. She was grateful at least for that.

Amanda had heard the sea first and turned toward the sound to find the opening of the path she'd been on. The path she was now below. She'd headed toward it briskly, knowing she'd be able to find her way from there. She'd stopped in the opening, awed by the beautiful sight. The sky so alive with stars, making it the most amazing thing she'd ever seen in her life.

She'd closed her eyes, having one of those epiphanies that seem to come only once every so often. Those times when you just know something is so very right, so right you feel it entirely and commit it to memory forever. It felt as though she'd belonged right there, in that very moment and at that very time. As if all the answers were there for the taking. Amanda forgot about being lost, forgot about the party waiting for her, forgot about Robert even, and how he'd been acting odd as of late. And as feelings of peace and contentment rolled through her, lightning tore through the calm night sky. She'd laughed, wondering if it meant to prove or disprove her point.

Then she'd felt hands as they grabbed her, saw the venom in Robert's eyes as he looked at her, *into* her. She'd fought with everything she had, fought against the man she'd thought would be, if nothing else, protective of her forever. She'd heard horses then, the shouts and echoes louder as they came closer. Robert had been pulled off of her as she stood shaking, staring at the four men who sat atop the largest mounts she'd ever seen. The men had been huge, each wearing long-sleeved shirts and black capes secured by gold braided ropes at the neck and tall black riding boots. She'd been grateful at first, but then she saw their expressions and her fear came back with a vengeance. They looked at her with…with disgust?

The men had kept coming closer with each backward step she took. Their looks so menacing they terrified her. She didn't know them, but they seemed to recognize her—more than that they seemed to despise her, but how on earth was that possible? She'd never seen any of them before. Had Robert hired them? Was all of this because of Robert's greed? Did he really need more than what her father had generously provided? It had always been clear that Amanda would get the estate when her father died. What had Robert thought would happen? Was her life worth the pittance he'd inherit upon her death?

As the men on horses watched, Amanda had stepped closer to the opening and her feet slipped against the slick rocks. She'd only fallen a short distance, but her dress had caught and snagged on the rock wall behind her. She'd felt sharp cuts on her hand and stomach as she'd clung with all her might at any hold, all of them small and slippery. The ledge was no more than two feet wide, but she'd caught a glimpse of another cave's opening to her right. Quickly judging its distance, Amanda knew she could make it with a calculated leap. She'd turned as slowly as possible, pressing into the wall as she made her way to safety. Then she looked down.

Amanda had begun shaking so badly she couldn't hear the calls from above, only the rushing water eddying below her. Cast within the shadows, she'd thought perhaps the men above couldn't see her anymore. Hopefully, they'd think she'd fallen.

It had seemed forever went by until she regained her courage. Amanda took a deep breath and moved toward the opening she'd clocked on her right. She'd almost made it, too, when *he* arrived. The man who called her Rebecca yelled at her as if he knew her, hated her. He stood in the opening that a minute ago had been her escape. Now it didn't seem to be freedom before her but surrender instead.

"What game is this, Rebecca?" he demanded, his hair blowing back from the wind. *My God*, he was the most fearsome, yet compelling man she'd ever seen.

"Becca, I'll not ask again—give me your hand!" he demanded once more, somehow even angrier now.

Looking at his hand, she hesitated. She knew she had no choice, but an odd sensation settled over her at the same time. She felt—she *knew*—that if she reached for him, it would be more than her life she owed him. If she reached for him it would be far, far more.

"Your *hand*, Rebecca!" he yelled as a flash of lightning tore through the sky. Emboldened, she looked directly at him and saw something inexplicable pass through his eyes. The anger abated, just for a moment, as his eyes shifted into an expression of, what? Confusion? A softening of some sort, anyway.

That was enough for Amanda. She reached out, her hand shaking until he grasped it, and at that moment their eyes locked again, and the lightning storm seemed to electrify them both. He pulled her back with such force they fell through the mouth of the cavern and Amanda collapsed on top of him. Momentarily forgetting where she was, and who he was, she wrapped her arms around his waist and pressed herself against him, the full relief of her rescue taking over everything else.

For a moment, he embraced her, too, but only for a moment. Roughly, he pushed her away, startling Amanda.

"Rebecca?" he said again, holding her at arm's length.

Remembering the anger that had flooded his eyes moments before, and the intimidating men on horses, Amanda leapt up, backing away. Then she ran through the cavern, suddenly more scared than she'd been in her life, even more than when she'd clung to the cliffs only moments ago. Her heart was racing and not just in fear. He scared her, but…but something about the way he'd looked at her scared her more. It had been like he'd stared into her soul and was confused about what he'd found there. Amanda could hear his footsteps echoing behind her as she ran. She turned as the tunnel split, running down the darkened path, a scream escaping her lips as his hands grasped her shoulders. She tried to fight, but he was so strong. Then he whirled her around so fast it took her breath away.

They stood in the darkness facing each other, this handsome, terrifying stranger. His tone angry again, he asked, "What game do you play, Rebecca?"

She was too frightened to answer, too overcome by his anger, his forceful hold, his features. His face a mere inch from hers, his breath warm upon her face. She shivered.

"Answer me, Rebecca. Now!" he demanded, shaking her as if to drive the answer out. Amanda felt a tear fall from the corner of one eye and she squeezed both shut to prevent any more. As she did, the man swore under his breath. "What were you *thinking*, Rebecca? No matter how much we despise one another, Callesandra deserves a mother, even one who doesn't care."

Amanda remained frozen still, this time out of confusion. Who did he think she was?

"Bloody hell, Rebecca, what's gotten into you? You're never at a loss for words, and always have an excuse for everything. And running away? Now?" he said, his voice low, but his tone menacing. "Guests—*your* guests—are already beginning to arrive for the festivities, an affair you *insisted* upon! Personally, I hate these gatherings, Rebecca, and you know that. I think you actually enjoy that I hate them. Well, you win," he spat. "I loathe pretending to appear complacent while you flaunt yourself and dance with every willing partner. You know it's only for Callesandra—the only good thing to come out of marrying you—that I even continue the pretense of caring for you in public. We haven't shared a bed in *years*, and I know you've sought others."

Amanda tried to speak, to protest—he clearly thought she was someone else—but he was on a roll now, his dark eyes flashing with anger, not appearing to even see her as he ranted.

"No, Rebecca. *I* won't be the one gossiped about, at least not about infidelity. Callesandra will still have one parent she can respect. She's the only one I care about, which is more than you can say. And for her I won't play this foolish game in which you so love to engage," he said, his voice dripping with distaste.

Amanda shook her head, a gesture of denial. "I play no game," she cried in a whisper, once he paused long enough for her to speak. She clutched his arms in her desperation to make him believe her.

He seemed to react to that. His eyes softened and he seemed to be about to speak again when the sound of his men approaching caused them both to turn. The tunnel was suddenly cast in light and Amanda shivered as he stared at her, deeply, intently as if searching for something in her eyes. Then he grabbed her hand and she muffled a cry as he squeezed it harshly, pulling her out of the tunnel and onto the lawn. One of the men approached, leading a horse by the reins. Amanda stared at it, then at the men. For a moment she forgot her fear as she looked around the estate's Great Lawn, still familiar, but not quite as she'd left it.

The manicured grounds were being illuminated by at least four groundskeepers she'd never seen before. They were tending to the lampposts, one by one, setting them ablaze. Horse-drawn carriages, several of them, were making their way down the long drive toward the estate. Amanda rubbed the back of her head, wincing as she felt a bump.

"Did my staff hire you and your men for tonight?" she wondered aloud, turning to the man who'd saved her before she could stop herself. "I know it's a costume party, but seriously, your outfits are amazing." She touched the fabric of his breeches at the hip, then rubbed part of his linen shirt between her fingers. "Actually, I'd swear they're authentic."

The man looked confused and then scoffed, muttering something under his breath that she couldn't quite catch.

Fine, be that way, she thought, suddenly much less afraid now that she was back on solid ground and with so many other people milling about.

"Alexander," the man with the horse said, and the man who'd saved her turned. "It's getting late."

Ah, so that was his name. *Alexander*. It suited him, Amanda thought.

Alexander's expression tensed again, and he nodded to his friend. "Thank you, Gregor. Rebecca, get on," he spat out, looking at her expectantly. Amanda didn't move. "Get on, Rebecca," he repeated through clenched teeth. "Your guests have already begun to arrive."

Amanda looked back and forth between the horse and Alexander, and then toward the group of men, Gregor in front. Alexander glared down at her and a small bit of fear crept back. She tried to hide it, but she was too tired to make a real effort. She shook her head to prove her point. She was not getting on that thing. For starters, she didn't know how.

His men looked even angrier than he, like they despised her even more than Alexander, if that was at all possible. "Leave her, Alexander," another one of them said. "We'll see she gets back."

Suddenly Amanda didn't want Alexander to leave. She gasped, grasping his forearms with her hands. He was frightening, yes, and a stranger still, but at least he'd saved her life. "Go ahead," he ordered his men, keeping his gaze fixed upon hers. "We'll follow shortly." His men grunted in unison, then turned and left in the direction from which they'd come.

Once again, they were shrouded in darkness.

"Take the mount, Rebecca. I'll walk back," he offered, as if the only thing holding her back was that she didn't want to ride with him. He turned then, leaving her alone, and began walking. Amanda had to hold back a laugh. Okay, so he *wasn't* going to hurt her. He might hate her, but he *was* trying to help. She watched as he retreated, patting the horse absentmindedly. She could walk it back, she supposed, but she'd prefer to wait until Alexander and his friends had gone completely.

After a few minutes, however, she was startled to see him marching back her way. "Rebecca, take the mount!" he shouted in frustration.

"I don't know how," she whispered, suddenly embarrassed.

He threw his torch to the ground and grasped her shoulders, hauling her around to stand before him. "Cease your games," he said, seething. "You love horses. More than anything. They're probably the one thing you *do* love besides yourself."

Amanda had no idea what to do; she couldn't get on that horse, but she found she couldn't pull away from this man, either. Never mind that he towered over her, never mind his apparent anger, she felt safe with him. Like she somehow knew that he wouldn't harm her. At a loss for words, and so confused she'd already forgotten what he demanded, she only shook her head.

He looked down at her then, with a curious expression. Amanda stared back, momentarily forgetting that she didn't know him, that she'd almost been murdered, and that she still had a piano performance to give. Then his expression changed into something even more startling: desire, very real and oh so raw. A flush went through Amanda as she felt it too. He continued to stare into her eyes and then at her lips. They stayed frozen like that for a moment and then, as if this was what everything had been leading toward, his hands palmed her head and his lips covered hers.

They each made a sound at the contact; the sensation was electrifying and seemed to hit each of her nerve endings. He pulled back then as if stunned and stared deeply into her eyes, looking at her features as if they were new to him. With a look of confusion, he shook his head then pulled her close once more. She may have met him halfway.

My God, this man could kiss.

Rational thought fled Amanda's mind as he all but devoured her, feasting upon her with such need he took her very breath. Lost in sensation he pulled her against his body, crushing her breasts to his chest. A groan escaped his lips as she wrapped her arms around his neck and kissed him back.

Alexander, suddenly, seemed to be an anchor, not someone to be afraid of, and she found in him, what? Salvation? Was this where fate had been leading her ever since that moment in the opening of the cave, the moment when everything had felt perfect and right? Whatever it was, this kiss felt like none she'd had before. Demanding, powerful, and so consuming she didn't realize her feet dangled above the ground as her hands moved up to cover the back of his head. Too late she was lost again, lost in his strength and his thick hair now tangled between her fingers.

Suddenly he pushed her away, swearing under his breath, "Damn you."

It was all he said, then she remembered that he hated her, or the woman he thought she was. For some reason that realization hurt more than the others she'd been crassly exposed to tonight. Before she knew it, he picked her up roughly and placed her on the saddle. She grabbed the knob, terrified of falling, and when he came up behind her, she breathed a sigh of relief and leaned back against him. He didn't say anything but made a clicking sound and tugged on the reins to urge his mount forward.

They wound along the path for long, tense, seemingly endless minutes before the gardens came into view. The marble veranda stretched across the back of the castle was now filled with people, the tall iron lamps casting a glow. Everyone was dressed impeccably, and she was again taken aback by the opulence of everyone's costumes. Men in formal tails and cravats and snugly fit trousers tucked into tall polished boots. And the women in beautiful dresses like she'd seen only in history books. Tight-fitting bodices, bell skirts, and ornate jewels fixed around their necks and even laced in their hair. Who were these people?

Amanda scanned the faces around her, but none of them were familiar. None of Robert's friends, none of her own guests. No, this was not the party she'd left earlier!

Alexander spoke then, "Why do you shake? You love these gatherings."

"I hate parties," Amanda corrected him, still focused on finding at least one person she knew, and definitely still tingling from their kiss moments earlier.

"You've tried my patience enough, Rebecca," he snapped. "Dress quickly. I'll retrieve you once I've changed."

He dismounted then reached for her. His hands encircled her waist as he pulled her down, then he let go quickly as if burned by the touch. Disappointed, she followed him through the doors, knowing she had no choice but to go inside. The sights in front of the castle were just as unsettling as those behind it. Carriages circled the large courtyard, footmen helping guests as they stepped to the ground below.

Amanda held back a gasp as she stepped through the doors. The entrance took her breath away—a foyer grand and opulent with marble floors and glowing chandeliers. This was also not the castle she'd left earlier.

A woman came forward and quickly took her hand. "M'lady, hurry. We must get you dressed." Amanda was pulled up the stairs. The stairs themselves were familiar, as was the basic structure of everything else around her, but the runner was covered in burgundy and gold. In fact, all of the décor was different, the furniture, the art. And the lights that had been dim this evening were ablaze with oil wicks and candles.

Alexander followed from behind. He hadn't looked at her again, which was probably a good thing, because if he did, scowl or not she'd step right into his arms. They reached a landing at the top of the stairs and turned left up another short flight. She was led into the first room and watched from the corner of her eye as Alexander disappeared down the hallway.

Amanda was ushered across the threshold into a room that was not her usual bedroom here. Dresses were everywhere, strewn across the bed, the couches in two sitting areas, and there was even a privacy screen. The room was in utter chaos. It was decorated in hues of blue and gold with sitting areas on either side of the bed, a large full-length mirror in the corner, and two large armoires on either side of the bathroom door.

"Where did this garment come from?" the woman asked, not bothering to hide her disgust as she pulled Amanda's sundress over her head. Amanda was about to retort when she noticed the scratches on her hands and the one on her stomach.

"Dear Lord, what on earth happened?" the woman asked in shock and Amanda couldn't think of what to say.

Within minutes, her wounds were covered with ointment and strips of linen and covered again with a soft sheer material that matched the dress she was stepping into. Confused, she let the woman put it on her. What else was she supposed to do? By now she'd realized that something was very, very wrong, but until she worked out exactly what was going on, she'd decided to play along. It could be worse to fight back. The ties were secured behind her back and her hair roughly brushed before being plied with jewels and ribbons. Then her feet were encased in heeled shoes that buttoned on the sides.

"Check yourself, quickly," the woman hastened. "Then choose a necklace." Amanda walked to the mirror, looking at her reflection. The gown was beautiful. Blue and in style with those she'd seen earlier. Her hair looked wonderful pulled back, but too severe and with far too many stones set in it. It simply wouldn't do.

She pulled the jewels from their placement and loosened the ribbons. Her hair fell gently around her face now, wavy lengths cascading down her shoulders.

"M'lady, you instructed me earlier to fashion your hair as such. I apologize 'twas not to your liking," the woman offered, her voice shaking, almost like she was afraid of Amanda. What was going on?

Another woman came in. "Mother? Alice?" She quickly corrected herself when she saw Amanda. "Callesandra is asking for you." The new girl, obviously Alice's daughter, looked at Amanda cautiously. Like she was waiting for Amanda to berate her and praying she wouldn't.

"I'll be just a minute," Alice called over her shoulder. "Come, Lady Rebecca. We must choose a necklace." Amanda turned, looking at the jewelry Alice held. She was Rebecca to these women too. There was something familiar about that name now, something she hadn't had time to realize when she was fighting for her life on the cliff, but that now tugged at the edge of her brain. Alexander and Rebecca. Where had she read those names in conjunction before? Amanda saw then that Alice and her daughter were still watching her, Alice holding out the necklace. Amanda only shook her head. She wouldn't wear any of these pieces. Not only did they look as though they weighed ten pounds, they were truly gaudy.

"No thank you, Alice," Amanda said, patting her arm. "They'll weigh me down."

Alice looked at Amanda like she'd lost her mind. Then she turned in surprise as the door opened again. "Callesandra, I'll only be a moment. Go now. Quickly," Alice said.

Amanda looked to the door then, too, and an angel stared back at her. The child could be no more than five and Amanda knew at once that she was Alexander's daughter. She had his dark eyes and determined mouth, though oddly her hair seemed to be the exact shade of Amanda's own.

The little girl bit her lip and then turned to leave. "Wait!" Amanda cried out. She didn't want her to leave. She looked so scared. And feeling the exact same way, Amanda suddenly wanted—no, needed—to help her. Callesandra came back then, her face cast down as she approached. Her nightgown had a soft ruffle tied at the neck while another danced around her little toes. They were the sweetest toes she'd ever seen.

Callesandra stopped when she stood right before her, acting like she had no choice and bravely accepted the challenge. Amanda bent down but still the child didn't look up. This little girl was scared—*of her*. Hoping to ease her fears, Amanda sat on the floor, and gasps sounded behind her as Alice and the other woman watched.

"Callesandra?" Amanda spoke softly, coaxing her to look down at her.

"Oui, Mama?" Callesandra whispered hesitantly.

Amanda almost fainted. First Rebecca and now this? Mama? Did this child truly think that she was her mother?

Obviously this child was not hers, but she most certainly was Alexander's.

He stood in the open doorway then, filling its space completely. His formal attire was tailored impeccably, and his hair was tied back with a leather thong. The features of his face were strangely comforting, ranging somewhere between confusion and anger. At least that hadn't changed, she mused, biting back a smile. She looked to the little girl and reached out to hold her tiny hands. "Callesandra, it seems I'm in a bit of trouble," Amanda said quite truthfully. "Do you think you could help me?"

Callesandra looked up tentatively, her eyes barely making contact. "Oui," she whispered.

It was then, when Callesandra looked up at her, her eyes so earnest, that everything clicked into place. Well, everything except for how Amanda had ended up in this place. As she looked around the room at the ornate furnishings, the old-fashioned dresses, at the fearful maids, she realized the significance of the names Alexander, Rebecca, and Callesandra.

Amanda had been so fascinated when her father first brought her to the rocky British coast estate, she'd researched everything she could about it. She'd found a few ledgers and journals with miscellaneous records. Some familial and some legal in nature. She'd read them over so many times, she'd committed much of the information to memory. The most intriguing story she'd found was of the original owner's great-great-great-grandson, Alexander Montgomery. He'd been born in 1738, titled, and uber wealthy. He'd become a Royal Admiral of the White, whatever that was, and upon returning from his last commission had suffered an arranged marriage in 1767. And suffered, according to the records, was putting it mildly. From what Amanda had found, and unfortunately there wasn't much, his wife was the cruelest of the cruel. Their first child recorded as a girl, Callesandra, and their second, a boy, not named because he'd died during childbirth. The rumor was that Alexander's wife, Rebecca, had killed him, just to spite her husband. That's how utterly vicious this woman was supposed be. There was never any mention of this extension of the family beyond 1774. It was as if they'd vanished, and Amanda had looked. Hard. The occupants of this estate—Alexander, his wife, and their only living daughter—mysteriously had never been written of again.

Amanda shivered involuntarily, and it was only Alexander clearing his throat that brought her back to the present. Or to the past. Or wherever it was, *whenever* it was she was. She turned back to Callesandra—this historically disappeared little girl—and gave her her warmest smile.

"It seems I need a necklace," Amanda explained in a conspiratorial whisper, risking a glance toward Alexander still standing in the doorway. He was watching her carefully. "But I don't really care for any of the ones Alice offered me."

They all looked shocked by her statement. Apparently, Rebecca had loved expensive baubles.

"But, Mama," Callesandra exclaimed. "You love jewelry."

"Jewelry is not something you love, Callesandra," Amanda corrected with a smile. She couldn't help but care for this little girl. She felt like she knew her already, and she kind of did, given how much she'd read about her and her family. "People, you love. I do however *admire* jewelry, but I would prefer something a little understated. May I borrow your necklace, please?"

Callesandra smiled then, not a full smile but the corners of her mouth lifted just a bit. "You wish to wear mine?" she asked, both awed and hesitant.

"I would." Amanda nodded. "May I? Just for tonight. After my performance I promise to return it."

Alexander snorted from the doorway, a derisive look crossing his face when she caught his eye. What was that about? She turned her attention back to Callesandra, who bent her head to let Amanda unfasten the simple silver chain that held a heart-shaped locket. She placed it around her neck and still sitting on the floor looked up again at Callesandra.

"Well, what do you think?" she asked.

"I think you look more beautiful than I have ever seen, Mama," Callesandra whispered.

"May I have one of your hair ribbons too? You can tie it around my wrist."

Callesandra reached back and gently pulled one free. "I can't tie, Mama." She shook her head and bit her lip as if she waited to be reprimanded. Amanda turned her around and sat Callesandra on her lap. They both faced Alexander now.

"I'll teach you," Amanda said, hugging her against her chest. "Just a simple loop," Amanda explained. "Would you like to learn?"

Callesandra nodded and Amanda patiently helped Callesandra tie the ribbon until she got it right. Then she wrapped her hands around Callesandra and hugged her tightly. "You did it!" she praised. "Thank you, Callesandra. I'll return them to you later, I promise."

Alexander came forward then, giving Amanda another curious look. At least she understood it now; her behavior must be terribly strange to him. Based on what she knew, Amanda was nothing like his wife, Rebecca—someone who she apparently looked very much like. Peculiar circumstances aside, her fear of Alexander subsided. Perhaps she could fix this.

"Come, sweet," he said, taking her in his arms. "Papa shall tuck you in."

Amanda watched Callesandra wrap her little arms around Alexander's neck. Then she gifted her a smile as she peeked over her father's shoulder. A real smile. *My God*, the most amazingly sweet smile she'd ever received. Amanda blew her a kiss, then laughed as Callesandra caught it.

Alexander came back a few minutes later, presumably after settling Callesandra into bed.

"I don't know what you were thinking!" he snapped. "But you will *not* play games with Callesandra. She's but a child."

My God, he was furious. And what had she done that was so terrible? Made Callesandra smile? *Ooh, capital offence, Alexander!* At the end of her rope, Amanda snapped back, "I'm not playing games, Alexander! And I would never do so with a child. Any child!"

He snorted in disgust. "Come. You've kept your guests long enough. I know you wish nothing more than to give your *grand performance*."

To be honest—which she was so not doing—Amanda really didn't enjoy grand performances and almost told him so. Instead she kept telling herself to play. *Just play, Amanda, and then it'll all be over. You obviously hit your head harder than you thought and this is just some weird hallucination or dream. Serves you right for being so obsessed with reading about mysterious disappearances!*

But somewhere in the back of her mind, Amanda didn't want it to be over. Toying with Alexander, watching him vacillate between hating her and kissing her, was remarkably entertaining. Okay, if she was being honest, she wanted to at least stick around until he kissed her again.

Oblivious to her thoughts—thank God—Alexander led her into a ballroom. He looked down in surprise as she latched her hand around his forearm. She narrowed her eyes in return, warning him silently and in no uncertain terms that there was no way she was letting go of him. If she'd ever needed an anchor it was definitely now as she stood in the entrance to the ballroom, an enormous high-ceilinged room ablaze in light from exquisite candlelit chandeliers. The woodwork was painted to a high shine, the walls decorated with gold leaf and breathtakingly lush draperies. Tables filled the room, covered with flowers and candelabras, and the dance floor was alive with people as they moved to the music an orchestra played to perfection. French doors lined the back wall, open and leading to the marble veranda she'd seen earlier, couples stepping back and forth between them.

"My God," she whispered under her breath.

"Not what you expected?" Alexander returned, glaring down at her.

Amanda looked up then. She was getting used to that stare of his, that "I'm your superior keeper and you're my inferior subject" look. Irked, she glared back for just a second, then her features softened, and she rubbed his forearm beneath her fingers. It was an unconscious gesture, almost like she was trying to put him at ease instead. She held his gaze and answered him honestly. "It's not at all what I expected, Alexander." *And neither are you.*

He regarded her a moment before the anger returned. Then he cut her to the quick. "Life is seldom what we expect, Rebecca. As you well know." He stared at the spot on his arm where she was still brushing her fingers against him. Then turned his face away and dismissed her. "Go. Have your amusement, Rebecca."

"I don't want to go, Alexander," Amanda whispered, meaning it. She was in no way prepared to play for these people, hallucination or not.

Alexander sighed before turning to her again. "You make no sense tonight, Rebecca. Go," he said again, this time more firmly. "Have your performance. Dance as you love too. Just remove yourself from my arm. Now!"

The orchestra stopped then and feeling as though she had no choice, Amanda released his arm. "Should I play now?" she asked.

"It's what you love most, Rebecca," Alexander said, shaking his head, looking almost like he was repulsed by her. She'd have to work on that. "Play to your heart's content." He made a sweep with his arm in a grand gesture to encompass the room.

Amanda shrugged and headed toward the musicians to his left, paying no attention to the guests as they spoke to her. One person at a time she could handle, but pretending to be the evil Rebecca to dozens? No, she'd rather lose herself in the music. When she reached the pianist, Amanda tapped the man's shoulder, whispering in his ear that she'd like a turn. The pianist bowed as he stood, ceding her the bench. A hush came over the entire crowd and she began to play.

This was more like it. This she could do. Amanda let go as her haunting music filled the room, nearly forgetting where she was. She continued until she could play no more, keeping her eyes closed until the last note had disappeared into silence. When the room erupted into applause, she opened them and looked through the crowd, fixing her gaze upon Alexander. The intensity of his stare gave her chills. The good kind this time.

She stood and walked through the expanse of the ballroom, ignoring every compliment called her way. She looked only at him, holding his eyes until she stood before him.

"My performance is over," she said firmly, quietly, and with a deadly seriousness. "Good night, Alexander." Then she left the room.

Glancing back, she saw him shake himself out of his stupor. Just as he turned and made a move to follow, Amanda hurried forward. She heard him behind her, but he didn't reach her until she entered her room. Grabbing her arm, he twirled her to face him. He studied her closely, shaking his head as his hands gripped her arms.

"Who are you?" he whispered in question and accusation.

Amanda, ready to wake up from this hallucination, decided now was the moment for honesty. It's not like any of this was real, anyway, no matter how real it felt. All of her obsessive reading about the Montgomery estate had apparently manifested in this crazy way in her subconscious after hitting her head. Entirely because that selfish idiot Robert had tried to kill her. And then physically *being* on the estate must have been the reason she'd imagined Alexander saving her life, not once, but twice. Thanks to her penchant for authoritative, powerful men for conjuring this vision of a man. Exquisite, elegant, masculine. Maybe also why being kissed by him may have been the single most enjoyable event of her life. And Callesandra. Amanda had always wanted children, but never found the right person to have them with. Had Callesandra been hers she would have cherished her. Such a sweet girl. It broke her heart that they both had been treated so poorly by Rebecca, that the stories she'd read had been true. For a moment, Amanda felt a strong pull toward this life, wishing it were real, for Alexander to be her husband and Callesandra her beautiful daughter. Wanting to touch him one last time before this was over, Amanda fingered his lapels before flattening her hands against him.

"Tonight, I am your wife, I suppose…and the mother of your daughter. But I have never seen any of you before in my life."

CHAPTER
FIVE

FEBRUARY 21
NORTHERN CALIFORNIA

"All I see, Evan, are flashes of my estate in the British Isles." Amanda shrugged, reluctantly turning back from the sun warming her face. It had been the first moment of real calm in the weeks since she'd returned home. "Callie and I leaving. Sam. Stan." She opened her eyes and looked down. Scratch-like scars marred her ring finger and the top of her left hand. Her wrist was another story. She'd obviously had surgery but couldn't remember any of it. She turned then and saw him as he came through the French doors.

Montgomery. *Mr.* Montgomery.

He stared right at her. Rooted her to the spot, actually. He had that effect on her, unlike any other man she'd ever known—or could remember knowing, at least. With barely a nod to Evan, he walked over to her and looked into her eyes. Deeply, penetratingly. This level of scrutiny was a bit uncomfortable, but she liked the seriousness in which he watched over her and her family. She'd never experienced anything like it in all her years of fame and stardom, any of the years she'd needed to hire protection, yet something about it felt right. She couldn't explain it and honestly wasn't sure she wanted to. Amanda chalked it up to a karmic tie because nothing else could explain the deep sense of connection she felt with him. For what could have been the hundredth time now, as she was obviously counting, she knew what he asked without him saying it aloud.

"I'm okay," she said, answering his unspoken question. His eyes softened. "It's nice to be outside." She crinkled her nose. "Even with you know who"—Amanda motioned with her head toward Evan, who was sitting at the large table on the terrace—"as my constant shadow."

"It's necessary." He reached out to inspect each of her wrists, his fingers skimming the discoloration, which had lightened to a pale yellow. Then his large hand wrapped around her shoulder and gently squeezed. "Would you care for a reprieve?"

"Oh, yes," she returned, rather animatedly. "Please."

"Come." He led her back inside, nodding to her in-house psychiatrist as they passed him.

"We'll speak later, Amanda," Dr. Childress called after them.

"Of course we will, Evan," she answered back.

Helen was reading quietly on the sofa in the large sitting room adjacent to the kitchen. A Moses basket lay atop the large coffee table in front of her, with Zander sleeping inside. Amanda and Mr. Montgomery reached for the baby at the same time. His long arms beat her to it, but after a quick press of his lips to Zander's crown, he placed her baby in her arms. Nestling him perfectly in the crook of her neck and at the proper angle for her to wrap her arm about him. Amanda turned to check the time where an oversized clock hung above the fireplace.

"O-seven hundred."

Amanda grinned. "Thank you, Admiral." She watched him pour a large mug of coffee, then look over his shoulder at her and raise an eyebrow, gesturing with the mug. At her "Duh," he chuckled and brought it to her.

Callie came padding into the kitchen then, her favorite stuffed doggy in hand and blanket trailing behind her. "Morning, Mama...morning, Admiral." Mr. Montgomery picked her up, his lips brushing her forehead. Callie settled her face on his shoulder and added two fingers to her mouth as her eyes closed.

It was the sweetest picture. If Amanda had a penny for each tender moment her house seemed to be filled with of late, she'd be a very wealthy woman. Not that she wasn't already, she thought, laughing a bit to herself. Her thoughts were interrupted when Sam came in next.

"Morning," she said, and Mr. Montgomery poured another cup of coffee, added some half-and-half, and held it out as she passed him. "Thanks, Alex." Sam took a seat in one of the kitchen's two large overstuffed chairs.

Stephen, finished his morning run on the beach, came in through the French doors and took the coffee his brother held out for him. "Hi, monkey," he said to Callie, who opened her eyes and smiled.

Rosa bustled in then and got busy making a fresh pot of coffee and breakfast.

"Well, now that the gang's all here," Amanda said, smiling brightly.

"Did someone say gang?" Stan made a dramatic entrance from the terrace, doing his best TV cop impression. Callie giggled, which was the whole point, and he reached out and tweaked her nose. "I'm out for the next eight," he said to Stephen. "Want me to wait 'til you're showered?"

Stephen peered through the window where two more of their guys were stationed out back. Amanda had seen them earlier. Her estate had become a veritable fortress since the brothers Montgomery took over. Not that she hadn't felt safe when it was just Stan in charge. She had. She equated the uptick in security these last few weeks quite frankly to Mr. Montgomery. He was, after all, the owner of a company worth hundreds of millions of dollars. She could only imagine what his net worth must be. Of course, the man who offered protection, and the best at that, needed to be protected too.

Stephen shook his head. "We're good. See you tonight." He held the door open and they all moved back out to the terrace, giving Rosa room to get breakfast together.

Sam lay down on a chaise and pulled up the throw at the end. It was still a bit chilly, and windier than normal. "Did you see the invite, Ammy?"

Amanda knew she was referring to the Night of the Stars charity event. Art Fisher had founded and chaired the gala for over ten years now, honoring and raising money for retired military personnel, wounded warriors and their families, as well as those who lost someone in service. She'd often performed in the past. This year, however, Amanda was supposed to help with the festivities. Her name wasn't listed just in case she wasn't ready to come out of hiding, but Art had been hoping that after the baby was born, she'd start to take her place once again in society. "It seemed like a good idea at the time," Amanda breathed on a sigh. "Didn't it?"

Sam chuckled, "Yeah, at the time it did."

Mr. Montgomery leaned against the railing as the sun rose behind him. It was quite the picture. Jeans or trousers, a button-down or a T-shirt, the man may as well be perennially stepping off the cover of *GQ*. "Night of the Stars? I actually have a table for the event," he told her. Then he smiled and shook his head, his thick dark hair rustling in the wind. "Art made me sign a contract that I would continue to be the benefactor and cochair moving forward, until, of course, he decides to retire. At which point, I'll likely be the official chair." His phone rang, then and after taking the call he said, "Seems I'm heading to the office early."

Amanda frowned, a bit sad that he was leaving already. She watched as he knelt by Callie, who was now resting on the chaise with Sam. He'd taken to dropping her off at school on his ride into town most mornings. Amanda couldn't say it bothered her—she absolutely hated the chaos of school drop-off—and besides, her daughter couldn't be in better hands. Callie smiled brightly at something Alex said to her, not that Amanda knew what since they often spoke in another frigging language. Though, it actually *was* quite comical. Her giggles subsided, and he lay his large hand atop Callie's head a long moment before coming her way.

"Grab something to eat on the way out," Amanda said as he stopped to look down at her and gently squeeze her shoulder. He didn't move and continued to stare. She finally rolled her eyes and smiled again, "I'm fine. Really." He smiled back, nodded, and went back inside. Stephen walked him out and before she knew it, they were having breakfast and getting Callie ready for school. Then the day passed in a whirlwind.

While Callie was at school, Amanda went down to her dance studio. It was just in the lower level of the house, but it was the first time in the weeks since she'd been home that she'd done something like this. Turning on some music, she smiled as One Republic's "Secrets" started playing. She hit the auto-repeat button and lost herself in the music for close to an hour, wondering just what her secrets were and when she would remember them.

Later that afternoon, Amanda drove with Stephen to pick up Callie from school, elated to resume some semblance of her routine. Evan's constant assurance to pick up where she'd left off and continue to let nature take its course helped. They ribbed one another, but she really did like him and knew he wanted only what was best for her. Callie was so happy to see her when her class came outside, she ran the entire way to the car, where Stephen lifted her inside and buckled her in. Amanda wasn't sure how the name Stephen translated to "Aboon" with Callie's speech impediment, but it was really cute all the same.

"Can we go swimming after I finish my homework?" Callie asked.

"Of course, sweetie." Amanda cupped the side of her face. "Now, tell me what you learned today."

A few hours later, they did just that. Sam joined them, of course, but so did Stephen, and then when Stan came on shift again, and Callie asked him to come in, he didn't resist. It was a veritable late-afternoon pool party. There was only one person missing. Al—Mr. Montgomery, she self-corrected. Lately, he'd been the one to pick Callie up from school, always just so happening to be on his way back around that time. Callie, Amanda knew, loved it. She had a beaming smile each time he lifted her down from the truck just before she'd run to tell Amanda all about her day. Then Mr. Montgomery and his brother would adjourn to the living room, kitchen, or terrace to discuss work before they all had dinner together.

Amanda thought back to one of the first times she'd come upon him after he and Stephen had finished one of their afternoon meetings. She'd just come downstairs to find him sitting at the bar, and found she liked that he was so comfortable at her house. Jeez, there were times when she thought he was *more* comfortable in her home than she was. And again, she'd noted how much she was drawn to him—it was more than just that he was incredibly handsome, but she didn't know what. Yet. She'd watched him then for a moment before he sensed her standing there. He always caught her when she was looking.

"Rough day at work?" she'd asked casually in an attempt to hide her embarrassment.

He'd smiled and fingered the files in front of him. "It's not the work. It's the contracts I seem to have a problem with."

He'd rubbed his eyes and motioned to the stool next to him in invitation. She'd needed no further prodding, happy for his company, and took a look at the documents. She flipped through the first of what had to be twelve three-inch-thick document bundles.

"Alex," she'd ventured, only the second time she'd called him by his first name, "you have a whole staff of attorneys."

"I do. But Chris advised me that Montgomery Enterprises should be our parent company and Calder Defense one of our holdings," he'd said wearily.

That he shared something so significant made her feel a part of it too. Which really was how being under the protection of the brothers Montgomery made her feel anyway.

"And you're reading these," she'd said, holding one up to clarify, "from cover to cover?"

"It's our family business, Amanda. Are you telling me that's *not* what I'm supposed to do?"

"I realize you're British," she said, patting his hand as she used his heritage as a silly explanation of his behavior, "but do you have a law degree?"

"No."

"Look," she'd said, leveling with him. "Anytime I have to sign a legal document, my attorney explains what

I'm signing. Informs me if any changes were made to the original contract, and if so, what they were. Then I sign it. That's why I hire an attorney. They're liable."

"Shouldn't I know exactly what I'm signing my name to?"

"Well, yeah, but that's why you have Chris and a staff of attorneys. I have to tell you, what's written in twelve lengthy paragraphs, they can sum up in a sentence or two."

"You're remarkably smart," he'd said, which had made her blush.

"You always surprise me," she'd said, feeling suddenly self-conscious as his fingers had skimmed the side of her face to move an errant wisp of hair behind her ear.

"How?" he'd asked, his voice quiet, fingers still in her hair.

She'd caught herself a moment too late leaning into the touch. She'd been so comfortable with him in that moment that she'd answered his question honestly. "I expect you to be arrogant. You're so not."

Zander's cry jarred her from her thoughts and Amanda excused herself from the pool party to take him upstairs for an early evening feeding. While he rested, she showered and changed, eager to rejoin everyone for dinner. She smiled as they started back outside, hearing voices, one in particular. She had to admit, she was becoming more than fascinated with the man. Odd that it happened to be another Alexander Montgomery who held her interest.

⟨⟨ ⟩⟩

"I smell meat," Amanda announced as she walked out onto the stone patio, closed her eyes, and inhaled deeply. "Mmm."

Alexander smiled at the display. She was wearing one of her favorite cashmere lounge pants and hoodie sets. Her hair was pulled back, her face freshly scrubbed, and she was barefoot. Helen was on her heels, Zander in her arms. It had been three weeks since he'd brought her home. Between her memory loss, exhaustion, and the rigors of their very demanding son, she seemed to acquiesce to the new order of things without much of a fight.

Just as he'd hoped, she'd accepted his presence easily given that Stephen was assigned as her full-time security detail. Amanda assumed Alexander came over early to go over schedules and paperwork with his brother. By the time Amanda realized he'd been taking Callie to school each morning on his way to the office a week had already passed. He'd started to explain he was just as capable as Stan or Stephen, when she'd actually stopped him midsentence, stood right in front of him, and said, "You travel with fifteen men, a five-truck convoy, you're all armed, and you"—she'd reached out and touched his arm—"I trust you, Alex." He knew she'd been about to say "And you brought me home," but "I trust you, Alex" was better and also the first time she had called him by his name. Most afternoons—at least until today when Amanda resumed fetching their daughter from school—he'd timed his return to pick Callie up on the way home as well. Then a couple hours later he'd come back for dinner. Amanda liked how close he and Stephen were. She actually encouraged him to come and stay. It was brilliant.

"What's for dinner?" Amanda asked.

He rolled his eyes at her. "Really?" If he was grilling, it was steak and she knew it. Thank God she'd slept through his first attempt a few days after he'd brought her home. He'd nearly lost his hair and blew up the house. Callie thought it was hysterical. Michael and Trevor too. Despite their training and understanding of present-day life and gadgets, there were obviously still some intricacies they had yet to learn.

Amanda smiled at his sarcasm then sat down on the sofa overlooking the pool deck. She held her hands out for Zander. "Hi, baby. Mama's here." Helen fussed with the pillows behind her and pushed her down so she was reclining. "Seriously, Helen?" Her nurse only smirked, loving her job—one, Alexander had to admit, she excelled at. He had to keep from laughing when she actually told him so in French, then Stephen joined in their conversation.

Alexander watched as Sam and Callie walked back from the pool and headed toward Amanda on the sofa. Callie ran over, gave her a kiss, and placed a big wet one on her brother before skipping over to Alexander and latching on to his thigh. Out of the corner of his eye, Alexander saw Amanda notice and smile to herself.

Sam gave Amanda a look as she grabbed a drink from the cart. "They are so rude."

"Tell me about it."

Probably to show how annoyed she was to be left out of the conversation *en français*, Amanda took that moment to turn up her music—loud. Alexander bristled. "If I Die Young," by, if he remembered correctly, The Band

Perry. Beautiful music but he hated the lyrics. His wife's love of music had spurred his own, and a soundtrack of her favorite artists always played in his mind now. One of the first things he'd done in the twenty-first century (after figuring out what a computer even was, let alone how to turn it on and download music) was seek out all the artists he'd remembered her telling him about as they sat by the fire, or that she'd played for him on the piano. He nudged Callie, who was still barnacled to his leg, and motioned with his head. She grinned and skipped over to her mother. Amanda snaked an arm around her as Callie bent to kiss her and snatch her phone at the same time.

"Callesandra Eleanor!" Amanda undoubtedly knew what she was up to, and knew he put her up to it. She faked being angry for a moment before dissolving into laughter. Alexander loved seeing her so happy, so lighthearted. It was like they were a whole family again. Well, almost. He had to admit, life was better here—*now*—in this time. There was a freedom, a difference on every level of what could be. Simplicity of their former life aside, there was this inexplicable sense of ease. Which may seem ridiculous considering he now ran a multimillion-dollar conglomerate. But where his family was concerned, they were beginning to display a carefree-ness that he'd not experienced before, even when Amanda became his wife in the past. And it was nothing like the grim notion of family he'd been brought up with. Callie trotted over and brought the phone back to him. Rosa came and grabbed the platter of steaks he finished grilling. As Amanda watched him, he winked at Callie and hit the song he wanted to play. "Anytime" by Journey. Amanda snorted. Loud. Alexander laughed, picked up Callie, and danced her back over to her mother.

"How can you be cross with such an adorable child?"

"Oh, she knows," Amanda teased. "I'd run if I were you, Callie. You know Mama means business when you break the rules."

"I think her *mama's* the rule breaker," he muttered in response.

"Oh, tomato...tomahto..." Amanda said with a casual wave of her hand.

"Is that your answer for everything?"

"Listen, Mr. I-Know-What's-Best-for-You-and-Your-Family...I have a very sound parenting plan."

Alexander knew the look on his face conveyed just how ridiculous he found that statement. "Just so we're clear, sweetheart—you think chasing your daughter and tickling her until she cries mercy is a brilliant discipline technique?"

Amanda grinned, obviously ignoring his sarcasm. "Of course."

"Bloody hell."

Callie yelled for the swear jar as he put her down. He chased her and tickled her 'til she cried mercy, then nudged her toward the supper table.

"See?" Amanda told him.

He grinned in response and approached her to pluck Zander off her chest so he could help her up. She stepped on his foot and thumped right into him. Brilliant. He wrapped his free arm around her. Pulled her in tight to steady her. "Alright?" he asked.

Amanda nodded, gripping his shirt for balance, but didn't attempt to move. Her head tilted ever so slightly as her eyes closed and she inhaled deeply. The gesture seemed reflexive on her part. A deep primitive instinct triggered by having your mate in your arms. He felt exactly the same. She remained completely still, making him wonder if there was something there—some memory, perhaps? Bloody hell. His nostrils flared as his body responded to her. She smelled amazing. It felt so good to have her pressed up against him. He was loath to remove his arms from around her back.

"Are we going to eat, Montgomery?" she said after another moment, finally looking up at him from beneath her lashes.

He smiled. "Yeah, Marceau, there's a porterhouse with your name on it." He nudged her toward the table, thinking that maybe it really was better for now to not say anything. He could feel the connection between them; it was alive and strong. Option two, most definitely. Still, he worried that if she found out in the wrong way, this game they were playing could blow up in their faces.

CHAPTER
SIX

Early the next morning, earlier than she'd risen in ages, Amanda took the stairs carefully, smiling as she held the railing with one hand and Zander in her other. She felt like a little girl at Christmas. Seriously. She had a house full of people now and it made her kind of giddy. She loved having everyone around, and they were around, like literally all the time.

It was still well before dawn, but she was getting tired of everyone doing so much for her, treating her like a fragile china doll. Not that she wasn't grateful for their help, but she needed to be more in charge. Of her own life. Of everything. The oddest thing she'd felt lately was that even with her memory loss, something inside her still felt whole. She couldn't explain it, and she'd tried.

In the kitchen, Amanda hit the brew button on the coffeemaker and sat with Zander on the sofa. As soon as she heard the machine sputter, she laid Zander in the bassinet and went for her first glorious cup of joe.

◁◁ ▷▷

"Where's Helen?"

Alexander watched Amanda finish pouring coffee, then reach for another mug. She turned with a conspiratorial grin. "I snuck away."

Bloody hell, she was adorable. Alexander took the coffee Amanda held out for him. He meant to chastise her for being up and about with no help, like she should forever more be wrapped in cotton and protected, but her smile disarmed him. That and the fact that she was wearing pajama shorts and her beautiful long legs and prime rear end had been the first thing he'd seen when he walked in. Instead he took a large sip, placed the mug back on the counter, and asked her why she was up so early. It was barely five. She'd already brushed out her hair and put it up. She looked fresh faced and ridiculously gorgeous.

"I guess I'm starting to feel better," Amanda told him. "My head's clearer. I feel rested." She shrugged. "And really, between Helen, Rosa, Sam, not to mention Stephen, Stan, and *you* there really isn't much for me to do. It felt so good to wake up before everyone today, tend to Zander by myself, watch Callie sleep. Jeez, I even brushed my teeth and hair all without anyone standing over me like I'm going to break. Mentally or physically."

Aside from the security detail outside, the house was still quiet and empty this early. It would be at least another thirty or so minutes before they'd have company.

"I got to come downstairs with Zander and start the coffee all by myself." She grinned again. "The coffeemaker had just sputtered to a stop when I put him down in the bassinet. Are *you* usually here this early?"

She knew he came over every morning to visit with his brother, but normally she wouldn't have seen them until later. He and Stephen usually talked business quietly between themselves. "I am," Alexander answered. He wouldn't miss checking on his family each morning for anything. Besides it being a luxury he'd lived without for so long, it seemed a necessity to his well-being. Taking over the estate next door made it terribly easy. "Would you like to go outside?" he asked. "It's warm enough already."

Amanda nodded. "I'll grab the mugs."

"I'll get the boy."

He lifted Zander from his bassinet and settled him against his chest. As he started for the French doors, Amanda stopped him. "Wait." He turned around. "Are you hungry?" she asked.

Alexander smiled down at her, shook his head, and told her that breakfast was in an hour, just like every day. He turned toward the doors again then almost knocked her over when he turned back to ask if *she* was hungry. He quickly reached out to steady her, but the only thing he could do with Zander in his arms was grasp her shirt. The material twisted in his hand, so he brought her closer and waited until she found solid purchase. This seemed to be happening often lately, and he couldn't say he was upset about it.

She stared at him, still holding their mugs steady, her head tilting slightly to the side. He waited, hoping perhaps she was remembering something. She looked at him so closely. *Come on, sweetheart, you've got this, I love you, you're my wife, we have two beautiful children, and I crossed centuries to be with you.* She finally shook her head, as if to clear it.

"Am I what?" she asked.

He smiled down at her. It took him a moment to remember just what it was he had asked her. "Hungry?"

"Why? You gonna cook me breakfast?" she teased.

His hand still fisted in her shirt, he brought her in a bit closer, and got right in her beautiful face. "I would hunt—kill—skin, clean, and cook for you."

"Bloody hell, Montgomery, why have we been going to the grocery store?" she whispered.

"You haven't answered my question, sweetheart."

Her eyes widened and she blushed adorably. "What did you ask me?"

"Are you hungry?" he reminded her.

She shook her head. "Coffee's good for now." This time she motioned for the French doors that led to the terrace.

They settled on the sofa. Alexander took up a considerable amount of space at one end, stretched out his legs, and adjusted Zander. Amanda leaned back against the cushions on the other and pushed her feet beneath the cushion next to him.

"So, *Mr.* Montgomery. How did you end up in the security business?"

Because I couldn't find you. "Military background. Like most."

"Great Britain?"

"Yeah."

"Do you miss it?"

"Great Britain?"

Amanda laughed. "Yeah, Great Britain."

He shook his head. "No, Amanda. I don't." Bloody hell, he never wanted to set foot on British soil again.

"I don't know why, but it scares me."

She'd said that so quietly. He tilted his head as he looked at her. "Britain?" he asked, to clarify.

"Yeah, Britain."

"How?" Because he absolutely knew why.

"You'll think I'm crazy…but…I feel like I left the biggest piece of me there. I mean we used to go all the time, but for some reason now…I feel like I…I…despise it."

"Not crazy, sweetheart."

Evan walked outside. "Well, good morning. I see we're all up before the rooster crows."

"Morning, Evan," Amanda told him brightly. Then she whispered she was going to tell Evan that she was going to shave her head and join the circus.

Alexander chuckled as he looked at the face of his watch, then said, "Why don't I give you some time together? It's still well before breakfast." He stood and reached for

Zander then made his way back inside. He turned after he'd closed the terrace door, watching as his wife closed her eyes and began her session with Evan.

◁◁ ▷▷

Amanda smiled as she walked outside, marveling again at just how content she felt, despite all that had befallen her. After another large family dinner alfresco earlier this evening, she'd found Callie standing on top of the stones by the fountain, singing as she hopped from one large boulder to the next, all the adults serving as her audience. Stephen and Sam were laughing as she belted out A Great Big World's "Rockstar." Alex was leaning against the balustrade, sipping a scotch. She noticed he liked the Macallan she had in endless supply behind the bar. It suited him. The sun was just starting to set, and she'd just approached the balustrade when Alex reached his long arm out and touched her. She stopped by his side, seeing he had a perfect view of Callie, still singing but now jumping to the ledge of the fountain.

"I was thinking of taking a walk on the beach. Game?" she asked.

"Undoubtedly." He reached out and fixed her hood. She wasn't sure it needed fixing, but the man had a penchant for physical contact. He had uber large hands that were actually very gentle. Each time she stood in front of him lately, she'd noticed that he touched her. Brushed her hair back, fixed her collar, steadied her. "Is something bothering you?" he asked.

He was also perceptive. She didn't want to say what was bothering her. Because what was bothering her was that she really enjoyed his company. She liked having him around. Yes, she liked having everyone around, but him most of all. The worry, however, that had been slowly creeping through her thoughts, more so that evening, was that despite her feelings of contentedness at the moment, she worried it may end.

She'd talked to Evan about it. Like, how did she maintain this feeling of security when the last person she had a relationship or whatever with obviously left? When she didn't even know if she could trust her own goddamned *brain* not to erase all her memories?

Beside her, Alex took another pull of scotch and offered it to her. She accepted the glass from his hand, considering its contents. "I think..." She tilted her head to the side, while he waited quietly. When nothing came to mind, she shrugged and took a small sip of the amber liquid. "I have four cases of the stuff and have no idea why."

He smiled, nudged the glass, and called out to the others below that they were going to go down to the beach. Amanda took another sip of the scotch while Stephen grabbed a couple blankets from inside the ottoman and signaled to Michael they were all heading down.

Callie went ahead with Sam and Stephen while she and Alex followed at a slower pace, winding their way down the stairs toward the path. Dusk was well upon them, making it difficult to see pebbles and rough spots. She lost her footing at one point and Alex grasped her hand to hold her steady. Maybe it was the scotch talking, or just her own daring, but she latched her other hand through the belt loop of his jeans for support. After a second stumble, he stopped and knelt. "Up, sweetheart." Gladly, she climbed on his back, wrapped her arms around his neck, and laid her chin on his shoulder as he carried her the rest of the way down.

Sam, Stephen, and Callie were still walking, but had left the blankets out not far from the path. Alex pulled a flask out of his back pocket and grinned. She laughed as he opened it, took a sip, and held it out in front of her. "Amanda," Alex said once they'd arrived and he'd set her down on the beach. She waited for him to say more, but he just shook his head and gave her another of his deep, penetrating looks.

"Can you see that cluster of stars?" she asked after another long moment, pointing toward the sky.

"I can."

"I can't remember what it's called. It's right on the tip of my tongue but I just can't retrieve it." Which itself was really weird because Amanda didn't think she'd ever been into constellations before. And it wasn't like she was looking at the Big Dipper.

"Canis Major," he said, knowing the answer right away.

Oh my god, he was right. "And that one?" she asked.

"Camelopardalis."

He continued to name each one she pointed to, and when he stretched his arm and started naming even more constellations and stars, she had the most incredible feeling of déjà vu. His knowledge of astronomy was impressive. There was also something about the cadence of his voice that calmed her and made her feel safe. Who was she kidding, *he* made her feel safe. She loved listening to him. No matter what language he spoke. That, and his ridiculous British accent.

"How do you know so many?" she whispered.

"It was part of my studies," he told her.

"What else did you study?"

"Astronomy covered a lot," he laughed. "Physical science, mathematical law, philosophy. Latin."

"You know Latin?" Amanda said, incredulous.

He chuckled. "Yeah."

"And then why astronomy?"

"I had to learn how to look up to the sky and know where I was. How the cycles of the moon would affect the tides."

"Oh, of course—ships," she said, smacking her palm to her forehead. Duh, he was an admiral. "Did you ever get caught in storms?"

"Often," he said, chuckling at her gesture.

"Were you scared?"

"I didn't have time to be. I had men depending on my knowledge and instincts to get them to port or safely home."

She nodded. "Determined."

"What about it?"

"It describes you perfectly."

"I'm human, Amanda. I've had my moments."

She laughed then. "I'm not so sure about that. Are you sure you're not a superhero in disguise?"

He sighed. "Superheroes don't always win, sweetheart."

She shook her head. Vehemently. "They do, Alex. They might struggle and even seem to lose ground, but they always win. In the end, they always win."

CHAPTER
SEVEN

FEBRUARY 28
NORTHERN CALIFORNIA

"Did you see Papa?" Callesandra asked sleepily when Amanda checked on her shortly after midnight. So stunned by Callie's innocent question, Amanda pivoted her head as if she'd been struck. *Papa?* "Who, Callie?" Amanda asked to be sure she'd heard correctly.

Callie rolled over as she whispered, "The admiral, Mama."

Alex? What had given Callie that idea, that *he* was her father? She supposed he had been around a lot, like all the time—and had been very affectionate with her daughter—but she'd never heard her call him "Papa" before. Poor thing, all of this must be so hard on her, too, her own mother barely remembering things. It's no wonder that she'd cling to him. Didn't she herself admit she'd latched on to him too?

Amanda sat down on the edge of Callie's bed, her daughter still looking at her with her bright, earnest eyes. Eyes that Amanda had always loved, though she could never see herself in them. Suddenly, Amanda froze. *Those eyes.* Surely, they couldn't be…no. Could they? Amanda let herself consider just for a moment—for a crazy, in-no-way-is-this-possible moment—that Callie *wasn't* mistaken. That Mr. Mont—Alex was her father, her real one.

She rewound as far back as she could. The hospital. He'd written a check for her release, AMA, against medical advice. The way he'd touched her wrists, the reverent sweep of his thumbs as he brushed over her bruises, once he'd removed the restraints before his large hands clutched her. In the moment, she'd been so woozy she'd barely noticed, but now she could almost *feel* the caress and possessiveness of his grip as she pictured it. How he'd almost ripped the manacles from the bedrails that secured her ankles. *Bloody hell, sweetheart,* he'd said. *I'm taking you home, Amanda.* The way he'd held her in the truck on the ride back. Sure, she'd been under the influence of drugs and traumatized and exhausted, but he'd held her. On his lap. In his arms. She vaguely recalled now burrowing into his neck. Why had she done that? He'd rocked her. And she'd felt safe. Really safe. When she'd awoken at home that night, he'd been there, at her bedside. Holding Zander. Jesus, her son looked like him, too, same coloring, same hair. No wonder Alex was so easily affectionate with Callie and Zander. And no wonder Callie was so comfortable with him. Could it really be true? From the moment Amanda remembered meeting him, Callie had always called him Admir—then her mind whirled again as an image, barely a second's worth, of Alex on the cliffs of Abersoch, windblown and reaching for her flashed through her mind—

"Mama? Did you?" Callie said again, jarring Amanda from her swirling thoughts. She pasted on a smile and brushed the hair from Callie's face before kissing her brow. Yes, she had his eyes, Amanda realized again. How had she missed that before? Callie had an uncanny resemblance to her, people had always remarked on it, but the similarities stopped at her eyes. Looking at her now, something else crystallized in Amanda's mind, causing her heart to break just a little bit. Callie was not her biological daughter. Out of nowhere, she realized that was true. And yet she loved her like she was. It seemed crazy—Amanda had seen Callie's birth certificate, her passport—but deep down Amanda knew Callie was not technically hers, sure as she knew anything else. In fact, six years ago was when she'd won her first Grammy. She could remember the awards circuit from then clearly. And she'd been dating someone who turned out to be a real jerk. She'd let herself forget all of that, but there was no denying it. Jesus, Callie even had that similar strange cadence to her speech that Alex had. How had she been so blind?

"I did, sweetie," Amanda said, turning to Callie, keeping her voice light. "He just left." She tucked the covers more tightly about her and kissed her precious little face again, realizing just how much she loved this child, *his child.* "I'll see you in the morning, baby."

As she leaned against the back of Callie's bedroom door, reeling from too many thoughts and emotions to count, what she couldn't fathom was why they hadn't told her. None of them. *Why?* She'd seen movies and read novels where characters had amnesia, but not one had a scenario that included keeping that person in the dark. Unless they were trying to gaslight them. Or worse. Was something nefarious happening? She shivered, terrified for a moment. What else were they not telling her?

Callie's innocent question spurred Amanda's next move. In fact, a series of moves that would forever change her life as she'd known it—or at least as she thought she'd known it. Cue the gears moving in her head. Not a firm landing yet, or anything close, just another piece of the puzzle that belonged on the board but was still set to the side.

Two hours later—after Amanda had torn the house apart looking for evidence of Alex before he'd taken her from the hospital, or any kind of relationship she might have had with him—Amanda picked up her phone and dialed, tapping her foot, frustrated and still thinking of more places to look even as the phone rang. There had been no evidence. Nothing made sense. Nothing explained why no one, Sam especially, told her Alexander frigging Montgomery was the *father* of her children. Or, if this ridiculous but increasingly plausible idea was the truth, then why there were no pictures of him or them together anywhere, even in a drawer or an album? She'd checked. Everywhere. No pictures, no love letters, cards, mementos, an old T-shirt of his in her closet buried under her things. Nothing online, nothing in the house. Nothing at all.

"Derek?" she said when her longtime private jet pilot finally answered.

"Amanda?" Captain Morgan said, obviously surprised to hear from her at two in the morning.

"Are you in town?"

"I am."

"I need to go to Chicago. I'd like to leave as soon as possible."

She heard fumbling in the background. "I'll call the guys and have her ready by four. Good?" he said, and Amanda breathed a thankful sigh of relief. Captain Morgan—always reliable.

"Perfect. Thanks, Derek." It would take an hour to get to the small private airport where they kept her G5 anyway.

She had one more call to make. She knew it would break the new current protocol, but at the moment she didn't really care. She needed to take control, and this seemed like the right move. The only right move. Stan's voice was clear as a bell when he picked up. "You okay?"

"I need you to pick me up."

"Amanda?"

"I need to get out of here, Stan. Please."

"I have to tell him," he said. Stan had been with her longer than he'd been with Montgomery, so Amanda knew that if she pressed, he'd be loyal to her, though it would pain him. Stan loved rules.

"No," she said firmly. "You don't. In fact, when we get out of here, you need to tell *me*. I still don't know what's going on, but I'd bet my last dollar that you do."

"Amanda, I have to let Alex know—he's my boss."

"I'm taking the kids and Rosa regardless. If you don't come, I'll go alone." She hung up the phone and glanced at the clock again—2:07. She knew Stan well enough to know he'd be here by the time she was ready. He'd never let her leave alone, too worried for her safety. In this house of cards, Stan was the only person she still trusted, and even that with caveats considering the circumstances.

Why hadn't anyone shared the truth with her? The question had run across a marquee in her head all night. They'd taken advantage of her good nature. It made her mad. And made her feel like a frigging idiot. She'd begun to bond with him. Jeez, they...*she'd* felt like they were becoming friends. Friends who liked to be with each other. A lot. Who gave each other longing glances—don't think she hadn't noticed. What, was she deemed too delicate to handle the truth? Well, screw that. She refused to be the Amanda who needed to be treated with kid gloves. Bring it on, people. Now she'd take the upper hand. She was taking charge.

Filled with renewed determination, Amanda grabbed a weekender and started packing, not sure how long she'd be gone, but knowing that staying *here* right now was not an option. God, she'd been stupid. It seemed so obvious now. The way he always looked at her, so deeply and so seriously. The way he always touched her when she was in front of him, brushed her hair back, fixed her hood, or checked her bruises. The way he spoke to her, and, she hated to admit, how his voice made her feel. And what security company's CEO was around *that* much, took *that* much personal interest in their clients, no matter how famous they were or how much they were worth? Amanda thought about how he always seemed to take cues from

Evan before broaching a subject. Like he was asking Evan's permission for it. Permission about how much she could handle. Of the truth. That made her angrier. She could handle anything, she thought, just give her a frigging chance. And Sam! That was the betrayal that hurt the worst. Why on earth couldn't her friend, her *best* frigging friend, give her a clue? The next time she called her that cutesy name, Ammy, she might just slap her.

Over feeling like a victim while waiting for her memory to return, Amanda marched past Sam's room, her anger turned to fury that she'd kept something this monumental from her. Fifteen minutes later, she had Callie and Zander packed. It was only a three-and half-hour flight, so whatever essentials she didn't have for the baby she'd send for. Amanda was smart enough to wait in the foyer, avoiding the men who were stationed outside.

Stan circled the drive at 2:37, behind the wheel of one of Montgomery's rotating fleet of Navigators. Stan must have said something to placate the men stationed out front since other than a cursory nod from the guards, they were left alone. Amanda carried a sleepy Callie and Rosa held Zander while Stan transferred their bags, then helped them get settled. Not wanting to further upset the applecart with the children and Rosa in the car, Amanda remained silent. It wasn't easy; she had a million questions swirling through her head.

By the time they pulled up next to the plane, Captain Morgan had the jet ready. Amanda settled the kids in back. Callie safely strapped to the sofa, Zander in his car seat next to Rosa. Amanda took her usual seat, always port side.

Her father had taught her years ago that it moved the least. Stan took the seat across the aisle from her. Lift-off was but moments later. She thought of Callie's sweet, innocent question about seeing her papa as the lights faded from below. Jesus, Alexander Montgomery. The father of her children. Where had they met? *When* had they met? How long had she known him before—seriously! It didn't feel like she'd lost that much of her memory, but here she was, missing an entire relationship. She looked at the scars on her left hand, but she couldn't remember how they'd gotten there. She was traditional in some regards, always had been, so she would never have had Zander without being married. But she couldn't remember any of it. She racked her brain for those lost memories, and her mind settled upon Callie's first day of school. She'd never forget it because that was the first morning her jeans hadn't fit since she'd gotten pregnant with Zander, and it wasn't like she could have arrived pants-less. Thank god for mommy blogs and the genius behind the rubber band trick for buttoning up your jeans. She remembered how cute Callie had looked in her litt—wait. Something else. Amanda remembered being so sad that day. Sad that he couldn't see it. Alex. Actually, she'd been more than sad, she'd been distraught. She'd hated that he wasn't there, but why? Had he been working for his government? Off on some secret mission? Had they just broken up and he went one way and she the other? Why would he have left Callie with her, especially when it was clear how he cared for her?

It took about twenty minutes for Rosa to fall asleep. Amanda had been waiting for this moment, wanting to question Stan. He must have been waiting, too, because not more than thirty seconds later, he crossed the meager aisle and took the seat facing her.

"Why didn't you tell me?" she asked before he had a chance to speak.

"I work for him now."

"That hurts."

"I know. Me too."

"Tell me what in the hell is going on, Stan? Can I trust you? Am I safe? Is he after the children?"

"Whoa, whoa, whoa. Amanda, all of this"—he made a circular motion with his hands—"is because of what happened in the hospital. Alex wanted to come clean. I wanted to come clean. But Evan has told us repeatedly that your memory is going to return, but until it does, it would be more harmful to overwhelm you. It's jacked-up complicated and I may in fact lose my job for taking you to Chicago, but you know there isn't anything I wouldn't do for you, or your family. Ever." Stan folded down the small airplane table between them and set his laptop on it. "The files are right here," he said as he clicked on an icon. "I took you underground, Amanda, last year when we moved from New York to California. The press was too much at the time, and with Callie and the baby on the way, it was just easier all around. On all of us. For a lot of reasons. Anything you read here has been wiped from the internet. Our team under Art and now Alex handles the daily sweeps. It's only the bones, Amanda. I really need to talk with Evan about the rest, if that's okay with you."

"For now, you can keep the color commentary to yourself."

Her eyes hurt from exhaustion and studying the screen so intently. Clippings from newspapers and tabloids with headlines that read things like "Amanda Marceau, Famous Songwriter, Heiress to the Marceau Fortune, Mysteriously Disappears," all dated from a little over a year ago. One article went into the specifics of where she was last seen. Apparently, it hadn't been known if it was in the States or abroad. Almost as strangely, Amanda read that her stepbrother, Robert, their usual family spokesperson, also couldn't be located for comment. Another article announced her return, which had apparently been just as mysterious. "She's Back! Amanda Marceau in the Flesh." Amanda shivered. It was eerie reading about herself like this, things she had zero memory about. This one drew attention and possible speculation of a family rift as Robert *still* wasn't available for comment. Frankly, Amanda didn't care whether or not Robert was ever "available for comment" again, but his absence was weird. He loved the spotlight, always had. An *In Scene* magazine cover showed pictures of her holding hands with Callie on the beach in the Hamptons, walking among the shops and eating in town. Sam, Stan, and two others, obviously part of her security detail, were pictured as well under the headline: "Marceau Part Deux—Where Did Amanda Keep Her Love Child and Little Clone?" There were countless more articles and magazine clippings. The latest featured a screenshot of that awful viral video under the headline "Can She Pull It Together for Awards Season?"

The next file Amanda opened gave her a shock. Various passports and birth certificates for not only her, but Callie as well. Each had corresponding mother-daughter names, aliases, and numbers. Adoption papers for Callie. An amniocentesis she'd had while pregnant with Zander. The documents drew attention to the fact that Callie and her unborn baby were related by father. Amanda realized she had been holding her breath as she clicked through these files and let it all out in one whoosh. Who was this person? What had she been up to that she needed so much illicit documentation? She'd actually traipsed the black market. Why? Had she *taken* Callie? And now that he knew she couldn't remember, was Mr. Montgomery making his move, coming after them again? But then Sam surely would have said something. Stan too. Forget that, Art would have killed him if—did they know? Maybe he cleverly worked his way back in? So many questions, and as of now, so few answers. Still, how had Callie come to be hers and not Montgomery's? They'd obviously been on the scene alone together sans Alex last year. What the hell had happened?

They landed at 9:30 a.m., Chicago time. Amanda gathered her children and what remained of her loyal retinue. They climbed into the waiting Range Rover at the private airport outside the city proper. The sun was just climbing as Stan navigated the downtown traffic to her penthouse. She felt like a character in one of those spy movies, trying to keep one step ahead of the other players.

⫷⫷   ⫸⫸

Alexander Montgomery didn't consider himself a man quick to anger. However, when he'd arrived at Amanda's early that morning, his blood shot up a hundred degrees.

"What do you *mean*, they left with Stan?" he asked the men stationed outside the front doors. Were they fucking kidding? After going to the kitchen and pouring a cup of coffee, he'd realized how oddly quiet the house was, even at this early hour. He'd taken the stairs two at a time and quickly discovered that Amanda and his children were gone. Helen was none the wiser as to their current whereabouts or that they had in fact left at all.

"At 2:39 this morning," Jason confirmed. At least the man had the decency to look a little sheepish that it had taken them this long to catch on to the fact that they'd been duped by their comrade.

Alexander called Stan. "Did you actually have the temerity to take my wife and children from their home without telling me?"

"Boss, I—"

"Bring them the fuck back *now!*" he shouted, not caring who else heard. Bloody hell, Stan had taken his family from him. And presently, he couldn't just jump on a plane and go after them. Alexander glanced at the dial of his Breitling; he had two important meetings today, one at nine, the other at six, in New York. Amanda knew it, too—he'd told her of his schedule yesterday, so she would know not to expect him for dinner. She'd made a cute comment about having only seven for dinner and what was a girl to do. It was adorable. Or, it had been.

"She's really mad," Stan said.

"About. What."

"You, sir." So Amanda had figured it out. She knew. He didn't know how she'd done it, but she was a fiercely intelligent woman. He felt his muscles relax, if only slightly. But if she knew what had happened, why had she left?

"Did she disclose any details?" Alex asked through gritted teeth, trying to retain what calm he could.

"At this point, I think she knows only that you're Callie and Zander's father."

Bloody hell. *Some* information could be terribly misleading. Without much of a choice, he relented. "One day, that's it," Alexander said. He rubbed his temples. *Bloody hell.* "You have until the morning. I want them in the house by lunch. Understood?"

"Copy that, boss," Stan said before hanging up the phone.

"Well," Alexander said, turning his gaze to Sam, who had come into the kitchen while he'd been on the phone with Stan.

"She didn't tell me anything, Alex. I swear." She held up a hand to enforce the point. "I'm as surprised as you."

"Well, *someone* has my wife's ire," he mused, pouring himself a cup of coffee. He couldn't be sure what was going through that terribly clever head of hers, but he'd assume it wasn't good, considering she'd up and left. With his children. Bloody hell, he finally had them under one roof—two, counting his temporary residence next door—and he was more than displeased they were gone. But he knew the longer they put off telling her, the more likely something of this sort might occur. Too bad it happened in the middle of the night when he was none the wiser.

Everyone looked to him expectantly where they gathered in kitchen. He motioned with his head. "Move. Stephen, you're with me today."

"Wait!" Sam called. She stood up from the large overstuffed chair that was her favorite. "You can't just not do anything about it." Her face was crestfallen.

"Not do anything about it?" he repeated, incredulous. "Samantha, I've given them thirty-six hours, of which I will count each second. If they're not safely back here, in this kitchen, by lunch tomorrow, I will move heaven and earth to retrieve them. And I can assure you, if that happens, they will wish the hell I hadn't."

"If you hear anything—" she started, but Alexander cut her off.

"I'll let you know. I expect the same."

The mood was grim as their caravan wound along the Pacific highway. Alexander's mobile command center, a black XL Navigator, drove as always in the middle of four others. All of the trucks in their fleet were customized to some degree, but his was completely tricked out, as they said in twenty-first-century lingo. A sectional in the back wrapped around the cab with ample legroom in the center. Computer screens and outlets for countless gadgets were everywhere.

Always driven by Gregor, with Trevor riding shot gun, he and Michael sat in back. Stephen was with him today, too. Calder Defense's offices occupied what had been JDL Security *pièce de résistance*, a stunning state-of-the-art eighteen-story glass building with ocean and mountain views. A new logo was now affixed to the building, which looked amazing. While there was a perfunctory street entrance, this particular facility was equipped with underground parking. They packed into two of the four elevators in the garage and arrived seconds later to the top floor, which housed their personal offices.

"Katie," he said, nodding to their receptionist, who'd worked under Art's tutelage for well over ten years. She greeted him in kind and handed him a clean schedule, identical to the one she'd sent to his phone. Sure, she looked like the typical modern-day professional working at any office, but Katie, like all of their employees, had military training. So, while she could smile and answer the phone, emails, and arrange any number of tasks, she was also trained in Krav Maga and a skilled marksman to boot. Should trouble darken their doors, Katie was a brilliant first line of defense.

Stephen hadn't been here since he'd had their new furniture delivered, so, momentarily distracted from his runaway wife and children, Alex eagerly ushered his brother inside his corner suite with stunning views, eager to point out the improvements. Alexander left Stephen behind his desk a few minutes later, where he was diving into some new instructional videos Trevor had put together for him. There was never enough for them to learn, including ever-evolving technologies and current business practices. When this business with Amanda was over, Stephen would take

Alex's place at Calder Defense, or somewhere within the confines of Montgomery Enterprises. Whatever he wanted was okay by Alexander. He only wanted his brother to be happy. And as Stephen felt guilty, misguidedly so, for what had ultimately happened that day they'd lost Amanda and Callie, his brother's well-being and satisfaction was paramount.

Alexander checked on Gregor next, but didn't find him in his office, even though Alex had had a wall of flat-screens installed for him. Irritated, Alex went back out to reception and— "Bloody hell, Gregor." Alexander stopped halfway down the hall. Gregor was leaning over the counter of the reception desk, trying once again to charm Katie. Alex grabbed him by the collar as he passed and pushed him forward.

"I'll call you later, Katie," Gregor said, trying to turn around and look at her.

"You don't even have her number," Alexander reminded him.

"Not yet, Alex," Gregor said, shaking his head. "But it's just a matter of time, my friend."

"Of course it is." Alexander rolled his eyes, then watched Gregor do a ridiculous He-Man impression—or the Hulk, he couldn't keep them straight—when he saw the new flat-screens set up. He held up his hand however when Gregor tried to go in for a chest bump. Not Alexander's style. The TVs weren't for business. Gregor loved sports. And not just the big leagues. He had a penchant for anything fast and competitive. And some not so fast. He'd already switched the TVs on to sixteen different events when Alexander left him. All on silent, of course, since Gregor actually had a real job. They had all decided it wasn't enough to sit around and collect interest on what they'd brought with them, that they had to earn money as well. Besides, they were all former military men, so what better than this? As his wife would say—*Seriously!* Bloody hell, he missed her and he wanted her—*them*—home. Now. He checked the face of his Breitling again; thirty-three hours, twelve minutes—yes, he was counting.

Day by day, Alexander was beginning to understand just what it was that his company did. Between Art explaining the mechanics of the overall operations and Trevor and Michael helping him with specifics, he *was* catching on. He had the personality, the cunning, and the command down, but in order to learn even more of the fundamentals of today's business practices, he'd sat in on the training of some of their most recent administrative hires. All of them wounded warriors. Just because someone was disabled or disfigured didn't disqualify them from performing a job. Comrades beget comrades. And what better than something within the realm of the security and surveillance business? He wasn't learning code or anything of the sort but understanding which buttons to push and when *had* helped.

After a few more perfunctory hellos, he entered his office, a large space filled with a massive desk and a sitting area. Large couches and chairs, a sixty-inch plasma TV, and a table for smaller meetings. He had his own bathroom, which was outfitted with a shower, two sinks, a comfortable chaise and table, and a private toilet room as well. Stephen's and Gregor's suites were the same.

Settling behind his desk, he looked at the stack of paperwork in front him. Mostly contracts that needed his signature. He was just about to call Chris, who was in New York waiting for them, when Stan checked in again. It was his hourly perfunctory text: *Amanda and the kids are well.* At least he was giving him that—bare minimum though it was.

They left for the private airport after his call with Chris. They had a six-hour flight, a two-hour dinner meeting, and then six hours back, including travel to and from airports. They'd be exhausted and back in California around midnight.

"Well?" Alexander asked Trevor. He hadn't seen him since they'd arrived at the offices earlier and now in the truck, he wanted to know what he'd been able to find.

Trevor held up his laptop and shook his head. "Stan's disabled his tracker, and must have done the same to Mrs. Montgomery's and Callie's as well."

While Alexander knew Amanda and the children were safe—Stan would make sure of that—he preferred to know exactly where they were at all times. Bloody hell, was that too much to ask? He'd feared the unfathomable for so long and thought the trackers he'd put on their phones would have been enough, but now he wished he could have them all chipped like he'd heard people did with pets. Leave it to Stan to give her the modicum of privacy she needed. Still, Trevor pointed out excitedly, Stan hadn't disabled the systems on her Range Rover or that of the penthouse in Chicago. The team knew when she arrived safely at her residence and when they were buttoned up snugly for the night.

When their caravan arrived at their Manhattan operations, they were filmed by a few news crews entering what was now Montgomery Enterprises Inc. headquarters, which had been happening with increasing frequency lately, now that the acquisition had made headlines. The meeting was over by ten and then they headed back home. Jesus, it was a long day, but at least as they settled on the plane, countdown was at twenty-three hours, six minutes.

Back in Cali, Alexander walked through his foyer, passing the long hallway to the left that led to the kitchen. He continued beyond an enormous powder room, then entered the living room. It was a beautiful house, but what he wanted was a home, with his wife and children. He poured a scotch and then stood in the terrace doorway that faced Amanda's property. He hated seeing it so darkened. Devoid of his family.

Early the next morning he hit the lights in the gym, taped his hands as he'd been taught, and instructed Siri to play "Dream On" on repeat. Then spent the next hour beating the hell out the bags that hung from the ceiling in a line. He lay spent on the floor afterward, wondering how life could change so very drastically in what was a relatively such a short period of time.

The remainder of the morning involved pacing the courtyard, foyer, and terrace on Amanda's property. Lunch came and went. An hour later, Alexander, his men, and Samantha boarded the Calder Defense jet, intent on bringing Amanda home.

I am so coming to get you, sweetheart.

CHAPTER
EIGHT

1774
ABERSOCH, BRITAIN

Amanda stood before the window in Rebecca's room. The sea churned as did her thoughts and emotions. On the heels of her declaration to Alexander, he'd grabbed her arms and pulled her in close, scrutinizing every inch of her face, which had been as terrifying as it had been exhilarating, then he'd abruptly let go and turned away. But really, what had she expected him to say? She'd told him she'd never seen him before in her life—and while that was one-hundred-percent true, to him, she looked just like his wife.

Relieved at least that for now they wouldn't be sharing a bedroom, she'd entered what was to be her chamber and kicked off her shoes. As she fought with the buttons of her dress, Alice returned to help her out of it and then into a long nightgown; a sheer, white confection with ties in the back. Amanda's gratitude must have been a bit over the top since her servant stammered and blushed throughout the whole thing. She'd finally left after pulling a brick from the fireplace, unwrapping it from its sooty cloth, and placing it at the foot of her bed.

Tired as she was, Amanda wasn't ready for bed. She couldn't do anything. Left alone with her thoughts for the first time in hours she was struck by how *insane* this all was. What the hell had happened? How had she come to be here, here in this castle that was no longer hers but apparently Alexander Montgomery's? Alexander Montgomery of the eighteenth-century Montgomerys. It didn't sound any less nuts the more she thought about it. And on top of it all, he was *hot*.

The longer this hallucination went on, the more Amanda was starting to feel that it wasn't a hallucination at all, that she somehow had fallen back in time. Everything was so real. The castle, the estate grounds, the weight of her dress, the feel of Alexander's hand on her—no. She wouldn't think about it, about what had happened, or at least, almost happened. Actually, she reasoned, if this *were* a hallucination, if this were something she was making up in her own comatose brain, Alexander wouldn't have pulled away the way he had only minutes before. No, she'd have let things progress much further, she was sure of it.

Alone, Amanda felt even more sure this wasn't a dream. She'd pinched herself so many times her arms were covered with red marks. She'd even pulled her hair. It didn't work. She actually wanted to laugh; *my God*, this was a fantasy come true: a mysterious time, a handsome husband who reeked of authority, and an adorable daughter. Strangely, she felt safe being here, safe being far away from Robert, and comforted in the most bizarre way to be a part of Alexander's and Callesandra's lives. She'd read so much about them already it was like she did know them, on some level.

Seriously, though, it was a dream, it had to be. She pinched herself again. "Ouch."

"Do your hands pain you?"

She turned, startled by Alexander's voice, soft-spoken as it was. Her heart started beating faster again. How could she reconcile, justify, rationalize her reaction to him? She didn't belong here, wherever here was, no matter how oddly safe and comforted she felt playing as Alexander's wife and Callesandra's mother. Would he want to sleep with her? Would he notice the difference? He was leaning against the door frame dressed in just trousers, his hair free of the leather tie that had held it back earlier. His broad chest, even in repose, was impressively sculpted. His powerful arms showed a marking across his left bicep she couldn't quite make out. A tattoo? She wanted to be wrapped in those arms, to lose herself in his strength. To lose herself in him. She'd never felt anything close to the attraction she felt for this man, and it had come on so quickly, so strongly. And this man couldn't even stand her. Or the woman he thought she was.

"My hands are the least of my worries," she answered, turning to look out the window again and avoiding his stare.

"Rebecca?"

She wanted to tell him that wasn't her name but couldn't. Not yet. "Yes, Alexander?"

"When did you learn to play the piano?"

"When I was five," she said. She'd tell as much of the truth as she could. Would telling the truth bring more harm? Did he know something was different? He must; it would account for his odd, he likes me, he likes me not behavior. Amanda heard him move closer, felt his heat when he stopped just behind her. "Should I be scared, Alexander?" she asked, knowing she was putting her trust in him. He was all she had after all, for whatever reason, and she was comforted by that, by him.

"You've never been scared before, Rebecca. What scares you now?"

"Everything," she whispered, pressing her forehead to the glass of the window.

"I don't have the heart for more games, Rebecca," he said, his voice turning to a sneer.

"I don't play games, Alexander." And truthfully, she wouldn't know how.

She felt his hands then as they brushed through her hair, pushing it over her shoulder. He had large hands, gentle hands. But the man's actions were so confounding—he ran hot and cold and she could never predict which it would be. There was this pull, connection, attraction, or whatever it was that was between them, and she liked being touched by him. He traced his fingers over her neck and she shivered from the soft caress. Oh God, what should she do? She wasn't his wife, wasn't the mother of his child. She had to tell him, try to make him understand. She turned slowly and lifted her head and froze. He was looking at her so closely she couldn't move. His hands cupped her face as he looked down and then he moved closer, just as he had before.

She met him halfway. The hell with talking.

She searched his eyes as he tilted her face up toward his, trying to read the swirling mix of emotions she saw there. Lust, definitely, but confusion, tenderness, and yet still a flash of anger. Then, all thought stopped as he touched his lips to hers. A soft sigh escaped Amanda's mouth. Somehow, nothing had ever felt so wonderful, so right.

She wanted to close her eyes, but Alexander was staring at her so intently that she couldn't. They watched each other, taking turns with their lips, first his capturing hers then hers doing the same, stopping after each gentle pull to gauge the other's reaction. A test. Of them both. Her head was cupped in his hands, her own splayed wide across his chest.

Then, suddenly, he pulled away and turned without saying another word.

Reeling, Amanda sunk down onto the bed, absentmindedly fingering the spot on her neck where his hands had been only moments before. It was then she realized she hadn't returned the necklace and ribbon to Callesandra. She'd promised she would, and she wouldn't have the little girl mistrust her.

She picked up a small oil lamp and peeked through the doorway to make sure no one was around. Thankfully the large hallway that wrapped around the second floor was empty. She stared at the line of doors running down the walls on both sides of the landing. It was such an odd sensation. She was at once so at home here, and yet it *wasn't* her home, not anymore. Or, she corrected herself, not yet. Amanda knew what was behind each door in her present day estate, but now she wasn't sure by whom they were occupied. She knew Alexander's room was just beyond her own suite. She'd heard the door close each time he'd left her. In fact, Alexander's current room was actually *her* suite in her own time, but obviously not now.

All thoughts of Callesandra swept from her mind, Amanda knocked softly on his door. It opened a moment later. She felt Alexander's eyes on her but found she couldn't meet them. What was she doing here? Staring down at his bare feet, she realized even *they* were beautiful. Large, wide, perfectly proportioned. Was there anything about him that wasn't perfect?

《《　》》

Alexander looked down, surprised to see his wife in the threshold, though if there was ever a night to expect it, it was this one. There was something strange about her tonight—it was almost as if she wasn't truly his wife, but was some beautiful, lovely imposter. He'd left her chamber with the intention of putting as much space between them as possible for this woman had him thinking he was bloody mad. Torn between grabbing her and kissing her again or slamming the door in her face, he reached for the oil lamp instead. She was shaking so badly she'd start a fire.

He'd been stunned to hear the knock upon his door at all, soft and tentative as it had been. Callesandra never knocked, always just entered, which was the reason he always slept in his breeches. His daughter knew she was welcome to join him anytime she wished. She obviously wished it often for most nights she crawled in beside him, whether or not she started the evening in her own bed. His men, when they wanted his attention, sounded two clear raps before they were bid entrance, so his wife's knock had been unusual, unexpected.

He lifted her chin. "You've never knocked upon my door, Rebecca. Never."

She met his gaze finally before speaking. "No, Alexander. I never have."

His gut clenched at her statement. Bloody hell she rattled him, it was as if she knew just what to say to infuriate him—and even worse her confounding replies were said guilelessly and in a damn near challenge.

"What is it?" he asked impatiently through his teeth, his wife's behavior confounding him yet again, not to mention how rattled he already was by his reaction—and attraction—to her.

"I don't know where Callesandra's room is."

Bloody Christ, how much of this could he take? Another admission that cut him to the quick. He could see tears in her eyes, too, but she refused to shed them. This woman was brave. And he knew to his very marrow that somehow, she was honest as well. Still, he had too many questions he wasn't ready to seek answers to just yet so instead he lashed out again. "Why would you?" he asked, unable to keep the bitterness from his voice. "You've never had time for her."

"If I had a daughter," she said evenly, "I would always find the time for her, Alexander." *If* she had a daughter? What did Rebecca mean by that? Before he could respond, she held out her hand, Callesandra's necklace and ribbon upon her gauze-covered palm. "Please return them to her."

Not knowing what else to do, Alexander took them from her. Then she whispered good night, and turned to go back to her room. He watched from the hallway as she felt her way. She'd not taken the lamp that he held in his hand.

◁◁   ▷▷

Amanda awoke to sounds in her chamber. She opened her eyes slowly before sitting up and looking around. She was actually relieved to find herself still in the eighteenth century, if that's really where she was. Her dreams last night had been like none she'd ever had before, filled with images of Alexander and Callesandra. They were the best dreams she'd ever had.

Alice was in the room, too, opening the drapes, sunshine blazing through the windows as each was pulled aside. It was a beautiful room, but it wasn't hers. And none of the things inside of it were hers either, which was somehow creepier than being here.

Alice helped her into a burgundy dress with delicate gold braiding and ties. This one was much more comfortable than the one she'd worn the night before. No bell hoops in the skirt and it fit loosely, as did the shoes. Each just a little too big. Alice said nothing of her ill-fitting clothing, so when she turned around, Amanda removed the shoes. The hem of the dress covered her feet; hopefully no one would notice they were bare.

When Alice started making the bed, Amanda stood before the mirror staring at her reflection, which was apparently identical to Rebecca's. Were they so similar? As she pulled back her hair, she turned toward Alice and asked to see Callesandra, her voice muffled from the hair pin in her mouth.

When Alice made no indication that she'd heard, Amanda repeated a little louder, ending with, "Would you bring her to me, please?" She finished securing her hair and was playing with the strands when she saw Alice still hadn't moved. "My daughter, Alice," Amanda reminded her as if she'd been doing it all her life. Seriously, this part of the charade was easier than she thought.

Alice nodded, rather curtly Amanda noted, and returned minutes later holding Callesandra's hand. Just seeing the little girl, imagining she was actually hers, boosted her spirits immensely. Amanda smiled and motioned for Callesandra to come closer. Callesandra was only a little hesitant as she moved forward to the bench where Amanda sat before an ornately crafted vanity. As soon as she was close enough, Amanda picked her up and hugged her tightly.

"Good morning, sweet baby girl. I missed you," she said, even more surprised to find she really had. She felt safe with Callesandra, as safe as she'd felt with Alexander, regardless of his moods.

"Your hair looks pretty, Mama," Callesandra said tentatively.

Amanda closed her eyes as she hugged Callesandra closer. When she opened them, Alexander was staring at her from the doorway. She looked him over from head to toe, unable to stop herself. His features seemed softer today, his hair still damp from a bath, water probably dragged in from a well somewhere. Gone was the running water, the plumbing her family had installed. There were only basins filled with fresh, warm water—and a commode she'd grimaced through using in the middle of the night when she could hold it in no longer.

This morning, Alexander wore a white long-sleeved linen shirt, the neck slightly opened and parted from ties that hadn't been fastened, and black trousers tucked into tall polished boots. Over it all was a devilish knee-length black cloak, which only enhanced his dark looks. Finished with her inspection, Amanda dragged her gaze back to his face, blushing as he raised a brow. Was that amusement she saw in his eyes? Then she watched as he gave her the same once-over. And just as closely.

《《　》》

Alexander stood in the doorway of his wife's bedroom, though the woman he stared at appreciatively was not his wife. It couldn't be. Whatever sorcery had transpired the night before, he was glad for it. Bloody Christ, his entire body had responded to her inspection. He'd never responded to Rebecca like that before. And not that she wasn't beautiful—she was—but Rebecca's beauty was only skin deep. But this woman. This woman shone from beauty so deep, bloody hell, it blinded him. And as similar as they were, today the differences were startling clear.

Her hair was a shade or two lighter than Rebecca's. Thicker, too, and shorter, falling between her shoulder blades. Her skin was paler, exquisitely flawless. Her nose was straight, devoid of the small bump that had marred it before. Her lips were fuller, softer, and sweetly innocent. And then there were her eyes. Her eyes were the most startling shade of blue they took his breath away.

This woman's neck was long and graceful, and her body slim. Her breasts smaller yet so full, he could still feel them crushed against his chest as he'd held her in the tunnels. Though he couldn't see her legs, he knew they were longer for she was in fact taller. He'd noticed it when she'd stood barefoot before him last night. And she stood barefoot again, her toes peeking from beneath the dress she wore, toes painted with the color red. He'd never seen that on a woman before, and he found he liked it.

He could make no sense of the reality before him—where had the real Rebecca gone? But he found he didn't care. He kept his face expressionless as he brought his gaze back to hers. She hugged Callesandra as though her life depended on it. She hid behind her, just as *he* did. But the warmth in her eyes held no manipulation, no malice.

"Papa, doesn't Mama's hair look pretty?"

He looked at Callesandra's "mama" as he answered, "Yes, angel. Your mama's hair looks very pretty. Callesandra, go with Alice now. I'll come see you before I leave." Callesandra hugged the woman holding her more tightly, rewarded for her efforts with tickles that sent her into a fit of laughter.

"Listen to your papa, silly goose," she said as she laughed with Callesandra. "I'll spend the day with you after we've talked, alright?"

Callesandra nodded and then took Alice's hand, following her out the door.

And then there were two.

"We must speak," Alexander said, at almost the exact same time as Rebecca spoke.

"There's something I need to talk to you about—" she began, before quieting.

Alexander was stunned to find they'd virtually spoken the same words. Somehow, he'd not expected her to do so. It was a foolish thought for if he knew anything about this new woman it was that she was both forthright and honest. Before he could say anything, she stood and walked toward him, stopping a step or two before she reached him, laying her hand upon his arm.

"Listen, Alexander, I'm not sure where—"

But he couldn't wait any longer. They could talk anytime. Kiss now, talk later. He had to have her. It had been some time since he'd been with a woman—he didn't like taking lovers, and he never slept with the same one more than once—but his body was responding as if it was just yesterday. With those thoughts in mind and little else he started moving forward and she back toward the wall, bracing herself against it and into him. They moved in perfect symmetry, mouths fused, hands finding purchase. His behind her back and cupping her head, hers on his chest and tangled in his hair. Just as he was about to press his entire body to hers, she reached out, grabbed his shirt, and pulled him in. So. Bloody. Sweet. Truthfully, he hadn't meant to kiss her at all, but when she'd come to him and placed her hand on his arm, when she began speaking and his eyes fixed on her mouth, he'd thought of nothing else.

The act was completely brash, but seemingly pre-destined. From the moment they'd touched it'd been like dry tinder igniting. Her clever mouth nearly had him out of his mind. In the minute they'd been lip-locked she'd kissed him practically a hundred different ways. Each one deliberate in its delivery. He'd never met a woman who kissed like that, who took charge the way she did. Suddenly he wanted to kill every man she'd ever practiced on. Jealousy gripped him as she sucked his bottom lip, taking a bite before plunging back in to swipe the roof of his mouth. She grabbed his shirt, fisting it in her hands, and pulled away.

"If you ever kiss anyone but me again, I swear I'll kill you," she warned breathlessly.

Alexander was so stunned by her words and the fierceness of her expression he threw his head back and laughed. Bloody hell, he laughed! She was obviously feeling the same as he. Looking back down at her, he saw that she wasn't quite so charmed.

"I don't know what you find so amusing," she said, her mouth pulled in a scowl as she glared at him.

"Presently," Alexander returned, "you." This woman was infuriating, but he found that he liked it. Seeing a devilish determination in her eyes—for what, he didn't know—he brought her flush against him once more. He pulled her top lip between his, biting and then brushing his tongue beneath it. He felt her knees buckle, and the knowledge that she was responding to him this way thrilled him.

Alexander chuckled again, pulling her closer. This time she didn't seem to mind his laugh so much. In fact, her reaction was empowering. Her hands fisted his shirt again; her short breaths warm now upon his neck. Then she burrowed in deeper and sighed in pure contentment. He palmed her head and pulled her away.

"Tell me who you are," he demanded in a whisper.

"Oh, now you want to talk," she said mischievously.

"Truthfully," he said with a grin, "no."

She smiled, then frowned. He could almost see the gears turning in her head. "Just how many women have you kissed?"

"Jealous?" he teased.

"Insanely."

He smiled. "Good." Then he bent to kiss her again, his question forgotten.

A loud knock sounded on the door. "Alex!"

Alexander swore under his breath. Leaning his forehead against the wall, he snapped impatiently, "What?"

The door opened and Alexander turned, fixing Gregor with a look of supreme irritation. Then he noticed his man's mouth agape in shock. Alexander couldn't blame him. He'd never stood in his wife's room before, let alone embracing her as he did so.

"I must speak with you," Gregor demanded after a moment. "Privately."

Alexander bent his head and whispered to the mystery woman, "Don't move from this very spot."

She nodded against Alexander's neck then braced the wall with her hands as he stepped away. Alexander tore himself from her gaze and followed Gregor into the hall, crossing his arms over his chest as he waited for him to speak. Gregor's words were hushed.

"We found her body, Alex. Below the cliffs. She had marks around her neck and was dressed in riding clothes."

"Whose body?" Alexander asked, momentarily stunned with such information.

"Rebecca's body!"

Bloody Christ, how could he have forgotten? He'd been so mesmerized with this new woman that he'd barely given thought to just what in the hell was happening. He ran his hands through his hair trying to assimilate this disturbing news. "Are you sure it's Rebecca?"

Gregor narrowed his eyes. "Aye."

Alexander stormed back into the room; his look murderous as he turned to the woman who robbed him of his wits. He blamed her now for his foolishness as well as his weakness. "Have you anything to do with this?" he demanded when he stood before her again. She cowed under his gaze, looking confused, shocked, and hurt. He had to admit to feeling the very same swirl of emotion.

"With what?" she finally asked, her voice small, meeker than he'd ever heard it.

"Are we back to games?" Alexander said, almost sneering now, feeling his eyes narrow.

"Wh-what happened?" she stammered, her fear appearing genuine.

"It *seems* my wife's body has been found," he ground out through his teeth. "And as you," he said, jabbing his finger at her, "are not she, I ask you again—have you anything to do with this!"

The woman just stared at him, shaking her head mutely. Furious that he'd been duped, Alexander grabbed her arm and pulled her roughly from the room. He led her down the hallway where he all but threw her into his chamber. *Let her be scared*, he thought as he turned his key into the lock, closing her in.

‹‹ ››

Alexander brought his mount to a halt besides the outcropping of rocks along the shore's edge. Stephen waited some distance away atop one of the shoals. As he neared the site, his fury escalated. Rebecca's body lay in a gruesome display—broken upon the rocks, already distorted from the waning tide. He reached out, albeit futilely, and pressed his fingers to her neck. Her skin was bruised, swollen from the strangulation that had obviously caused her death before she'd been cast from the cliffs.

"She's an imposter, Alexander," Gregor accused of the woman he'd left in his chamber.

Alexander pivoted on his heels, eyes narrowed. "For what purpose?" he questioned, surprised that he felt the instant need to defend her. On the ride out to the cliffs he'd tormented himself with wanting to believe her but seeing no way that he could. "What would be her gain?"

"Her gain?" Gregor repeated. "The same as your wife's!" he shouted. "The life of a queen. The trappings of wealth. A title she couldn't live without!"

Alexander stood, turning toward Gregor, gesturing for him to continue.

"What more proof do you need, Alex?" Gregor went on. "She was found just after we followed Rebecca into the tunnels. What if she killed Rebecca herself? Or worse, what if she had an accomplice who's still out there?"

"When we came upon her, Gregor, a man was overpowering her," Alexander reminded him, wondering if he was just trying to convince himself of her innocence.

"Have all these years left you so desperate that you can't see what's before you? It was a trick, Alex!"

Alexander grabbed him by the shoulders. "Cease!" he bellowed. "She ran last night. From you and from me. If she's an imposter, she's not a very good one. She's. Nothing. Like. Rebecca," he said, each word carefully enunciated through clenched teeth.

"And if she is?" Gregor returned.

"Then I ask you again—what is her gain?"

"And I ask you again—who is she!"

"Enough!" Alexander threw him aside. Bloody hell, he could only take so much! He had enough problems, one in particular, without this current dissension among his men.

"Alex, I've watched you suffer for years at her cruelness. If you're finally free of her, then for God's sake just be free!" Gregor pleaded once again, picking himself up from the ground.

"What am I to do with her, Gregor? Send her off? Where?"

"We'll find her family—give her back. Alex, please don't make the same mistake again."

"I saw hope in my daughter's eyes for the first time last night, Gregor. Hope that her mother might love her. I'll not take that away from her!" It was but half the truth.

"Your love has always been enough, Alex," Gregor said, his voice softening. "Callesandra's loved by all of us. You know that." He paused. "Will you listen to reason?"

Alexander pivoted on his heels. "You listen to reason!" he shouted, knowing how menacing he sounded and not caring. "You saw her last night, she has not one of the same mannerisms as Rebecca did—she played the God damned piano! An imposter wouldn't do such things. And if whoever did this to Rebecca," he cautioned as he motioned toward her body, "realizes a woman who looks so very much like her is alive and living within the walls of my holding, then she is in danger too!"

That at least brought the quiet he so desperately needed. "Think—all of you," he said, emphatically looking to his men. "If she wished to assume the sorry life of my wife, she could have done so easily, at least for a time. Though I appeared by her side, I never looked at her, not really. None of us have, and you know it to be true. But she sought my help last night—on more than one occasion. She looked to me—right in the eyes—for guidance. I tell you—she's no imposter."

They seemed to come to a silent agreement, then looked down at the body of the woman for whom they felt only contempt. None of them wished her dead, but they'd not miss her spite, her cruelty. They waited until dark before moving her from the shore and buried her behind the chapel. Stephen said a prayer as they covered her grave. They left the area completely undisturbed. No one must ever know what happened.

◁◁ ▷▷

Amanda spent the day trapped in Alexander's room. It wouldn't have been so terrible if he hadn't looked at her with that expression of betrayal nearing on hate. Somehow, she just wanted to make him happy. Something she knew he wasn't. At least not before. But she knew the few times, the very few times they were together, she *had* made him happy.

She paced for hours with nothing to do but admire his décor. It was completely masculine, completely him. His bed was covered in dark linens and filled with pillows; the posts wrapped with black silk. The floors sported rugs rich in design, their colors the same that ran throughout room, black, burgundy, and gold. The drapes over the windows hung from at least twenty feet above the floor, cascading from rods with ornate finials. The chairs in front of the fireplace were a dark shade of red, so dark, they appeared to be black. The leather was soft, decorated with gold nail heads. Another sitting area was arranged in front of the bathing chamber—a table, chairs, and large chaise covered with a throw. There were even baskets filled with toys she knew he kept for Callesandra.

She'd tried to keep the fire going throughout the day, but her attempts were futile. By evening, she had a pounding headache and was so hungry she had that sick, empty feeling in the pit of her stomach that wouldn't go away. What had she done?

You assumed the role of his wife, that's what!

Nothing made sense about how she had gotten here, but she was here. And oddly, that *had* made sense. Until now. Cold and hungry, she curled up by the fireplace and covered herself with a throw from one of the couches. She fell asleep wondering where she would be when she woke up. In the back of her mind, she wanted it to be here, but Alexander seemed to hate her again, just as he had before.

Her dreams weren't pleasant like they'd been the night before. They were nightmares of the man who despised her. Again.

‹‹ ››

Alexander kissed his daughter before heading to his
chamber. He'd told her before he left that morning that
her mother was feeling poorly. Her crestfallen expression
had made him add that perhaps tomorrow they'd have
some time together. Until he had some answers, he
wouldn't jeopardize her safety. Alice had orders to stay in
the nursery, and his chamber was to remain undisturbed as
Lady Rebecca was ill. She'd voiced no questions. Alice and
her own daughter, Beatrice, were newly employed and paid
generously for their service.

Rebecca always had the house in such a state of distress
the servants were constantly turning over. Her last waiting
maid left only a week ago, taking Callesandra's nanny with
her. Alice and Beatrice hadn't been here long enough to
realize things were so very different. A small blessing.

He slipped the key from his pocket, imagining the state
his chamber would be in when he entered, and was surprised
to find it was undisturbed with not a single item out of place.
Alexander couldn't see the woman, and truthfully was shocked
she'd not been waiting to throw something when he opened
the door. He wondered what her name was. Wondered too
if it was her lover that he'd rescued her from in the tunnels.
She'd kissed him eagerly enough, though. Bloody hell she'd
kissed him almost witless. Each and every time.

The room was completely dark, the fire long since
gone. He lit an oil lamp and searched his chamber. He
found her shaking on the floor in front of the fireplace.
Bloody hell, she'd lain freezing on the floor instead of
seeking the comfort of his bed. She was nothing like his
wife, who would have taken all she wanted without a

second thought. She was, in fact, nothing like any woman he'd ever known.

She sat up as he neared her, and he plucked her from the floor almost violently. He was furious, but this time, with himself. She wrapped her arms around his neck as he cradled her, pressing her face to his shoulder. Her silent tears soaked his shirt. He tightened his hold as he moved toward the bed. Bloody hell, she was chilled to the bone. Holding her easily with one arm, he pulled the duvet back and carefully placed her on the mattress, before covering her with a thick blanket.

He saw to the fire next, restoring it to a warm, crackling blaze. Then, unsure of what to do, what to say, he sat on the edge of the bed, bent over with his head in his hands. Did he really want answers to the questions that plagued him? As he pondered just how to proceed, he heard his door creak open, followed by the patter of Callesandra's feet. When she stood before him, he lifted his head, smiling in spite of his mood at his daughter's temerity.

"Can I sleep with you, Papa?"

"Yes, angel." He reached out to capture her little head in the palm of his hand. "You can always sleep with me." She threw her hands around his legs and he picked her up, hugging her tightly as he swung her toward the bed. "You get to sleep with Mama as well."

"But Mama never sleeps with you, Papa."

Alexander turned, looking at the woman in his bed. "She does now, angel." This new woman faced him now, quickly wiping the tears from her eyes. Her hands reached out, waiting to enfold Callesandra. He handed his daughter to her, the action somehow feeling right, and safe. He watched as she hugged her just as lovingly as he had, then stood and unfastened his cloak and removed his shirt. Callesandra remained buried in the woman's arms, her face hidden against her chest. The woman watched as he undressed, leaving only his breeches on.

He came silently into bed, looking at the two of them taking comfort from each other. "Mama, you're so cold," Callesandra whispered. "And you still have your dress on."

She answered his daughter while staring into his eyes. "I didn't feel well today, Callesandra. I was too tired to remove my dress."

"Papa said you were ill. Take your dress off, Mama, sleep in your shift."

"I'm fine. Hush now, angel, go back to sleep."

Alexander sighed. His daughter was right. "Sit up," he ordered softly, and she did.

He turned her to face the other way and undid the fastenings of her dress, pushing the material from her shoulders. It was then he saw the bruise on her back and those on her arms.

Callesandra gasped. "Mama, what happened?"

"I fell, sweetheart. It doesn't hurt." She smiled over her shoulder at Callesandra.

Alexander knew she lied for the sake of his daughter. He helped slip the dress down, then freed it from her feet. He tossed it to the floor at the end of the bed, smiling as Callesandra giggled.

They both lay down again, looking at each other, eyes filled with regret, but both for different reasons.

"Your name?" Alexander finally whispered when he was sure Callesandra was asleep between them. The woman lowered her eyes, but didn't speak.

Alexander bristled and repeated the question.

"Amanda," she said after a long moment.

"Where are you from, Amanda?" he asked, relief flooding his body.

It took a long time for her to answer. "Far from here, Alexander. So far I'm not sure if it truly exists anymore."

"Is there something or someone you're running from? The lover I pulled from you last night?" The thought not only sickened him, it angered him.

"No," she said, her face open and earnest. She was telling the truth. "I've never run from anything, and he was not my lover."

"You ran from me," he reminded her, suppressing a relieved smile. "You chose the cliff wall rather than the protection of my men."

"I'd never seen them before, Alexander. How was I to know they wouldn't harm me?"

"My men would never harm you, nor would I."

"You hate Rebecca. And if I am she, then you hate me too." Her voice was small—she looked almost scared.

"I didn't hate her. That would imply that I loved her at one time. I only hated her actions, her cruelness, especially to my daughter."

"Is Callesandra only yours, then?"

"No, Amanda. She is ours." It sounded right. He hoped she would agree. He'd only just met this woman, Amanda, but something told him she was the only woman for him.

"What of your wife, Alexander?" she asked.

"Well," he said, slowly, measuring his words, not sure how much to say. "It seems as you said last night: you are my wife, and for the sake of my daughter you shall remain."

"I don't know if I'll be able to stay," she said.

"Have you somewhere else to go?"

"No."

"Is there a letter you wish to send, a relative you have need to contact?"

"I wouldn't know where to send it, and there'd be no one to receive it."

"Then as I've said, Amanda, you shall stay—for the sake of my daughter,"

"And what of yourself, Alexander? What of your sake?"

"I have no sake, I have only my daughter."

"You're very lucky then, Alexander, for I have nothing—at least not here."

Amanda turned, taking Callesandra with her. She faced the wall, failing to hide the tears that fell down her face. Alexander wrapped his arms around her, pulling both her and Callesandra into his protective embrace.

"You have me and my daughter now, Amanda."

Alexander tucked her head under his chin, holding them even tighter. They slept that way the entire night.

CHAPTER
NINE

MARCH 1

CHICAGO, ILLINOIS

Actually, Alexander Montgomery decided he *was* a man quick to anger. Bloody hell, how much was he supposed to take? And *where* in the hell was Amanda? His five-truck convoy, just south of Oak Street, sat idle. He shifted in his seat and looked at the face of his Breitling again, thirteen hundred. "Sam?" he said into his transceiver. It was the third time he'd questioned her. Normally he would have smiled at her audible sigh, since it reminded him of Amanda—he wondered who had picked it up from whom. But these past ten months since arriving in this century had taken their toll, and to have finally found Amanda and Callesandra, to have them virtually in his grasp and now to *not*—well, he was just done with it all. He wanted to beat the hell out of Evan for thinking it was best to let Amanda draw her own conclusions. This would never have happened if she'd just *known*. Known who she was, who he was—who they were. Maybe he was angry with himself for momentarily being satisfied with just being close to them again.

Samantha made him wait ten long seconds before her voice sounded through his earbud thanks to technology—which, despite its new ubiquitous presence in his life, still amazed him sometimes. "Maybe she had to change a diaper, Alex. Besides it's a beautiful day, so unseasonably warm," she told him. "She'll stick to her routine. Something just held her up a few minutes." It was the third time she'd given him this same explanation from inside the nearby truck where she sat with Stephen and three of his men. In his own defense, he hadn't been in such a snit when he'd arrived at Amanda's penthouse two hours ago, just forty-five minutes after they'd landed. Once he'd realized Amanda and Stan had left the Range Rover behind in lieu of a stroll through the city, he'd become angry. Frustrated, and just the other side of furious, he'd headed out to find them. This time locked and loaded. All of them. Overkill? Absolutely. Stan wasn't going to be pleased by the turn of events. To be honest, he really didn't give a continental fuck. He wanted his family back. And he was taking them. Today. The only thing presently helping Stan's case was that he'd requested two men from their Chicago offices to ensure his family's security while taking to the streets. Not that he'd told Alexander that, but the Chicago office had informed him—*some* employees were loyal.

The hairs on the nape of his neck stood a second before Amanda turned the corner pushing a carriage with Callie by her side, as though his body had sensed her coming. As he watched them move down the block, his hands flexed, and his heart constricted painfully, just seeing them. Just seeing her. Bloody hell, she was beautiful. Even buttoned up in light winter gear, she may as well have stepped right out of one of the store windows. He watched as she stopped before a storefront obviously for Callie's sake as his daughter skipped right up to it and pressed her face against the glass. Alexander tapped the window and Gregor and the rest of his team merged with traffic, slowly inching their way down Michigan Avenue. Stan and his men saw their convoy approaching—which was exactly how Alexander wanted it—and instantly moved in on Amanda and his children. Trevor, who was seated across from Alexander, gave a thumbs-up to indicate that he'd hacked their transmitter frequency and were now able to listen to their verbal communication. Stan and his men must have figured it out immediately, as they went silent right away, switching to hand signals. Alexander tapped the window again, barely waiting for the truck to stop before he got out. The wait was over.

Alexander started forward as his men took their positions, effectively shutting down half a city block of prime Chicago real estate. Stan and his men had Amanda surrounded. And he had them surrounded. Alexander listened as Gregor told Stan to stand down. Stan was pissed as hell. Said he'd had it handled. *Welcome to my world, son.*

⟨⟨　⟩⟩

FIVE MINUTES EARLIER

"Callie, come on, sweetie," Amanda called. It was well past lunchtime and she needed to get Zander home. It was unusually warm for this time of year, so they'd stayed out longer than normal. She'd just turned the corner onto Michigan Avenue when a storefront caught her daughter's attention and she had indulgently waved her toward it, grateful for a moment of pause, anyway. A minute or so later, Callie turned from the window she'd been peering in and grinned. Amanda's heart melted. She held out her hand and waited until Callie grabbed it. Something about being in Chicago, just the two of them—well, Zander and Stan aside—was so freeing. It helped ground her anger and the uncertainty she'd been feeling about so many things. Like who in the hell Alexander Montgomery was and where in the heck had she met him. Why was he gone from their lives for the entirety of her pregnancy—which she also didn't remember—and now back again? The only thing she was sure of right now was that being away from home was the best move she'd made.

Of the many calls she'd received, there was only one she'd accepted. Evan's. She had no beef with him and honestly, she liked him. He was professional and kind and he only wanted to help her and to ease her memory's return in, if at all possible, a constructive way. And now more than ever that was something she wanted too.

"Are we going home today?" Callie asked.

Amanda smiled down at her and started pushing the stroller again. Callie had overheard the conversation she'd had with Stan last night. Al—*Mr. Montgomery*, she'd decided to go back to formalities—had apparently told him to wrap things up and bring her and the children home. To California. By lunchtime, which was...hours ago. She smiled inwardly. Heck, she grinned outwardly. It felt good to fight back. "No, sweetie." Jeez, she actually had a spring in her step. "We're staying until Sunday, just like I said."

Callie giggled and covered her mouth with her hands before she told her, "He's gonna come, Mama."

"So you keep reminding me." Amanda thought she'd said it under her breath, but when Callie pulled an overly exasperated face, she realized her daughter had heard her. With a sigh she knelt and held Callie's shoulders. "I know you miss your papa, Callie." Oddly, Amanda felt like she *had* missed him too. She didn't remember him, at least not before he brought her home from the hospital, but some part of her thought she really had missed him. It was also surprising how easy it had been to slip into calling him her "papa," though she hadn't yet settled on "husband" for herself. "Do you remember what I told you? Think really hard, it's super important."

Callie pursed her lips, a determined look crossing her face. It wasn't much longer before she said, "You said no one would ever take me away from you."

Jeez, out of the mouths of babes—that was *not* what she was referring to, and in fact Amanda had no recollection of saying that to Callie. What she'd told Callie was not to worry, that they would figure everything out. Now, however, Amanda grabbed her and pulled her in tight. Was she—*had* she been on the run from Mr. Montgomery? When—and why—had she felt the need to tell her little girl something like that? "You listen to me, my sweet baby girl, *we*"—she motioned between them for emphasis—"are going to keep on going just like we have been." She kissed her cheeks, hugged her tight, and reminded her, "I'm pretty good at making the rules, aren't I?"

Callie laughed out loud. "You're good at breaking rules, Mama."

"Oh, tomato, tamahto… Come on, your brother's fussy."

Amanda had just reached down for Zander when she heard Stan swear behind her and Callie whisper "Mama" as she latched on to her thigh. Stan was telling someone to back off. Obviously on his earbud since he wouldn't be saying that to her. She picked up Zander instinctively and Callie said "*Mama*" again, this time with more force.

"What, sweetie?" she said distractedly while turning to Stan. Jeez, he looked furious. The other two men guarding them closed in. Really tight. Callie shouted this time, drawing Amanda's full attention, and pointed toward the street. Amanda felt a moment's hesitation before turning. And when she did, she gasped.

She'd seen this picture before. Last night, as a matter of fact. She'd been preparing dinner while Callie sat on the sofa in the kitchen. One second the TV had been muted, then it was blaring. Amanda had startled at the noise then turned. Callie was standing on the coffee table, her whole body shaking with excitement, remote in hand. She'd rewound whatever had caught her attention and listened as the TV news anchor spoke. "From our business desk—exclusive and rare footage of billionaire Alexander Montgomery, president and CEO of Montgomery Enterprises. Mr. Montgomery is seen here, leaving his New York headquarters. His entrance to America happens to coincide with a masterful power grab of JDL Security." They showed a caravan of black Lincoln Navigators pull up to a prestigious Manhattan address. The cameras of course focused on *him*. The impressive, handsome man in question stepped from his vehicle. He ignored the press as he and his entourage entered the building. The newscaster continued, "While still in London, Mr. Montgomery amassed a brilliant staff, hand picking, if not plucking, some of the savviest technical, military, and medical minds. He's apparently settled in the States indefinitely."

Callie had thought it was so cool to see him on TV, but when she'd skipped over to her and asked if she could call him, Amanda's heart broke a little. How was she supposed to know what to do? She didn't want to keep her daughter from her father, but there were still so many things that didn't make sense to her. And she'd had Stan remove whatever tracking gadgets had been placed in their phones or on their persons and belongings. She just needed some space. "For now, sweetie," she'd said, trying to calm her juiced-up daughter, "let's just make it a mommy and babies' trip. On Sunday, we'll go back home." Then she'd figure out what to do and how to handle things. She didn't want to promise a visit, or dinner, or quite frankly anything for that matter. At least not yet. She'd held her little cheeks and told her, "I don't want you to worry about anything, understand? Mommy will figure it out."

Stan swore again, jarring Amanda back to the present as the caravan came to a stop. The doors opened in unison and Mr. Montgomery and his men emerged. Callie was right, her papa had come. And jeez, they meant business today. All in black suits. All wearing sunglasses. And she'd bet her life that they were all armed. They were large men and had a way of taking up the most space possible with a stance. Using hand signals to communicate, his men formed a perimeter, shutting down the street as he continued toward her.

Something about the way he looked now—dressed to the nines, storming so powerfully toward her, so totally in command—set her body thrumming right there on the street. Seriously, Amanda Abigail Marceau! How did you forget *him*? He was her every girlhood fantasy come to life. All six and a half feet of him. Tall. Broad. Dark. And so wickedly handsome. Straight nose, strong chin, and a mouth, she would swear, that was made to give orders. In fact, she watched him order Stan and his men just now to stand down as he walked right up to her. Like almost touching right up to her. She had to tilt her head back, which wasn't something she was accustomed to doing, not at her height. He stared at her a good few seconds, his eyes softening just a bit, before saying quite forcefully, "It seems there's a security problem."

"Wh…" Amanda had to wet her mouth; it had gone bone dry at his accent. She did after all have a thing for his voice, and apparently after just two days without it, it worked its magic on her again. She tried once more, "What security problem?"

"I'm in charge of your security," he shouted as he got right in her face, "and you're my problem!"

Callie giggled, obviously not afraid of her father in the least as he knelt to pick her up. Amanda was about to tell him to put her down, but he'd motioned with his head and told her, "Move!"

"Excuse me?" It wasn't so much what he'd said, but how he'd said it. That jerk of the head was one she used. Repeatedly, with Callie.

"Bloody hell, Amanda! Get in the God damned truck!" he ordered again as Gregor came forward and grabbed Callie, leading her away.

Instinctively, Amanda reached out for Callie with her only free hand—a futile gesture, it turned out. She was losing control of the situation completely and started to panic. Sensing her stress, Stan reached for his gun. Okay, so not the right thing to do under the circumstances but seriously it was turning into a big boy pissing match and had made Montgomery absolutely furious. She watched as he beat him to it, pulling out his own gun.

"I told you to bring them home, Finch. You had your orders. Yesterday," he shouted, twisting the barrel against Stan's temple.

"Old habits, eh, Montgomery? Think we're going to duel right here in the street?" Stan said, which made the larger man snarl. Amanda had no idea what he meant, but had no time think, either.

"It's not his fault," Amanda cried, reaching out, positioning herself in front of Stan. "Stop, please. We'll go. Right now, if you'd like."

Shaking, Amanda gave a silent plea to Stan to cooperate as Montgomery said, "Are we done here?" At Stan's "Yes, sir," Montgomery removed his weapon and waited for Amanda to start forward. When she didn't, he ushered her toward the truck he'd stepped out of earlier. Callie was already inside. Amanda hesitated again, her eyes darting from her daughter to the street. "Bloody hell, Amanda, my plane's leaving in two hours," he told her. "You and my children will be on it." Her first instinct was to shake her head. "It wasn't an invitation," he informed her, confirming her thoughts about his mouth being made to give orders. "Jesus Christ, Amanda." He shook his head and rubbed his hand across his forehead, suddenly looking worn and exhausted. "I would never hurt you or our children. Please." He reached for Zander.

She clutched the baby protectively, then whispered, "Are you going to take them from me?"

He shook his head. "I am not taking him from you. I need you to step into the truck." He reached for Zander again, but she was shaking so severely he had to unfurl her hands from around him. He held her arm as she climbed in and followed right behind her.

Still in shock, Amanda took little note of the custom appointments as Callie jumped into her lap. Instead of a bench in the back and seats in the middle, she sank into what looked like a plush leather sectional built around the frame. TV screens, laptops, and spyware were everywhere.

Stan sat shotgun. He looked back to make sure she was okay; she wasn't, but nodded anyway. Montgomery sat next to them, taking up a considerable amount of space. He stretched his long legs and settled Zander into the crook of his neck. Then he grinned at Callie, motioning her over. He threw his head back and laughed as she burrowed against him. Then he looked at her, "Bloody hell, Amanda, I wi—"

Yeah, she wished a lot of things, too, but the way he looked at her was so sweet, so endearing in that moment she just didn't know what to think and cut him off instead. "Are you going to put him in his car seat?"

"We're traveling four city blocks. At ten miles an hour. He has a better chance of getting hurt on the sidewalk." He gave her one of his deep, penetrating looks then, the one that wasn't guarded.

"Is there something you'd like to tell me, Mr. Montgomery?" Amanda asked pointedly.

"Yeah, Amanda," he said, leaning forward and gripping her shirt, bringing her in close, "I don't care for you to call me Mr. Montgomery."

"That's it?" Seriously, the way the man looked at her went right to her bones.

"Presently."

She shrugged and stared out the window instead. He had such a commanding presence; it was difficult to be so close. As if reading her mind, he made it worse, nudging his large foot in between hers and dragging her closer. She looked at him against her better judgment and was relieved to see his head was back, eyes closed, hands holding his children. The similarities to Zander were glaring now that she knew to look for them. Same dark hair, same skin tone, and looking at him now, she realized that behind his closed lids, their eyes were the same dark color. Amanda continued staring at him, boring holes into him with her eyes, trying desperately to remember ever being with him, married to him, knowing him. It was so frustrating, but it just wouldn't come.

Suddenly it seemed crazy to have left. The answers to all her questions were right here in front of her. But maybe she'd had to go away to see that. To see that he was the only one who could tell her what had happened.

"Did I leave you?" she asked. "Or did you leave me?"

"Neither, Amanda."

"*Ugh*," she groaned and started hitting the side of her head with her palm. Hard. This was just so frustrating.

"Don't!" He grabbed her hand. "That won't help."

"How do you know?" She knew she was acting childish. But honestly, she couldn't help it. As composed as she tried to remain on the outside, inside she was a mess. Mostly because when he'd grabbed her hand, he laced their fingers and hadn't let go. Intellect said tread with extreme caution. Her heart, maybe even her soul, said something entirely different.

"We don't have time for that conversation right now," Alex told her. They'd just arrived at Amanda's penthouse. Stan opened the door and Alex waited for her to get out first. Trevor was waiting, grinning from ear to ear. He really was sweet, and she'd missed him, all of them for that matter—well, almost all of them.

"Hi, Mrs. Montgomery," he said and suddenly Amanda wanted to smack him. Was she Mrs. Montgomery, really? How dare he just assume she could be that. She had to temper her reaction to the name; grinding her back teeth helped. "Your bag was under Zander's car seat in the stroller."

Amanda reached for her tote, keeping her inner commentary inner. He really had been such a sweet boy, until twelve seconds ago. "Thank you, Trevor. Can you—"

"They're bringing the base from your Rover up now. I'll have it ready by the time you're back."

Amanda remained rooted to the spot. She knew everyone was waiting for her to go forward but she wasn't moving. Yet. Then she noticed Samantha getting out of the truck. She was still so mad at her, and on top of what Trevor had just said, she freaked out. Again. She plucked Zander from Alex's chest, did a quick pivot, and started down the sidewalk.

She heard a bloody hell and a minute later felt Alex behind her. Then his large hands were on her shoulders. "Please, don't walk away, Amanda." His voice was gentle now.

She turned. "Why is Sam with you?"

"Probably because she felt lost without you and the children."

"I'm sure she was fine."

"Really? She's your best friend and she's been by your side for months."

"Some best friend for keeping an entire *husband* from me for over a month, but whatever." Amanda clutched Zander closer, turned, and began walking again. She felt him behind her the entire time. She couldn't keep what she was thinking inside any longer and finally turned. With her free hand, she smacked his chest and yelled, "We were married!"

He grabbed her shoulders, pulled her in, and got right in her face. "We *are* married!" he yelled back.

"There's no record that I was ever married." She went through the files Stan had showed her repeatedly since arriving in Chicago.

"I was there," he bit out. "So were you."

"But I don't even really *know* you, Alex. How am I supposed to remember any of that?" He took it like a slap, actually physically recoiling, but regained control a second later. *Well, bully for you.* Still bothered by another thought she said, "You tricked me!"

"I have never deceived you."

"You purchased JDL Security so you'd have access to your children."

"I purchased JDL to find *you!*"

If she was so important to him, if they were really married, where was her frigging wedding band? "You're wearing an eight-thousand-dollar suit. Two-thousand-dollar loafers. And word on the street is you're richer than Midas."

"And you're wearing three-hundred-dollar jeans, eight-hundred-dollar boots, and your jacket cost at least eleven hundred. What's your point?"

"I. Don't. Have. A. Ring." She held up her left hand to emphasize her point. Scars, plenty. Ring, no.

"Bloody hell, Amanda!" he yelled. "You really want to do this? *Now?*"

"Apparently!"

"You. Don't. Care. For. Jewelry," he told her.

Her eyes narrowed, true but... "What woman doesn't like jewelry?"

"You."

"Well, I would have wanted a simple band."

"You did."

"Where is it?"

"On a chain," he ground out, "around my neck."

"Why?"

"Why?" he repeated in a shout.

"Yes, Al—Montgomery." Oh, jeez, this was so confusing. Still, she spit out, "Why?"

"Have you seen your hand lately?" he shouted again, then grabbed her left hand and held it up. "What do you think caused this gash along your finger?"

Her eyes went wide. "You took it from me?"

"What?" He couldn't believe what she'd asked. "Are you fucking serious?"

She sucked in audible breath. "How dare you speak to me that way!"

"How dare I?" He lifted her right off the ground. Their argument had become so heated his men had surrounded them. Stan was talking to a police officer someone had called. "You want to know why your wedding band is around my neck?"

"Rich *and* smart. Just my luck." His eyes narrowed even more, his mouth settled into a fine line, and the muscles in his neck corded. She was literally right in his face. Nose to nose. He'd brought her there.

"You. Let. Go. For ten months those three words have haunted my every waking and sleeping moment. You let go, Amanda!"

He'd bellowed each word at her. The anger, she felt. But the pain in his eyes caused her to sharply inhale. She realized the gravity of what he'd just told her. She suddenly felt ill. It must have showed because he gently lowered her to the ground and scrutinized every inch of her face. She could see the marks on the inside of his wrist as he cupped her face and tilted it this way and that. There were four crescent-shaped scars. Like a hand had been there, holding on. She could barely hear her own voice when she said, "You're right. We'll do this later." She couldn't look at him anymore. Her head was spinning as she started walking back the way they'd come.

Alexander took Zander as soon as Amanda turned to him. They were just approaching the entrance of her building. She'd barely been able to enunciate the word *please* as she held their son out to him. Stan, Stephen, and Trevor were the only ones still waiting outside. Stan turned the key for the penthouse elevator. Once inside, Amanda pushed herself into the corner. Her hand was gripping the rail. She was staring at the now faint scars that marred the top. Scars he'd put there in his desperate attempt to hold on to her as she'd let go of his wrist and slipped through his fingers.

There was a scar along the inside of her ring finger as the band scraped the bone when it had come off in the struggle. She looked up at him then. Bloody hell, he knew that look. He passed Zander to Stan and stepped in front of her as she turned three shades of green. He palmed her forehead to keep her hair back just before she threw up in her tote bag.

She'd just completed round three as they reached her floor. Stephen cleared the elevator and waited outside the door. She finally dragged her hand across her mouth and shuddered. "Done?" he asked, reaching for the bag.

"Uh-huh." Amanda nodded. She closed her eyes as he brushed her hair back with his hand.

Stephen stepped inside for the second it took to grab Amanda's bag and hand him a water bottle. "Just enough to wet your mouth," Alexander said, passing it to her. She took the smallest sip and let her head fall back. "Amanda?" She had the strangest look in her eyes. And that was saying a lot considering. "What's going through that clever mind of yours?"

She shook her head as if to clear it. "Are you going to take her from me?"

"I would never take either of them from you."

"You could. You have the resources and enough evidence to lock me up. Maybe for good."

Bloody hell! She thought he'd use her breakdown in the hospital against her. "I'm not having you locked up, Amanda," he lied. Because he abso-fucking-lutley was. With him. And their children. And the gaggle of people he seemed to collect along his way. "Now that I've found you, I'm not going anywhere. Ever. Again."

"Why did you come back?"

"*Back?*" he repeated. "I. Didn't. Leave. You," he said, speaking evenly to keep the anger out of his voice.

"I feel broken, Alexander. If you didn't leave me before, you should now."

"Listen to me, Amanda. Very carefully. I will fix you. I *will*."

"You're too late."

"Story of our lives," he said. Would she ever remember? "Always too late."

"You should really work on that."

"I'm trying."

She took a deep, fortifying breath, then said, "Okay. Let's do this."

Alexander gave her a good once-over, tilted her face, and looked in her eyes. "You're okay?"

"Define okay."

He shook his head. "Can't anymore."

"Then all I've got is a big fake smile," she said, pasting one on, "and a 'ready'!"

The corner of his mouth lifted slightly. "That's my girl." He couldn't help brushing his lips across her forehead. She didn't resist. "Let's go."

As soon as they passed through the foyer, Amanda headed toward her room but ran into Rosa in the hallway. "Rosa, Mr. Montgomery is taking us—" She paused. She didn't know where he was taking them. "To be honest, I don't know where. Can you start packing—"

"I'm taking you back to California, Amanda. Backpacks and comfortable clothes for the ride, Rosa."

Alexander watched Amanda make her way down the hallway. She reached for the wall twice for support before she turned into what he assumed was her bedroom. Samantha was watching her as well, and he motioned with his head for her to follow and check on her.

When Sam came back a minute later, he was holding Zander while Rosa was on the floor with Callie preparing a bottle. "Angel, can you go with Uncle Stephen and get your backpack ready?" He waited until they turned into her room, then gave Samantha his full attention.

"She kicked me out," she said with disbelief in her voice. "She brushed her teeth, took off her shoes, looked right at me, and told me to leave."

"Give her time," Alexander said as he brushed past her, hoping he was right. He grabbed the bottle for Zander, a good prop, and headed for Amanda's room. He knocked as he opened the bedroom door. "Amanda?" Alexander called out. Zander fussed again. "Shh…shh…Mama's going to feed you," he promised his son. She came right out, looking adorable with her hair up and face scrubbed. She'd changed into cashmere lounge pants and a hoodie. She walked right up to him and plucked Zander off his chest.

"Mama's got you, baby," she cooed. "How much time do I have?" she asked.

"Twenty minutes good?" When she nodded, he grabbed the tote she'd put on the floor. "What do you need from the other one?"

"The one I threw up in?" she asked.

"Yeah. That one."

"My wallet. I'll get it."

"Rosa already fished it out."

"Tell her thank you," she said, a look of pure relief and gratitude passing over her face. "She'll know what else to put in it." He gave a nod and closed the door behind him.

Closer to twenty-five minutes later, Amanda walked into Callie's room where he was sprawled on her bed, Callie right next to him. She was showing him something on her iPad. He had her tucked in tight under his arm, loving the feel of his daughter curled against him. Callie had changed into a blue tracksuit. Alexander had changed as well, jeans and a T-shirt. Amanda looked like she was about to leave them when he held up his hand and motioned her over.

When she sat on the edge of the bed Alexander asked, "Ready?" She gave him her brightest smile.

Callie giggled. "Big fake smile," she whispered.

Alexander tweaked her nose. "I know, angel." Then he looked at Amanda. "Your mama's specialty."

"It's so strange to hear you talk about me like that." She shook her head. "It's true of course," she said, smiling at Callie as she reached out to touch her. "And it happens to be my favorite defense mechanism."

Callie giggled as his hand covered Amanda's thigh. "Let's go then. Everything but our phones and Callie's iPad is packed."

He lifted Callie in the air again, tickled her till she cried mercy, and watched as she scurried from the room. Then he stood and looked down at Amanda, holding out his hand to help her up. She paused, and he saw her notice the scars that marred the inside of his wrist and up the entire side of his thumb. She put Zander down against the pillows and looked at him questioningly from beneath her lashes. Slowly, she reached out again, this time with both hands to trace the marks. His breath caught in his throat, and he watched as she turned his hand over and held her own scarred hand up to compare. When she saw that he had no scars like she did, she rubbed his hand absently. Then she turned it back over and pressed her fingertips right into the marks on his wrist. Bloody hell, she was taking him right back to his nightmare, and she didn't even know it.

He wasn't sure if she'd meant to speak aloud but he heard her whisper "perfect fit" as she dug her nails in, not hard, but enough to know. Then her hand grasped his wrist. Reflexively, his did the same—just like that night when that was all he had to hold her by—and he clutched her back. It startled her. Her eyes widened, then he watched as she loosened her hold and looked to him with that same questioning expression. Sickened, he silently demonstrated, his fingers trailing her scars, from wrist to the top of her hand and finally along her ring finger.

She swallowed hard, then looked up. "I let go." All he could do was answer with a slow, deliberate nod. "Why?" she asked, fear darkening her expression.

Bloody hell! He did not want to do this right now. He scrubbed his hands over his face and sat down next to her. He picked up Zander and laid him down on his lap. Rubbed his little body with his hands. He looked right at her, and she shrunk back a little, which broke his heart. "Jesus, Amanda, it wasn't because you were scared of me!"

"Well, you don't have to have a coronary!"

"Sweetheart, I've had nearly a dozen since I've met you."

"Do you...do you have a condition?" she asked with genuine concern.

"A condition?" he repeated. "A condition, Amanda?" He got right in her God damned beautiful face. "Yeah, I have a condition, Amanda—it's called *you're fucking killing me!*"

Alexander watched Amanda bite her lip just before she smiled up at him. "You don't scare me."

"Bloody hell, *that* I know."

"First of all, there's a swear jar in the kitchen. You can make a contribution on our way out. And secondly—"

"Swear jar?" Was she crazy? "You're serious?"

"Why does that surprise you?"

"Because my favorite swear word I learned from you!"

She sucked in an audible breath. "That can't be true."

"It sure the hell is!"

"I don't swear!"

"Oh, sweetheart, it may only be one word, but your mouth is filthier than any sailor I've ever been around. And I've been around a lot."

"You're lying!"

"I. Don't. Lie."

"I. Don't. Swear."

"Yes. You. Do."

"Well, maybe it's because of you."

"Oh." He grinned devilishly, looking at her in such a way that made her blush, like he was seeing right through her clothes. "I can assure you—it is."

"What are you trying to say?" she said, shifting in her seat.

"I'm not trying to *say* anything," he said, still taking her in, top to bottom. "I'm telling you—in the right circumstances, you swear!"

"Because you irritate me?"

He shook his head. "No. Irritating you is fun as hell." He got right in her face again and gripped her shoulders before running his hands up and down her arms. "*This* is better."

The implication of what he was telling her hit full force, and she turned three shades of red before she was able to speak again. "So...so..." She had to clear her throat. "When we made him." She pointed at Zander, hoping he wouldn't make her say the whole thing aloud.

Alexander put her out of her misery. "Yes." Bloody hell, their conversation was messing with his head. Literally. "Secondly?" he asked.

"Secondly?" she repeated.

"After you informed me of the swear jar, you said secondly."

"I have no idea."

"Good. Wheels up in forty-five. Let's go."

◁◁   ▷▷

Taking his family to the car from Amanda's penthouse, Alexander felt like an enormous weight had been lifted from his shoulders. They were going home. Amanda was quiet. Finally. Bloody hell, they were not the same two people they used to be. Maybe it was because she'd had her own life in the twenty-first century, while back in his, he and Callie *were* her life. How different things may have been if she could still remember him. Them. Zander was sound asleep, tucked beneath Amanda's chin. Rosa was talking with Stephen, and Callie was holding his hand, staring between him and her mother. Every now and then Amanda gave her a wink, then a big fake smile, which caused his daughter to burst into peals of laughter, her face rubbing his thigh.

Stan was downstairs making sure everyone and everything was ready. As Alexander stood outside the truck, he literally counted his ducks getting in. Amanda, check. Zander, check. Callie, check. As he checked Callie's buckle she asked, "Do you like to fly, Papa? More than ships?"

He covered the top of her head with his hand and told her, "I like anything that gets me to you."

"Hey, Callesandra," Gregor called out as he adjusted the rearview mirror to see her, "I love to fly!"

"I knew it!" she exclaimed with a fist pump. Amanda smiled, too, sharing a look with her.

It was a forty-five-minute ride to the private airport, and they pulled right up to the plane. Hank, his pilot, and the rest of the crew were waiting. Alexander couldn't help but check his family again as he helped them from the truck. Wife, check. Son, check. Daughter, check. Hank introduced himself to Amanda, Callie, and Rosa.

Callie ran onto the plane, turned around at the top of the stairs, and asked, "Can I sit wherever I want?"

"Anywhere but the pilot's seat, angel." He walked with Amanda to the stairs, his hand against her back. Callie had sprawled out on the sofa in back by the galley. She had three TV screens to watch and was already plugging her iPad and iPhone into the jacks. Stephen sat down next to her and she promptly threw her feet into his lap. Rosa took one of a cluster of four chairs with Stan and Gregor. Trevor and Michael took another cluster. Zander's baby seat was already installed by the front. Amanda sat in the seat next to it. Alexander spoke with the pilot and checked Callie's seat belt even though Stephen just buckled it.

He checked Zander's harness and Amanda's belt too. Satisfied they were tucked in tight, he finally sat across from Amanda. He looked at his watch; he'd said his plane was leaving in two hours. It was one hour fifty-nine on the dot. As Hank started to taxi, Alexander shared a look with Stephen. This day was a long time coming. They left the ground a minute later.

Mission fucking accomplished.

<< >>

Lights out and plane relatively quiet, thirty minutes later Amanda got up and went to check on Callie. She was sitting in Stephen's lap, looking rather content. She gave her a kiss and told her she loved her. Then went to check out the galley where she found a feast from Gibson's, her favorite Chicago steakhouse. She was just about to head back and ask if anyone wanted anything when she saw the bottle of Macallan. It was ridiculously expensive. In fact, one of the most expensive pours out there. The four cases at home, the bottles that lined the shelves above the bar, they were for him. She knew then she'd bought it for Alex.

She fingered the bottle, desperate for a memory of him, them, anything. Just as she was about to whack the side of her head again, he was behind her, his large hand covering hers. "Don't," he whispered.

"I can't help it."

"If I thought it would work, believe me, I'd do it myself."

She turned and looked up. "It seems logical, doesn't it?"

"Let me tell you something about logic, Amanda…"

Amanda waited for him to continue. And waited. He was just staring at her. "Well…?"

Alex shook his head. "It's complicated."

"It's supposed to be simple."

"Not when all the variables change. Not when the simplest way from A to B is no longer a straight line. I lived for *and* by logic, Amanda."

"What changed?"

"Bloody hell, sweetheart, that's easy." He smiled down at her. "You."

"Can I ask you a question?"

"You may."

Her eyes narrowed. "Did you just correct my grammar?"

He smiled, only slightly, and her heart hurt just then, realizing how much pain he was in. It was remarkable how well he seemed to push through things. "Not on purpose."

"Are you hungry?"

"Always."

"Good, let's eat."

As he was about to leave the galley, she called out to him.

"Were we happy, Alex?"

He turned and looked at her so intently, a million emotions crossing his face, before saying, "Deliriously."

"Really?"

"Swear to God, sweetheart."

CHAPTER
TEN

MARCH 2
NORTHERN CALIFORNIA

It was well past midnight by the time they circled Amanda's drive and subsequently piled through the front doors, which wasn't an exaggeration. Seriously, there were nine of them, and that number would have been larger if not for the late hour. On the ride from the airport, Alex had told her that he'd long ago leased the estate next door, and so whenever they knocked off for the night, that's where he and most of his crew went. Amanda had stared at him incredulously. How had she never noticed? No wonder they were always close at hand. Now that Amanda had some of her footing back and could see things a bit more clearly, she realized it was kind of ridiculous that she'd allowed the circus into her home so easily. The break had been good for her. She'd needed that burst of independence, even if it had been short-lived.

Exhausted, Amanda let Alex carry a sleeping Callie up to her room and tuck her in, following closely behind. She stood in the doorway, watching him, racking her brain again for a memory, any memory, *something*. He looked so natural with Callie, so much like he fit. At that moment, he turned, stood, and approached her. "Amanda, I—"

She reached out and laid her hand on his chest. It always surprised her that touching him was so easy, natural even. Was that a sign? She'd never been so immediately easy with a man before. And aside from when he'd dragged her closer in the truck and laced their hands together, he hadn't made any overt moves. Nothing romantic or particularly intimate. In fact, she'd even caught him a couple times pulling back, which she really appreciated.

"Can we do this tomorrow, Alex? Please," she asked, not ready for whatever other revelations he had in store.

He nodded. "I'll be back in the morning." He covered her hand, gave her an uncustomarily shuttered look, and said good-night. She could feel his hurt; it actually pained her. Not just emotionally, but physically. Half of her felt like the worst person ever for sending him away, and the other was just so confused and tired. Thank God for Evan, who had advised them to keep things as they were for the moment.

She stayed on the landing listening as Alex spoke quietly with his brother. Once they stepped outside, Amanda walked down the stairs to sit on the bottom step, watching as his taillights wound down her drive. Stephen came back inside a few minutes later, looking beat and a bit forlorn. Amanda watched as he shut the door behind him and paused for a moment, before banging his head against it in frustration and cursing silently, rubbing the spot. He hadn't seen her yet.

"I've tried that, and been told it won't help," Amanda said, feeling a sudden rush of affection for this man who, she realized with a start, was technically her brother-in-law. *So weird.* She could see the corners of his mouth lift a bit before he turned to look at her.

"Leave it to you, Amanda, to purposely hit your head."

"Does that surprise you?"

He gave something of a snort. "There was a time when you did worse, so a knock to the head? Not even this much." He demonstrated a smidge with his fingers.

Wow, she could actually feel the history—the familiarity—between them now. Not that she remembered it, but even the way he looked at her, spoke to her, she knew now beyond a shadow of a doubt, she really *was* connected to these brothers in a deep, inexplicable way. "What'd I do?" she asked, scooching over to make room on the step for him.

He sat down and held out his hand to her. Without thinking, she extended her left hand, but he shook his head. "Oh, the good one," she chuckled. "Lucky me." She rolled her eyes and placed her right hand on top of his. He turned it over and brushed his thumbs across the now-familiar scar that ran diagonally across her palm. She had a flash of Alex doing the same when he'd brought her home from the hospital. "Were you there?" she asked.

The sound he made was closer to a chortle this time, and he shook his head, looking up to the ceiling before returning her gaze. "I was always there when something happened to you, Amanda. Or at least not far behind. I had your guard at times then too. When Alexander was off, uh, on business. Apparently, I suck at it."

She smiled. There was something about the way he said that that warmed her heart. "We were close, Stephen, weren't we?"

He nodded. "Yeah, we were."

"Was it you who took me to the hospital?"

"A hospital." He shook his head. "No way, we would have never—I mean—had we even been able, it would have been too far. Alex had just returned from sea and… Christ, Amanda, you were bleeding like a sieve. I held you while Alex stitched you up."

"Wait," she said, pulling her hand back and looking at the scar. It was so smooth, and aside from the small dots that still marred her skin where the stitches had been, it was terribly clean. "Your brother did this?" She held her hand up to him just to clarify they were speaking of the same wound.

Stephen nodded. "Yep. He did. Mr. Cool as a Cucumb—"

"Oh my God," Amanda said, cutting Stephen off. "Something just came to me, someth—if you ever have a crisis," she said slowly, an image of Callie in an old-fashioned dress flashing through her mind. Had she been playing dress up? "He's the one and only person you need with you," she said, her voice trailing off a second before she finished. God, was this normal? Her *new* normal? "I don't know where that came from."

"Let's keep that between us, okay? I wouldn't want it to go to his head," he teased. The levity was a much-needed break from all the tension that had been filling the air, and she was grateful for it. "Back to your hand, he cleaned, stitched, and dressed it him—"

"Wait!" Oh God, she could see a glass filled with a white milky substance. She shuddered—a tactile memory of how horribly awful it had tasted. Alex was straddling an ottoman on one end and she was facing him with Stephen behind her holding her steady. There was something terribly odd about the memory. It looked like a room at the estate in Abersoch, but the furnishings were so old-fashioned. "I remember that."

"You do?"

She nodded. "He had the most serious look on his face—I mean more serious than usual." At this, Stephen smiled and nodded. "I think he was in a uniform." She hesitated. The uniform was more like the ones she'd seen in historical reenactments, but she supposed it was entirely possible Alexander was into those things. She narrowed her eyes as she tried to home in—her head was obviously a jumble—then shook her head and shrugged. "Maybe." It was gone.

"He was so scared you would get an infection, or that if he didn't get it closed just right, you wouldn't be able to play the piano anymore."

They both turned as Callie's voice sounded from the top of the stairs. Poor baby, traipsing to and fro the past few days had taken its toll. She reached out to Stephen. "Thank you for sharing that with me." Then she called to Callie, "Coming, sweetie."

So much had changed in the past few days. And while she didn't have her memories, at least not of her relationship with and marriage to Alexander Montgomery, she felt more secure, like there wasn't this big secret hanging overhead, being kept from her. It really helped her feel more in control. And bits and pieces *were* starting to come back.

She heard a soft knock on her door a bit later. She was in bed but still had the light on.

"Ammy?"

She turned as Sam pushed the door open and padded to the other side of the bed to slip beneath the covers next to her. "I'm sorry I didn't say anything. You have every right to be angry with me," she blurted out.

Amanda closed her eyes and shook her head. "I don't know what to think. Evan has assured me that my memory will return naturally. He really believes that." She rolled her eyes. "Seriously! Now I'm buying into what the company shrink says." They both chuckled. It felt good to laugh with her best friend again. And Evan's words felt more possible now that she had started getting vivid flashes of things, as strange and startling as they were. "I was just so mad and freaked out—you were an obvious and easy target."

"You and Callie, and now Zander, have been my life for these past months, Amanda. I would never let anyone hurt you. Ever." She came up on an elbow. "Like Stan would have to get the hell out of the way, because I would kill them myself."

Amanda's eyes narrowed as she tilted her head. "Wait, wasn't it *you* who told me Stan was the guy who would take care of everything?"

Sam rolled her eyes. "You were a mess that night, Amanda. Jesus, according to Stan, Callie was too. I was thousands of miles away when you called, and if I couldn't be there myself, I reached for the first name I could think of, and that was Stan."

"I can't remember it, but I'm glad it was him. I can't remember any of it." She shook her head, looking at her wrist and the scar she had from her surgery. She thought about Alex then, his stricken expression when she'd replayed whatever scene had happened with their hands. Finally wiped out, Amanda turned off the light and rolled over. She heard Sam flip the pillow and get comfortable. "I asked him if we were happy," she whispered a few minutes later.

"What did he say?"

"Deliriously."

"You know, I didn't meet him until Zander was born, but based on the way you spoke about him, I think you were, Ammy. I really think you were."

⟨⟨ ⟩⟩

Alexander walked back into Amanda's at o-seven hundred. It had been a long, restless night. Evan had given him an earful, going on about Alexander letting his anxiety—that was Evan's word—get the better of him. But the truth was

Alexander had been furious that Amanda had left and taken his children. Not that she wasn't capable or for that matter entitled to do what she wanted, when she wanted, but—and it was a but of monstrous proportions—he'd just found them again for Christ's sake, did she really have to leave? Deep down, he knew the answer of course—they'd kept her in the dark. And now, although she knew there was something between them, a big something at that, presently it felt worse. He checked in with Stephen when he decided to stop torturing himself and get out of bed. Stephen told him lights had been out in Amanda's house on the later side, as in way later, which meant no one was about yet, not even Helen with the baby. A quick workout later, Alex and the boys made their way over just as Amanda was coming down the stairs with the baby.

"Morning," he said. She gave a perfunctory hi in return. This new awkwardness between them was difficult even under the circumstances. "Callie going to school?"

She smiled then. "Well, since it's Saturday," she said, "probably not."

He swore under his breath; this was perhaps the first time in his life he'd actually lost track of the days. And considering his life the past year, which included two different centuries, that was saying a lot. "Amanda, I don't know what to do. How to—"

"Can we just go have coffee and breakfast? Like most other mornings?"

"Yeah, that sounds like a great start," he said, feeling his shoulders relax. He followed her into the kitchen where Rosa was getting breakfast together and poured coffee.

The boys, including Stephen and Gregor, had taken up residence in the sitting area adjacent to the kitchen. When he turned to hand her a mug, Amanda was just staring blankly. He softly called her name, but she didn't respond. He tried again, reaching out to grasp her arm. "Hey, where'd you go?"

She blinked, looking as if she'd just come out of a stupor. "Where did *I* go?" she repeated. "Where did *you* go, Alex?"

And so they'd continue. And not in private, either, apparently. "I didn't *go* anywhere, Amanda." He shook his head. "For the longest time I couldn't *go* anywhere."

"I don't understand, Alex."

"Until you remember, sweetheart, you won't be able to."

She shook her head, a look in her eye that Alexander knew well. She wasn't going to let this go. "Uh-uh, no, not good enough. I still don't know *really* what happened. You said I let go, which means you didn't intend to leave me, right? Bu—"

His head snapped back as if he'd been slapped, unsure he'd heard her correctly, he pulled her in closer. "Excuse me?" he said. Bloody hell, he liked her closer. She smelled so good, and her gorgeous blue eyes sparkled from the sun blasting through the kitchen windows, even as they narrowed at him.

"I said, I don't think you meant to lea—"

Jesus. "I heard you," he ground out. It sounded just as bad the second time. "I would have never left you, Amanda." Didn't she know, couldn't she *feel* what was between them? He felt the sting of tears. *Fuck.* Now was not the time. "I *never* would have left you and Callie alone if it could have been helped," he said evenly, forcing his voice to steady.

"I don't know what that means, Alex!" she said, clearly exasperated. "If *what* could have been helped?"

Bloody hell, the way she looked at him, he just wanted to tell her everything. But what? "Gee, Amanda, you see you and Callie fell hundreds of feet from the side of a cliff and traveled through time and well, um, then after me and the guys *also* time traveled here to be with you." Evan would love that. He sighed, hating that she couldn't yet know everything. "It means at the time it was impossible for me or my men to get to you. And by the time we could, you were under the protection of JDL."

Her brows drew together as she considered God only knew what else, but then she nodded, satisfied at least for now. "Did you know I was pregnant?" she asked, her voice smaller than before.

He breathed a sigh of relief. This one he could handle. "I'm not sure even *you* knew then. We were moving." Fleeing, actually. "The entire household was upside down that night, Amanda. It had been for days."

"Wait." She shook her head. "What household?"

"Abersoch." *Come on, sweetheart, you've got this*, he thought, hoping something, *anything* he might say would trigger her memory return.

She wrapped her hand around his forearm, nodding slowly. "Do you think going back there would help?"

"It might," he told her. Bloody hell, what if going to Great Britain was the key? What if seeing the estate again brought her memory back in a flash? But Alexander never wanted to set foot on British soil again. It was a different place now than it had been then, he knew that, it was just the principle of the matter. "But we're not going back."

"I don't mean right now," she said, rolling her eyes. "Duh, not like this second, bu—"

"We won't be returning to Britain, Amanda," he said firmly, feeling surer of that than anything right now.

"I meant at some point in the near future."

Bloody hell, when his wife became stuck on something, very little could change her mind. "We won't return to Britain, Amanda," he repeated slowly, evenly.

"Ever?"

"Ever." He could never go back to a place that had once put a price on his head for simply believing in the right to freedom, no matter how much time had passed since then.

"Okay," she said slowly. "Whatever happened, Alex, I know it must have been bad. I believe you. I've been having mixed feelings about Abersoch, too, though I haven't known why. I used to love it there. Maybe this is part of it. But what if Callie wants to go to Oxford? Or Cambridge? Or LSE one day? It's part of her heritage, Alex—it's not unreasonable she'd want to explore it."

"She won't," he said, though he hadn't thought of that. "You can't know tha—"

"Bloody hell, Amanda, ten months ago we were hellbent on leaving Britain. For good."

"I *know* that," she said, "but why? You keep telling me we're not going back, but what happened, Alex?" She clutched his shirt. "I used to love it there, so what was so awful that I have such strange feelings about it now?" He could only meet her stare, unsure of what to say. "Help me, please," she pleaded.

"It's complicated."

"Uncomplicate it."

"Jesus, Amanda." The gravity of his actions hit him then. For the first time he realized that everything, all of it, was his fault. He'd been the one to rebel, to join the other side. Why couldn't he just have been happy with the status quo? They could have lived their lives and been okay. Of course, he may have died anyway once the war broke out. He wiped his eyes.

"Just tell me already," she pleaded.

He thought of how best to put it. "There was a price on my head."

"What?" She stepped back. "You mean..." She came back in and whispered, "Like a hit? A contract?" She looked around as if there still might be danger. Her guess was close enough, so he nodded. "Who?" she asked.

It was easy to stick to the truth here. "The Crown."

She gasped, Zander stirring as she clutched him tighter. "Your own government! What—did you steal state secrets? Were you a rogue spy or—" Bloody hell, she started gasping for air.

"Amanda!" He led her to the table, sat her down, and knelt in front of her. "Breathe, sweetheart." He placed a hand over her chest. "Shh...shh..." he whispered, cupping her head with his other hand. "That's it, breathe." She shuddered and clutched his hand.

"That's been happening to me a lot lately," she said between shaky breaths. "These flashes of memory and they just…take over. Just now, I remembered a document. It was in a leather-bound ledger of some sort. Like some kind of legal accounting."

"Do you remember what was on it?" Alexander asked, every one of his senses alert.

She shook her head, but something in her look said she was holding back.

"Amanda, I wasn't—I wasn't executed." Though he shuddered now at the thought. "I'm alive and well. As are you and our children."

"Can you take him?" she asked as she started to stand. Then he watched again like an idiot as she thumped her forehead with her hands.

"Stop."

Callie padded into the kitchen then, latching on to Amanda's leg, and joined right in. "Papa, are you going to leave a lot again?"

"I have a new business and responsibilities, angel."

"Are you still an admiral in the navy?"

Amanda's eyes darted right to his. "No, angel."

"Are you still a spy?" she said, twirling her hair and examining it intently as she did so.

He kept his eyes on Amanda as he answered this question too. "No, Callie."

"Did those bad men take me and Mama 'cause they found out?"

"Wait, what bad men?" Amanda jumped in, wrapping an arm around Callie.

"The men who took us from the house, Mama," Callie told her, then went back to twirling. "You killed them, right, Papa?" Callie said absently.

"The bad men are gone, angel. I killed them," he said evenly, praying his daughter wouldn't say anything more. Not now.

"Papa?"

"Callie?"

"I have to tell you something."

"I'm listening."

"When…that night…" She looked down, worrying her little hands together again and again. "I was hiding under your desk."

"I know you were, I helped you get there." He gently moved her chin up to look into her eyes. "It's not your fault, angel."

"Do you remember what you told Mama when she came in?"

"*Bloody hell*," he whispered as he scrubbed his hand over his face. "I remember." He took a deep breath and gave Callie his full attention again. Knowing she would continue pressing unless he got the story exactly right, he tried not to look at Amanda as he continued. "First, Mama came in and said she had a bad feeling. And I said—"

"You said, *really?*" Callie interrupted, giggling. Alexander gave her an indulgent smile. "'Cause that's what Mama always said to you when you told her something she already knew."

"That's exactly why I said it," he replied, suddenly feeling very heavy. They'd excelled at being a family, and remembering the easy closeness they'd once had killed him.

"Do you remember what you said after that?" Callie asked.

He didn't take his eyes off her as he reenacted the scene, which was branded in his brain—the last hours he'd spent with his family before everything shattered. "I said, 'Twenty minutes, Amanda. That ship—'"

"Did you point to it, Papa?" Callie interrupted again. "I couldn't see from beneath the desk."

"I did...I said, 'Twenty minutes, Amanda.'" He lifted his right arm as he had that same night and pointed as if it were still there. "'That ship. We're on it. So if there's something you can't live without, you'd better fetch it now.'" Amanda looked horror stricken. *Jesus, I know, sweetheart. It's a living, recurring nightmare in my head that never goes away.*

"Do you know what it was she couldn't live without?" Callie asked eagerly.

"I didn't know at the time," he said, shaking his head, "but I'm guessing it was you, Callie."

"So it *is* my fault," she said, dropping her head dejectedly. The sight broke Alexander's heart. If he'd known this was where the inquiry was leading, he'd never have taken her there.

"No," he said at the same time as Amanda. "You were still hiding when Mama came back, weren't you?"

Callie nodded.

"Then you know that when Mama said she had to talk to me, *I* told her it had to wait."

"But she didn't think it could."

"She didn't say that, angel." Alexander shook his head.

"But, Papa, that's what she *meant*," Callie said, her voice getting more and more distraught. "I remember how she said it. That's why I went after her." She looked at Amanda. "Mama?"

"Oh, sweetie, I wish I could help you," Amanda said, hugging her. She looked at him then, shrugging her shoulders helplessly. Something about the gesture changed the dynamic, warmed his heart too. Amanda was trying to help him help their daughter.

When her mother couldn't add to the story, Callie continued. "By the time I caught up to you, it was too late," she told Amanda. "Do you remember how you roared, Papa? When you found us on the ledge?"

He swore under his breath then answered, "I do, Callie."

"And when I fell and then Mama let go of you...you roared again. I thought the first roar was fierce, Papa...but I'll never forget that last one. You roared like that 'cause you thought we were gone forever, didn't you?"

He couldn't acknowledge that particular question. Wouldn't. "I found you, though, didn't I?"

"I gotta tell you something else, Papa."

Jesus. "Still listening."

"I know why Mama can't remember anymore."

"Oh, angel. She got real sad in the hospital after Zander was born and her memory is taking a little break. You know that."

"Nuh-uh." Callie shook her head. "Mama thought *you* were gone forever, too. I remember. We were living in our big house in New York." She smiled then and looked at Amanda. "I liked it there, Mama." Amanda smiled back, mouthed *me too*, and started running her fingers through Callie's hair. "Mama used to light a candle for you every single night, Papa. Then when she thought I had gone to bed, she'd play the piano." She looked at Amanda again for reassurance. "You play the prettiest music, Mama." She turned back to him after Amanda gave her an indulgent smile, which masked the expectant tension in her eyes. "But Mama would always cry after, Papa, and then she'd stand in front of the window, like right in front with her head and hands pressed against the glass, and tell you to come home to us. I remember 'cause she did it every single night."

◁◁ ▷▷

"I did?" Amanda barely got the words out, her head was whirling, and she felt like a five-hundred-pound weight lay on her heart. She couldn't remember that, or so many other things. Poor little Callie, holding all these memories without her mother to take some of the burden. Well, there was that flash of the ledger, but nothing else. She remembered their home in New York, of course, and now that she was thinking about it, she was surprised they'd moved. She thought she'd loved it there, and from what she could remember, the things she *could* remember, they'd had a great summer. She'd seen pictures, thanks to Stan and the newspaper and magazine articles he'd shown her. "I loved our home in New York too, baby," she said again.

"But not after you saw that book."

"What book, sweetie?"

"The one that made you scream, Mama. I found it after Aunt Sam and Mr. Finch took you upstairs. Mr. Finch had to carry you."

Alex looked at her then. But she shook her head. She didn't know what Callie was talking about.

"What did it say, Callie?" Amanda asked gently, a bit petrified and baffled.

"It was open to a page that had Papa's name on it," she told her emphatically, nodding her head. Then Callie looked at Alex. "It said you were guilty, Papa, of *reason*. And you had to write a sentence about death. It took me a long time to sound that sentence out, Papa, but I repeated it a bunch of times, so that I would never forget it."

‹‹ ››

Amanda spent the rest of the morning vacillating between wanting to know more and just letting sleeping dogs lie for the moment. It was frigging exhausting. Evan was out of town for the weekend, but she had called him about it. It was one thing to have all these random memories, flashes, or whatever they were, but when she tried to place them in context, it was like the pieces of a jigsaw puzzle locking together. And the picture was sometimes terrifying. After

Callie's last declaration, Alex's phone had gone off. He'd looked ridiculously relieved, probably grateful for an emergency. The circus, minus Stephen, had piled out the front doors and hadn't returned for a few hours. She still had so many questions—more now than before—but for the moment, Amanda was happy for the reprieve. There was only so much a person could take in one frigging sitting.

◀◀   ▶▶

When the crew returned, Alex and the boys took up residence in the living room. Later, she passed him in the hall, both going in different directions to and from the kitchen, and Alex reached out to touch her. For the first time that day, he gave her one of those looks that she used to love, where she could see how much he worried about her wellbeing. She nodded and smiled, telling him, "I'm okay," before she reached out to keep hold of him. "You?"

"Yeah," he said as she was absently rubbing the material of his shirt between her fingers. "Soft enough?" he asked.

She smiled. "Considering the fortune you spend on your clothes, I'd expect soft, but your clothes are the *softest* I've ever felt."

"You always had a thing for my clothes," he chuckled.

"I did?" she asked, a second before Rosa popped in and handed him a stack of freshly pressed slacks. "I may be one sandwich short of a picnic, but I'm telling you now, I would notice if you moved in, Montgomery," she teased, knowing Rosa loved indulging Alex and the guys. And God it felt so nice right now to just *be* with him; she missed the easy rapport they used to have.

"You? One sandwich short?" He shook his head. "You happen to be a ridiculously intelligent woman. And you're not crazy, sweetheart," he said, touching her again, this time to tuck an errant wisp of hair behind her ear. "You're suffering from psychogenic amnesia."

"That's a lovely sentiment, Alex, but what I *have* is psychogenic amnesia, *caused* by my suffering."

"You just proved my point, clever girl."

The next hour she spent pacing the house. She'd been up and down the stairs and through the foyer what seemed like fifty times. On each pass, she stopped to look at him. Then thought better of it and walked away. Finally, Alex put his laptop on the table, threw his phone next to it, and started after her. Heart racing, she ran. He caught her in the hallway just before the kitchen and pulled her back against him. "What is it?" he asked.

"I don't know what to do," she whispered, a bit out of breath, fully in his embrace. It was a first, at least that she could remember. She was engulfed by warmth, and the most powerful set of arms. Something about it felt amazing.

"About what?"

Amanda turned in his arms. He had her so close there wasn't a lot of room between them at all. "About this." She wagged her finger back and forth. "About us."

"What do you think we should do?"

"I just told you, I don't know!"

"Then figure it out, clever girl."

"That's my girl, clever girl," she repeated the monikers from yesterday and today. "I don't know her! I don't know you!"

"*Her*—is *you*, Amanda."

"Do you miss her?"

His eyes narrowed. "How could I? You're right in front of me."

"I'm not the same," she cried out, confused by how she felt being held in his embrace, so close she could see small flecks of amber in dark, dark eyes. Her heart was racing and not from the run down the hallway.

"Neither am I," he told her as his hands snaked up her back to cup her head.

"What if…what—" She lost her train of thought. Oh God, was he going to kiss her? Suddenly that's all she could think about. Wrapped in his arms right now, so close to him, she knew—could feel it in her bones—knew that she was safe with him. No wonder listening to his deep, accented voice calmed her. Or staring into his dark eyes anchored her. And although she'd been pressed against him a few times now, too many of her other senses had been engaged or confused. "We lived, Amanda. All of us." He bent his head closer.

"We lived," she breathed, barely able to follow the track of their conversation with her heart racing. "You went to prison, Alex. I obviously thought you had been executed for reasons I don't think I can handle knowing about yet, and I had a nervous breakdown." She clutched his shirt, leaning closer.

"And here we are, sweetheart. Alive. With our children." Both his hands gently clutched her head now as he breathed, "You slipped through my fingers once, Amanda. Literally. That will not happen again." Then he kissed her, canted her head just where he wanted it, and covered her lips with his brilliant British mouth.

Seriously, how on earth had she forgotten that!

CHAPTER
ELEVEN

Alexander's phone rang at twenty-two hundred on the dot. He was standing in the doorway between the terrace and living room, leaning against the jamb. Scotch in hand, he'd been nursing the drink for the better part of an hour looking out over Amanda's property. Dinner was long over; he'd left Amanda's before bedtime tonight. She'd asked for some time, and unable to think of a reason why she shouldn't have it, he'd pleasantly said his good-nights. The boys had looked a bit crestfallen—how he felt, but hid—to be knocking out early. They usually liked to help the girls with whatever puzzle they were working on, or if their luck was right, Amanda would break out Yahtzee and things got competitive. And those were just the things that happened before the kids' bedtime, *after* they would usually retire to the billiard room. He was becoming rather proficient, Stephen too. Amanda just liked to be part of the gang and Sam, Christ, she was *good*, albeit a tad bloodthirsty. So yeah, leaving early was rough. Actually, it sucked. Especially since some of the awkwardness of the past few days had fallen away, as Amanda had finally worked out in her mind that he was a good guy and that what they'd once had was real. Just interrupted.

It had taken a week, and another blowup, to get there—Amanda was not one to be satisfied by a single round of questioning—but from where he was standing, even next door, it had been worth it. Early that morning they'd been on the terrace; she'd just wrapped up her morning session with Evan. She was still remembering only everyday life since her return to the States. Nothing about their time together in Abersoch, not of significance anyhow. Her greeting to him that day had been blunt. "How did you get out of prison? And by the way, does that make you a felon?"

"Good morning to you too," he'd said, giving a look to Evan, but the medical genius had only shrugged. So, while measuring his thoughts on which way to take this, Alexander had poured himself a mug of coffee, taken a long sip considering the coastal view, and had turned to stand in front of Amanda, finally having landed on an answer he hoped would satisfy her. "Stephen and Gregor broke me out, Amanda. And am I a felon? Technically, no. Any and all records of my activities are gone or have been destroyed." Which happened to be the truth.

"What'd you do, super spy, to make them disappear?" Yeah, she was huffy at best.

"You want to know the truth?" he'd asked her as she crossed her arms over her chest.

"I wouldn't be asking otherwise, wise guy." Her foot had started tapping then too.

"Your friend Samantha and the other super spy, wise guy"—he'd motioned with his head toward the kitchen—"Finch made the last of the records disappear."

"Bull."

"Bull?" he'd repeated.

"Yeah, Alexander, bull."

"Let me tell you something about the company you keep, sweetheart." It was time to get something off his chest that had been bothering the hell out of him. "That dear, dear friend of yours? Samantha Gilchrist, your sweet schoolgirl pal of yore who became a savvy esquire extraordinaire, gave you the name of one of the most notorious fixers in London."

"Fixer," she'd said, scrunching her face, not following. "Who?"

"Stanley Finch."

Her mouth had fallen open for just a second before her determined expression returned. "Just because someone's capable of taking care of things doesn't make them notorious, Alex. Maybe *you're* the notorious one."

Her naivety was frustrating at best, and he'd let her know it. "You hired Finch through a black-market ring of blokes so unsavory I'm surprised you and Callesandra lived through the night. *Why* you wouldn't just pick up the God damned phone and call Art Fisher or a reputable service to begin with I have no idea." He'd yelled the last part. She'd showed him her displeasure with a look. "Sorry. You were ridiculously lucky. At his core, Finch happens to be a great guy, and the best at what he does. So, in the end, while Sam may have been correct, it was precarious at best. And still gives me nightmares that it could have gone another way."

"You weren't there, Alex!" she'd snapped. "At least I had someone to help me."

It'd cut like a blade, sharper even than Stephen's dagger. Stan's voice of all people had sounded behind him then.

"He's right, Amanda. It could have been really bad. Thank God I knew Sam, or she knew me," Stan had said.

"Really, Stan? Whose side are you on?"

"Listen, I didn't meet Alex until he purchased JDL. But in the time that I've known him—shit, Amanda, I knew him from you too. Your own words, actions even. You poured a scotch every night, placed it on the piano, and played for that fucking glass. Consider yourself lucky you can't remember it, 'cause Sam was right, it was heartbreaking to watch. So as far as coming to his defense, yeah, I am. He's one of the good guys."

"He's got blood on his hands," she'd said, her voice exasperated, confused.

Stan had shaken his head. "Don't we all."

Alexander had watched Amanda digest what Stan was telling her, nodding as she accepted the story yet again. He knew she trusted Stan completely. Memory or not, it would be a lie to say it didn't bother him that there had been a time when she had trusted him completely and that he wasn't there anymore. That it was his fault for not telling her they were married to begin with. "Why did it take you so long to find us?" she'd finally asked.

"By the time I was able to start searching for you and Callie, Stan had you buried deep," he'd said. "After finding the surgeon who repaired your hand, and your home in New York, your trail went cold. Ice cold."

Stan had interjected then. "Before we left Great Britain, I made a call to Art Fisher. He hired me on the spot, and you became a client. We had Callie's adoption papers and accompanying files forged in case we were stopped by the authorities and purchased passports."

"Wait." She'd put her hand up. "I just…ugh." Her frustration had seemed to get the better of her. "Wait. That seedy back alley storefront outside of London." She'd looked right at him then. "You were there searching for *me*, weren't you? And Callie."

"Bloody hell, Amanda. I did nothing *but* search for you and Callie." He remembered when they'd shaken down the document forger in that alley, how close he thought he'd been to finding the key to tracking down his wife and daughter—and how devastatingly disappointing it was to find he knew only Stan's first name and little else.

"So we had already left?"

"When you realized you were pregnant, we left for the States," Stan had told her.

"New York?" she'd asked, and Stan had nodded in response. "Why didn't you come then, Alex?" she'd asked him as if it were that easy.

"By the time we found the surgeon and document lab you were gone from New York, Amanda. Not just Great Britain."

"But I thought you were a spy," she'd said, seeming genuinely confused. "Why couldn't you just, I don't know, find me?"

"From the moment you and Callie have been on your own, each purchase you've made has either been in cash or under an assumed name. Including the admission forms for Callesandra's private school. Callie's medical records. And yours. No back doors, Amanda. Encrypted. Sealed. Impossible to penetrate."

"Impossible?" she'd said, challenging him. "Yet here you are."

"Because I bought JDL, Amanda. After acquiring a slew more security and surveillance companies that you happened to *not* be a client of."

"I'm the reason you went into the security business?" she'd asked as if the enormity had just dawned on her.

"Yes, Amanda. I needed to be on the inside. Not that all clients require the services that you did for a time. But what use would those services be if another good sleuth could happen upon you? So, with Chris's help, we..." He trailed off. That part she didn't have to know.

"So with Chris's help you what?" she'd pressed. Alexander sighed. Never satisfied until she had the whole story, this one.

"With Chris's help, we purchased JDL Security, all its subsidiaries, and with the other business we had already acquired formed a corporate conglomerate."

"That had to cost an incredible sum of money."

"It did."

"How much?"

"It's not important, Amanda."

"How much, Montgomery?"

"Six hundred and fifty million dollars," he said, suppressing a smile when Amanda whacked his chest with a "Shut the front door." Then she leaned in closer and whispered, "You paid that much money to find me?"

"I would give all of my worldly possessions for you, Amanda, and then some." Callie had come outside then, ending their conversation.

She'd ruminated on this new information for the better part of two days, then called a truce. That she'd only snapped at him again that one time was really remarkable considering the pressure she was under. Not that *he* was pressuring her—at least not anymore. He'd gotten the message loud and clear after he'd gone all alpha and taken them from Chicago. At times he actually longed for their old life, nothing like eighteenth-century estate life to know where his wife and children would be at any given time. That, however, had come with its own uncertainties as well. War, disease, travel that had kept them apart for long periods of time. They were better off here. Amanda could actually have a life here, Callie too. And, Jesus, he liked it here. What wasn't to like? He had buckets of money and was charting his own destiny. He loved his new business, the people he employed and help they rendered. It beat the hell out working on behalf of the British Empire and having no choice in what was ordered.

So, once that bit of tension had gotten out of the way, there had been another uptick in tension, but now of the sexual kind. Jesus, just being near her since he'd kissed her was difficult at best. When he'd chased her down the hall and caught her, and finally held her fully in his embrace, it was all he could do to maintain a coherent thought. And when she'd turned and then looked up at him the way she had, all bets were off. As the saying goes, and he loved that saying now, he'd kissed her six ways to Sunday and back again, and it still wasn't enough. He wanted to drag her in close, kiss the hell out of her, and bury himself so deep inside her, he wouldn't know where she began, and he ended. He'd been on his best behavior though and was waiting again for a sign from Amanda.

He was still leaning casually against the door jamb, staring at Amanda's property when he answered his phone. "She's on her way over, Alex," Stephen said.

"What?" He wasn't sure he heard his brother correctly.

"She put the kids to bed, came downstairs, grabbed a jacket, and said, 'I'm going to Alex's, left or right at the bottom of the drive?'"

"She's walking? *Alone?*"

"Are you kidding me?" Stephen said, sounding insulted, then corrected, "Um, well, yeah she's walking, but two guys have eyes on her and I'm watching with my mon-knock," he told him, using an abbreviation for a night vision monocular—a handheld device used for surveillance.

Alexander swore, hung up the phone, and checked the app that monitored his property. And there she was, mama bear in all her glory approaching his drive. Jesus.

He opened the gates with a push of a button and ran for a shirt. He was on his way downstairs when he saw her pass the fountain in the courtyard through the enormous picture window above his front doors.

He almost tripped in his haste to get to the front door before she did. It opened in a whoosh, and she startled a second. "Hi," he said, feeling like a stupid schoolboy idiot.

"Hi." She looked gorgeous, no surprise there, cheeks flushed from the brisk air. "I thought…"

He reached out and pulled her inside. "Come in, please."

Her cheeks reddened more, flustered perhaps. "Alex, I…" She laughed nervously. "Jeez…" She fanned herself then and it was all he could do to not laugh at the lightness of the moment. He was not going to miss the opportunity. He *was* supposed to be working on his timing anyway.

"Amanda." He grinned as he backed her up the two steps it took to press her against the door. "Forgive me, sweetheart." Her arms were around his neck by the time he'd pulled her in, leaned down, and kissed her. Bloody hell, his head was spinning within seconds. She felt amazing. Tasted better. She made a sound as he nudged her with his head right where he wanted her. Her delicate hands wound around his head; her slender fingers moved through his hair and he kissed her from every possible angle. Then he did it again. She pushed against him a few moments later and he backed off.

"Alex, as good as we are at kissing, I didn't come over to make out with you." She blew a wisp of hair off her face, which was adorable.

"Sorry," he said, still smiling like an idiot. He was so giddy, he had to stop himself from actually jumping up and down. Instead, he calmly led her to the living room, stopping short as they passed the hallway to the kitchen. "Are you hungry?"

"Why? Something living in the backyard you can hunt, clean, and cook for me?" she asked with a roll of her eyes.

He laughed, bloody hell she made him laugh. "Listen, funny girl," he teased, "I will find something of the sort if you'd like. Otherwise, I have a refrigerator full of food. Trevor and Michael eat enough for an entire football team."

"Weren't you at dinner tonight?" she chided him. "Rosa prepared a feast. Again. I'm not sure who she's trying to satisfy more, me, or you and the boys." She shrugged. "My money's on you and the boys."

"There are snacks on the bar anyway," he said.

"Snacks!" she exclaimed, wide-eyed. "Really?"

Amanda loved snacks. "Yeah," he chuckled, "just wait."

"I hope it's not far."

He was still smiling as he pulled her forward. This had to be the best night they'd had in centuries—really.

"Ooh." Her eyes went wide as they passed through the living room threshold. The bar was covered with small crystal dishes, each filled with nuts, candies, and pretzels. She went right for a bowl of chocolate-covered peanuts. He knew they were her favorite.

"Inside or out?" he asked.

She looked around his living room, which, much like hers, housed a large bistro-sized bar, two separate sitting areas, and a grand piano. "Let's sit over there." She pointed to a cluster of chairs and sofas situated before the large picture windows.

"Drink?"

"Just a Diet Coke if you have it, please."

He had everything. Especially her favorite soda. After fixing hers, he topped off his. She took a corner of a sofa; he took the club chair next to her.

"Amanda."

"Alex." They'd spoken at the same time.

He gestured with his hand, giving her the floor. She took off her shoes and curled her legs up on the cushion next to her. He liked that she was so comfortable. A lot. "I wanted to ask you about something. I just can't seem to reconcile it in my head. And I'd feel stupid askin—"

"Whatever question or questions you have, Amanda," he said, moving to the cocktail table and sitting directly in front of her, "I'm here. Ask away."

She smiled when he moved closer. She was enjoying this, he could tell. Amanda wet her lips before speaking. They were hard not to stare at, but he focused on her eyes. "So, when we separated—"

"Whoa, whoa, whoa." He laughed at the mere thought of it, *and* that he could actually laugh at it. He leaned forward. "Let's get this straight once and for all— we did not *separate*, Amanda. We *were* separated."

"Isn't that what I said?"

"You said *when* we separated."

"Jeez, Montgomery." She rolled her eyes. "Are you splitting hairs or what?"

"It's a terribly touchy subject, sweetheart," he told her, smiling at their banter.

"I'll be more careful next time," she whispered under her breath, rolling her eyes again. God he missed talking to her like this. She was so quick, so much fun to be with. "So, when we *got* separated."

"You mean, when you let go." He couldn't help himself. And couldn't believe he was able to tease her about something so serious. But here they were, together, working toward *being together*.

"Are you for real right now?"

He shook his head; he wasn't sure what had gotten into him. He felt like a teenager who couldn't control himself. His wife, his beautiful, famous, talented wife was right in front of him, in his house. He was a bit delirious. That's what it was. They really had been deliriously happy. "I'm sorry. That was uncalled for."

"Where were we? Callie said we were on a ledge, is that true?"

"Yes, it's true," he said, sobering immediately at the memory. "We were in Abersoch."

"The cliffs?" she asked, and her eyes widened again. "We couldn't have been that high up though," she mused. "I mean, aside from my wrist, Callie and I are both okay." She paused, and Alexander panicked for a moment. How to explain? But then, thank God, she continued, dismissing the point instead for, "Why didn't you get us after?"

He reached forward, resting his hands on the cushion on either side of her. "Remember when you," he corrected himself quickly, "you used to tell me all about your favorite movies—rom-coms and action flicks, you called them." He'd watched them all. "In *Romancing the Stone*, Michael Douglas and Kathleen Turner fall down the side of a cliff, they race past trees, get swept away by what looks like a mudslide, and land in the water relatively unhurt and okay. And from the looks of it, they started out in a completely different area and ended somewhere else entirely."

"Duh, I remember the scene, Alex."

"Okay, what I'm trying say, and rather badly, is, bloody hell, please believe me, Amanda—where I lost you and Callie, and where you landed were two separate stratospheres."

"So—"

"Let's come to an understanding, okay?" He needed to keep the ground he'd gained of late. "Another truce if you will, since the last is going so well."

"Maybe," she said, eager and bright-eyed. "What did you have in mind?"

"Give it, *me*, more time. You're going to remember, sweetheart, I know it, and once you do, everything will make sense. I swear."

"So help me remember, Alex. Please."

He grinned. This he could do. He stood up and extended his hand. "Come here, beautiful."

She blushed as she stood. "Where are we going?"

"I'm going to dance with you, but first we're going on a detour," he said, grabbing her hand and leading her back to the bar. "Hey, Siri, dim living room lights three, four, and five."

He topped off his glass and Amanda laughed. "Drink a lot?" she asked.

"It's not just for me," he told her.

"You got a mouse in your pocket?"

He laughed. "Bloody hell, I missed you, Amanda."

He took her hand again and led her to the other side of the room, leaning her against the side of the grand piano. He took a long pull of scotch and smiled as she plucked it from his hand and took a sip. A large sip. "I told you, funny girl."

⟨⟨　⟩⟩

Amanda stared at Alex over the rim of the rocks glass. Her heart was beating so fast, it felt like her chest was going to explode, and she couldn't stop smiling. Jeez, she wasn't just smiling, she was grinning from ear to ear. There was something about being with him that tugged at her heart, body, and soul. God, she was in trouble here.

They were in such a different place now compared to last week. She still couldn't believe she'd snapped at him the way she had. She'd been so petulant, jeez, she'd called him a felon right to his face. His reaction was remarkable. Actually, something she couldn't forget. Watching him gather his thoughts, then answer everything she'd thrown his way, evenly and determinedly. It didn't escape her, either, that she'd given him a chance to scold her for the things that had been bothering him as well. And he'd taken it.

She couldn't blame him; she was the one who tried to push every button of his she could. Some of it was in reaction to that kiss they'd shared. Not just the kiss, the entire episode that surrounded that kiss. She'd almost screeched when he'd thrown his stuff aside and chased after her. And the way he'd grabbed her from behind and held her, forget the kiss, when she felt his breath on her neck and the slight scratch of his whiskers on her face, she'd almost dissolved into a hyperventilating fit right then.

And tonight, when he'd left after dinner. Because like an idiot, she had asked him to, she could think of nothing else *but* him. She'd been so distracted putting Callie to bed, she hadn't heard half of the things Callie had said, including the remark about letting go of the toothpaste so she could actually use it. Yep, it was then she knew she was coming over to see Alex. The anticipation from that point on had built until he'd opened the door and pulled her inside. And it was still building.

He reached out now to trace the side of her face, and she leaned into his touch. "I thought we were going to dance, Montgomery."

"Oh, we are," he told her, taking the glass back and putting it down on the piano. Then he led her to the space right in front of the windows.

She watched as he fished his phone out of his pocket, fumbling with it and chuckling at the same time. It was a charming display. She'd never seen him so relaxed, carefree. Or if she had, she didn't remember it. She touched his face to get his attention. "Did we dance together before, Alex?"

"Oh, sweetheart," he said, looking down at her so seriously. "Each chance we had."

Wow. The things he did to her. He turned his head and kissed her palm, then pressed the screen of his phone again, and swore, "Bloody hell—hey, Siri, play 'Amanda playlist.'"

"You named a playlist after me?" she asked, unable to suppress her grin.

"Yeah."

He took her hands and lifted them around his neck. Circled her waist and pulled her forward till she was so close she had to look up at him. Then he brushed his lips across her forehead and pulled her in just as Jason Mraz's "I Won't Give Up" started playing.

He whispered the lyrics as he slowly moved them around their makeshift dancefloor. She burrowed her head in the crook of his neck, not able to believe how amazing it felt. Three songs later, she pulled away to ask, "Do you think I had one too?"

"One what, Amanda?"

"A playlist. For you." He looked down, becoming otherwise occupied in putting her hair behind her ears.

"I think you did. I just...I think when things became too much for you, you—"

"You think I erased it?" she said, screwing up her face at the awful thought. God, had she been *that* heartbroken that she couldn't even keep a playlist of songs? She'd dated before, even been in love, but a man had never affected her like that. What had she and Alex *been* like together? Amanda shook her head. "No way, Alex. Where's my jacket?"

He gave her an indulgent smile, and used that same head motion, minus the "move" part. She turned in the direction he'd nodded to see her jacket hanging over the banister. Amanda went over to it and reached into its pocket, pulling out her own phone. Sitting down on the step, too impatient to wait, she opened up her playlists, chancing a glance up at Alex before she dug in. He stood, leaning against the railing, watching as she scrolled through. Everything looked normal: Workout, Meditation, Callie's Faves. And then she saw something that caught her eye and she paused, her finger over the screen. Amanda looked up at Alex. He raised a brow as she wet her lips, feeling breathless again. "I think I found it."

"*You did?*" His shock was real as he sat next to her. They leaned against each other while looking at the screen. She was terrified and excited at the same time. She'd never even thought to look at her music library. Some music professional she was. *Jeez, Amanda Abigail, you of all people should have known there would be a trail of this sort.* He saw what she did. "Bloody hell, sweetheart," he breathed, just as surprised as she was.

Yep, because there it was, the playlist she'd named "The Spy Who Loved Me." She looked at him then, and it felt like a valve released. She started to cry. She didn't mean to, it just happened. It wasn't an all-out bawl fest or anything, just a few tears shed in relief. And another piece of the puzzle clicking into place. A deeper layer too. This wasn't an image or a flashback. It was a tangible feeling right here, right now. And for her, a bit of evidence that everything she'd felt for Alexander Montgomery since he'd brought her home from the hospital was real... was true.

She wondered if it was just the title of the playlist or if that song was on it. "Hey," Alex said, wiping beneath her eyes. "You okay, sweetheart?"

"Did we dance to that song?" she asked before looking through the list herself.

He smiled, cupping her face. "Did we dance to it?" he repeated. "Amanda, you sang that song to me almost every night we were together."

"Can we—"

He nodded, and it felt like they were racing against time as he laced their hands together and took her back to living room. She was shaking when she started scrolling through her list, but then Alex shook his head, took her phone, and put it in his pocket. "Why'd you do that?"

"I've got this. Hey, Siri, play our song."

"No."

"Yes," he whispered, pulling her in flush against him as the keys sounded on the speakers, seconds before Carly Simon's beautiful voice belted out the song. And when Alex moved her around their dance floor again, she could only imagine what this man had meant to her. That song was akin to her dream song, like her every girlhood fantasy come to life.

"That song, Alex," she told him as he continued to hold her as they swayed back and forth. "I never—"

"Played it for anyone."

"It was—"

"What you imagined singing to—"

"The spy who loved—"

He shook his head. "Loves."

"You're really a spy."

"Was."

"Did I have secrets?"

"Not from me. And we didn't keep secrets from each other."

"You kept them safe?"

"I tried, Amanda. Bloody hell, I tried."

"Start it over."

He did, then he pulled her in close again, cupped the back of her head, and pressed her face into his neck. They both shuddered as he rocked her back and forth for the umpteenth time that night. Then he'd walked her home, holding her hand the entire time. They didn't talk about the kids, they didn't talk about the past; it seemed they finally found that middle ground they had been searching for. And as it happened, it turned out to be one of the nicest evenings she could remember. Including the kiss he gave her on her front steps. She watched him walk back down the drive, where he turned and waved one last time. Then she may have skipped up the steps, feeling like a teenager and floating on air the rest of the night.

CHAPTER

TWELVE

1774

ABERSOCH, BRITAIN

"Welcome home, Admiral."

"Goodly," Alexander acknowledged with a nod. He turned as his man reached for his overcoat, then raised a brow.

Goodly smiled, a twinkle in his eye, which belied his dry remark. "As our mistress fondly says, sir...wait for it."

Alexander hadn't heard that one yet, but could only imagine Amanda saying so, and not a second later peals of laughter came from the parlor. Alexander grinned. "Ah, Goodly, that's a sound to come home to."

"Sir." Goodly bowed his head in agreement as Alexander started down the hall.

His home had changed so much in these last few months and this particular commission had taken him away longer than intended. When he stepped inside the parlor, he nearly tripped over his own feet at the sight of Amanda and Callie. Bloody hell, she was dressed ridiculously. Though he supposed he should be getting used to that; they'd been corresponding by letter and she'd confessed quite charmingly that she'd ruined nearly half of his clothes, partial as they both were to soft breeches. A woman in breeches; he chuckled every time he thought of it. But that wasn't what had startled him. No, it was Amanda sitting beside Callesandra on the piano bench with her face pressed to his daughter's cheek. Her little hands were on top of Amanda's as she intently watched the keys they pressed.

He regarded them for a good minute, perhaps two before Amanda noticed him. When she did, she smiled, and when Callesandra looked up at her and asked, "Mama, why did you stop?" Amanda placed her hand on her cheek and said, "Your papa's home, sweet baby girl."

If he'd stopped breathing just then, he would have died a happy man. It was the most gratifying homecoming he'd ever experienced, and he'd experienced many in the time they'd been together. Callesandra squealed when she saw him and came running. He scooped her up and hugged her tight.

"Angel, what on earth are you doing in here?" he asked, even though he already knew. He just wanted to hear it from her.

"Mama's teaching me to play the piano, Admiral," she told him as he walked with her back over to Amanda. He straddled the bench, Callesandra still on his hip, so happy to be home with them.

Amanda reached out to touch his face. He rubbed his cheek into her hand, settled Callie in his lap, then dragged Amanda in close and kissed her. When Callie giggled, he pulled away and gave his daughter a little tickle before turning back to his wife.

"Your hand?" he asked anxiously. She'd injured herself with Stephen's dagger a few weeks ago, not realizing just how sharp it was. Thankfully Alexander had arrived home just as it happened. At the time, he'd never considered the possibility that he could hurt her terribly. His focus was on stitching her hand quickly and properly—first so she would not in fact die, and second so she could continue to play the piano. He did his best not to contemplate that a simple but clean wound such as it looked might be the death of her. God knows he'd heard of men dying over less. She could not die. Bloody hell, he would not let her.

He'd never seen to a task more diligently in his life. He'd tried not to show the worry on his face, but in the back of his mind he'd never let go of the fear that her cut would show an infection. She held it up for his inspection now.

"Stephen took out the stitches two weeks ago," she told him. "Thank you. You did a remarkable job."

Alexander lifted her chin next, looking carefully at her neck. The bruises were completely gone now, not a hint of discoloration. Only one had been particularly stubborn, the last hanger on, as a small yellowish stain marred her skin. He was sorry they'd found Robert's dead body shortly after they'd found Rebecca's. He wouldn't have minded killing the man himself.

Callesandra wiggled in his lap, eager for attention. "You know what else Mama's teaching me?" she asked.

Alexander had heard about that, too, from his wife's letters, but he gave Amanda a wink and played along. "No, angel, what else is your mama teaching you?"

Callesandra jumped off his lap then ran to the side table that held a music box. She turned the crank several times and when the music started, she showed him various ballet poses and finished with a twirl.

"Your mama seems to be newly possessed of the arts," he said conversationally but there was a question for Amanda in there as well. They were learning so much about each other, yet here was another piece of her he'd not been aware of.

"I spent three years in classical training before deciding it was the piano and songwriting I couldn't live without." Callesandra was still twirling all over the room. The music box played for close to eight minutes when fully wound.

"Where's Beatrice and Janey?" Alexander asked.

Callesandra bumped into his leg, dizzy from all the circles, and informed him, "We don't really need their help, Papa." Then for good measure she parroted what he'd heard Amanda say many times in her presence. "We're quite capable of taking care of ourselfs."

He wasn't sure what was more amusing, his daughter mimicking Amanda or her lisp. Then the gravity of what he'd heard set in.

"You dismissed them?" Alexander asked, fearing she actually had.

"Of course not," his wife laughed. "They're wonderful. And believe me, they're never far. But—"

Callie finished for her, "We are self supchishient."

Alexander grinned at his daughter's words, or rather Amanda's coming from her. He called after the women wondering if they really were close by. They nearly fell into the room, clearly having been waiting for just this moment, to be needed. He laughed aloud, grinning at Amanda. Bloody hell, his house had truly become a home. By now everyone adored his wife. He'd heard whispers from the servants about the change in their mistress's behavior. They'd called it sorcery, too, whatever had taken the cruel, thoughtless traits from her. But they weren't complaining. Amanda was considerate and warm, and there was no mistaking that.

"I told you," she said, rolling her eyes.

He couldn't help himself and kissed her again. "Janey," he said, turning to Callesandra's latest nanny. "Why don't you tend to Callesandra's bath."

"Mama gave me a bath," Callesandra told him.

"Did you have your supper yet?" he asked her.

She nodded. "I had supper with Mama."

"Why don't you have Janey read you a story, then?" he asked.

"'Cause Mama reads me stories," she told him, a little exasperated now that he didn't seem to be catching on.

Amanda laughed and finally took over. "Callie, go with Janey and Beatrice. I'll come up soon."

Alexander kissed the top of his daughter's head and watched Janey and Beatrice fawn all over her as they left the room. Then he turned his full attention back to Amanda. He slid her closer, rubbed his hands on her thighs, clad in another pair of his favorite breeches, which she'd hemmed and taken in. Then leaned in and told her, "I want my pants back."

"Down, boy," she teased as he closed the distance between them.

Alexander couldn't remember lifting Amanda to his lap, but there she was, and bloody hell, she felt good. He couldn't get her close enough. He'd missed her so much. His arms wrapped around her back, his hands tangled through her hair until he was holding her head just the way he wanted, then he pulled her in tight and kissed the breath from her. Once he started, he couldn't stop. Could not get enough. He canted her head just right and went in deeper—bloody hell!

His wife moaned as the heat and friction between them became combustible. She was so expressive, loving to touch and be touched in return. Her legs wound around his waist and sounds of their wet and carnal kissing intensified his arousal. Needing much more, Alexander stood. Easily. Standing wasn't the problem; the bloody problem was that he'd actually forgotten where they were for a moment. Amanda's legs were wrapped tight around his waist, her arms around his neck and her hands in his hair. He couldn't think between the noise of the blood rushing in his head and the low moans Amanda was making as she kissed him. He had to admit he liked how out of control she was. Then realized he was too. Thinking to...bloody hell, he couldn't think! Every time he took a step, his erection rubbed against her center. Actually, it wasn't just from the steps he was taking; his hands on her hips were moving her that way. Seconds later he'd pinned her to the wall, close to the entrance to the hall. Jesus, he couldn't make it out of the blasted room!

He held her there, his body pressed so tight to hers that if not for their clothes he'd be inside her already. Her legs stretched wide around his waist, the soft thin fabric between them providing little protection, and he could feel the heat as her moisture pooled between them. He knew he was in just the right position, and at just the right angle as he rocked against her. So inflamed, knowing he could play her, make her release, right here, right now. And loving to have that power over her, he kissed her most naughtily now, and gave her a long hard rub as his hand pressed up her body, cupped her breast, and squeezed. She whispered "Ohmygod" as her body started to coil against him. He felt it, as she lay just on the edge and repeated the motions again and again until she mewed into his mouth and broke into a thousand tiny pieces.

Alexander captured that bloody sweet sound she made as she released against him, and he slowed their kissing while he waited for her body to calm. Somehow, he moved them from the wall out into the hallway. Still kissing, her center, so wet between them now, and her legs wrapped around his waist, it was only seconds before they were back to their loud smacking sounds. Bloody hell! He made it to the landing of the stairs this time, another wall, another few moments of moans and grunts, as he kissed her hard, and she held him tight with those long strong legs. She was rubbing against him, and he honestly wasn't sure he'd last another bout of foreplay, but he couldn't step from the wall. He needed to get her upstairs. All the stairs. And into his chamber. Amanda was saying something, but he couldn't make out the words. She tugged on his hair and he finally came up for air. Bloody hell, her whisper had him moving as she used a word that he knew meant business.

He got the message, loud and clear, and seconds later, kicked open the door to their room. He kicked it just right, too, because no sooner had they passed through, did it slam behind them. He didn't take her to the bed, bloody hell, he laid her down on the floor as soon as they cleared the entrance. Both hands at her hips, he dragged off her trousers and somehow released himself from his. She trembled as he looked down at her, kneeling between her legs and using his hands to make sure she was ready for him. He touched and played with her a moment too long as she whimpered and motioned for him to come to her. Grabbing her knee, he moved it forward as he came over her and slid inside.

Bloody hell! He was inside her! So hot, so tight, so his! Her hands cupped his face as she wrapped the leg he brought up for better access around his hip, allowing him to slowly sink in deeper. His grunt of approval was met with a long, throaty moan as her eyes widened and he began to move. Slowly, watching her expressive face, knowing what he saw was a mirror of his own. He felt her body begin to coil, knew he was right there with her and with a final thrust released deep within her.

It took Amanda way more than a few minutes to come back down to earth. Her husband took her on the most exhilarating expeditions. She was so happy to be wrapped in his arms again, beneath the heaviness of his weight. She was of the firm mind that there were worse things than being stuck in the eighteenth century, married to her Royal Navy admiral who was also secretly a spy as the American Revolution was about to unfold, and absolutely nothing better. Finally catching her breath, she whispered, "Oh my God, how did that happen?"

He gave a half grunt from above her, elbows bearing his weight, his head on her chest. "Do you need me to explain it to you?" he teased, his voice low and raspy. Sexy as hell too.

"Well, yeah," she answered.

"The graphic detail part of it?" he asked. "Or that I swear it was predestined from the moment I first touched you, Amanda Abigail Montgomery."

"How about both?" she told him. He laughed then, as if something had dawned on him, and shook his head. "What's so funny?"

"Trust me, you don't want me to tell you." He shifted to lie next to her on his side and pulled her snugly against him.

"Yes, I do, Alexander," she argued.

"You really want me to tell you what's so amusing?"

"Is there an echo in here?" She pinched him to send the message loud and clear: out with it.

"Alright, but remember, it was you who asked." He started laughing then, so amused with whatever he was thinking.

"Alexander!" she cried, enjoying the push and pull of their conversation.

"We passed four servants and three of my men on our way up here."

"Shut the front door!" She whacked him, suddenly feeling herself go a deep crimson.

"Yes," he assured her, grinning wickedly, "we did."

"Oh my God," Amanda groaned. Then her eyes went wide as she had a panicked thought. "Did they...?" She trailed off, not willing to ask so directly if they'd witnessed her orgasm, as good as it was.

"No, Amanda," he assured her. "We were alone in the parlor."

Right, she remembered, some of the tension seeping out of her. She'd sworn, though, that when he had her pressed against the wall, they'd already reached the landing. "Did they hear?" she whispered.

"Our kissing?" he asked. "Bloody hell, Amanda, all of London probably heard our kissing," he told her quite honestly.

"That's not what I meant, and we're not *that* loud," she said, giving him a playful punch on the arm, even though she knew very well that they had been *that* loud.

He gave her a look that let her know he thought she was out of her mind. "If not our kissing, did they hear what then?"

"You mean the fact that I had to beg, b-e-g beg you to quit messing around and get down to business?" she said, rolling her eyes.

Shaking his head, he laughed and said, "That's not quite the way I remember it."

"Well, it was so long ago, who cares about the particulars."

He laughed and leaned down to kiss her. "Bloody hell, woman! I care about the particulars." He kissed her again. "And taking you on the floor but two steps from the door was not what I had in mind," he admitted. "I didn't even get out of my breeches!"

Amanda grinned. "But you did get me out of mine." Shaking his head at her, he stood and held out his hand. She took it instantly. Then he led her to the bed where he pulled off her shirt, removed his own clothes, and fell in beside her. They lay quietly for a few minutes, then Alexander rolled on top of her, nudging her legs apart and getting very comfortable. Skin to skin contact was amazing. She brushed her fingers through his hair, a luxury she'd come to cherish in such a short time. He lay his head on her chest and in that moment, she wished they could stay like this forever. She loved this man so much and he'd been gone almost three weeks this time. She worried over him terribly, knowing they were on the brink of war, and how dangerous this game of spying was for him. For all of them.

She'd been shocked when he'd confided to her his allegiance to the Colonists. Not that his allegiance was shocking. Alexander Montgomery, she'd learned of her time with him, was his own man, a free thinker, and very ambitious. She'd just happened to ask him point-blank why he was suddenly being so secretive, in his own home no less, while speaking with his own men. It seemed that overnight they'd all suddenly started looking over their shoulders. To his credit, he'd come right out with it. They'd shared so much between them, he'd not held back even a second. Apparently, he thought he'd been tailed after a dinner with a few prominent congress members, and she'd reeled a bit as he mentioned the names of some of America's founding fathers. While he'd told her he'd always planned to move to America, he warned that now it may be a case of fleeing instead. It would depend on whether his name was being bandied about in certain circles. If so they would evacuate and soon. She damned herself for not paying closer attention in history class. Especially now that she was *living* a part of that history. It had never occurred to her until this very moment that *this* could be why there had never been any mention of Alexander past the year 1774 in all her reading about him. Had leaving for America caused them to write him off as a deserter? She'd follow him, of course, but how sad it would be to leave this beautiful castle, her favorite home, no matter the century.

In fact, the last three weeks without her husband passed quickly. During the day she walked the flower gardens, had tea parties with Callie, and read some incredible classics from the estate's library. First editions, no less! She wrote letters to Alexander each night, a habit they had begun the first time he was called away. She actually felt heartsick. Who knew it was really a thing?

And with each letter she wrote, Alexander answered each time.

Stephen had removed her stitches as she'd told Alexander two weeks ago. He'd found her going through her closets with Beatrice and Janey while Callie lay on her bed giggling. She'd formed a truce with her lovely servants. Beatrice could "dress" her each morning, but after supper, all bets were off—as in time to rifle Alexander's drawers for more pants in that soft nubuck material she was becoming partial to. Stephen had watched, shaking his head and grinning at the display. "Come," he'd said, motioning with his hand. He'd straddled the ottoman and a second later she'd joined him and extended her hand. Her nose crinkled even now, remembering the anticipation she'd felt as he'd fingered the threads and inspected the wound. Once he'd declared it healed, Stephen had held her hand in such a way that she'd barely felt the pull as he removed each stitch. He'd spent another minute working her hand this way and that, before nodding, looking as relieved as she felt. She would be able to play the piano again. She looked at the scar now, knowing it would always be a memory of her time here, then tangled it back in Alexander's hair.

"I want to hear the particulars again," Alex whispered in her ear, pulling her out of her thoughts and back into the moment—this moment with her husband, in bed.

"You mean, quit messing around and get down to business?" Amanda teased him.

He shook his head. "Tell me, Amanda."

The seriousness and authority in his voice added to her excitement, and needing no further prodding, she kissed him back and whispered, "I need you, Alexander." But her husband wasn't finished with her. He stretched her arms above her head, then used his mouth and fingers to bring her this close to the edge again.

"Tell me," he demanded again.

"I need you, Alexander," she whispered, and told him again in detail just what she meant.

He pushed inside her with a hiss and waited for her to stretch her legs around him, allowing him to sink all the way home.

Amanda pressed her heels into Alexander's back, keeping him still while she adjusted to him. When she eased her leg muscles, he waited for her nod before he started moving. He was being so gentle now that she was getting a little frustrated, and she cupped his face and told him so. And what she expected him to do about it. She got a "bloody hell" in return and just what she'd asked for.

◁◁   ▷▷

Alexander lay on his back, his arm casually folded behind his head. Amanda was tucked into his side, sound asleep. They'd had a hot bath by the fire after their last bout of lovemaking, changed, and went to Callesandra's room. She was waiting for them; he could see her excitement when they walked in together. Given his absence over the last few weeks, he realized she'd so rarely seen her parents both happy, let alone both happy together and at the same time.

Her long auburn hair framed her beautiful face, and her white bedgown looked like it had been shortened to above the knee. She jumped on the bed, barely able to contain herself. Alexander had never seen her this way, and knew it was from the attention Amanda had been giving her. She gave him a hug when he got close enough and led him to just the spot she wanted him, sitting against the headboard that had been piled with pillows. She came and sat cross-legged facing him and arranged her hairbrush and some ribbons on the bed. Then she grinned at him; bloody hell, she was anticipating what came next and couldn't wait for him to see it, he realized. She was showing off for him, showing off her new mama. Amanda sat behind her and picked up the brush and gently started pulling it through her hair. He winked at his daughter, a clear conspiratorial *I know how you feel*, and started reading. He was halfway through when Amanda had finished this new routine and Callesandra's hair was pulled back and tied with a slew of ribbons. Then Amanda curled into his side and pulled his daughter between them. Three stories later, they left her tucked into bed while Janey knit before the fire.

He'd started back toward his chamber but stopped when Amanda tugged on his hand. She waited for his full attention. Looking at her, he knew just what she was thinking. Didn't she know he thought about their present circumstances more than anything else? He was anxious to sail for America and making their final arrangements. Until his family was safely overseas, he'd not rest easy. She'd just taken a deep breath and started to speak his name when Stephen interrupted them. This late into the evening, Alexander knew it had to be important. He kissed Amanda's forehead, promising to have this conversation later.

It was a habit that started shortly after Amanda became a resident in his home. Talking. Deeply. To one another. Bloody hell, who knew *that* was what could actually happen when two people respected and loved one another. Their bond only got stronger, especially after they married. One of many nights he would never forget. By then they'd spent countless hours and nights trying to figure out what had actually occurred, as in how did Amanda come to be here in the eighteenth century when as he could hear her say in his mind—shut the front door—she was born in the twenty-first, which was a year that seemed impossible to Alexander, certainly impossible to picture. He hadn't believed her at first, had actually thought that perhaps she was the sorcerer the servants whispered about, but after a while it started to actually make sense. Her strange way of talking. Her funny accent. The things she said existed in the future, there were too many of them and too detailed for her to be making it up. Then, of course, there were the breeches, which she said women wore all the time where she was from.

That night, he'd found her lying next to Callesandra as she slept. Not unusual as his business could carry on at any time. "Come with me, Amanda," Alexander had whispered to her. That had been eight weeks ago already. Time was flying.

"Where are you taking me?" she'd asked, after settling the covers around Callie.

"Downstairs," he'd said, taking her hand and leading her away. "There's a matter that requires immediate attention." At that, she'd stopped dead in her tracks. "Don't be scared, Amanda." He'd shaken his head and looked imploringly at her.

"Will you do something for me?" Amanda had asked.

"Of course. What do you wish me to do?"

"Close your eyes," she'd whispered. "Just for a second...please."

Alexander had done as he was told and waited. He'd felt Amanda step closer, wrap her arms around his waist, and lean against him. Had his eyes not already been closed, he would have done so now. Bloody hell, she'd just wanted to be held, and he'd wanted—still wanted—nothing more than to hold her back. He'd wrapped his arms around her and gathered her close, pressing his back to the wall, which had made her physically relax into him.

"I'm still scared, Alexander," she'd said after a long moment.

"Look at me, Amanda."

She'd slowly pushed away and tilted her face to look up at him. He'd pulled her back. "I didn't say to let go," he'd laughed. "I said to look at me."

His hands had splayed across her back, moving slowly to her neck, then through her hair. He'd only meant to kiss her quickly, reassurance to ease her fears. So many rugs seemed at the ready to be pulled from under them. This business of Amanda's being here, for one—was it permanent? they'd wondered. Add to that his ever-precarious situation between his false allegiance to the Royal Navy and genuine loyalty to the Continental Congress, who he was in fact in talks with about the creation of the Continental Navy. But as he'd pulled away, the loss was tangible. One kiss never seemed to be enough for him with Amanda.

His hands had still held her head, but his thumbs had begun tracing her face, brushing her features as he bent toward her again. Then he'd felt Amanda's hands move up his chest and tangle in his hair. She'd pulled him closer. So. Bloody. Sweet. He'd turned, pressing her to the wall as he took the kiss deeper. He could kiss her forever.

"Amanda," he'd finally whispered in between tugs.

"Mmm?"

"We have to go now."

"Okay, Alexander," she'd said on a sigh.

But they'd gone nowhere. In fact, they'd stood in the hallway so long Stephen had finally come and cleared his throat at the bottom of the stairs. Alexander had sworn under his breath; Amanda had laughed.

"Amanda?" he'd asked, putting a hand out to Stephen, unlike tonight when he'd done the opposite.

"Yes, Alexander?"

"Where do you want to belong?"

"Here, Alexander. I only want to be here—with you and Callesandra."

"And I want you to be here, Amanda. With me and Callesandra."

He'd kissed her one more time, looking into her eyes as he'd held her face between his hands. "Come with me, Amanda." She'd nodded and followed Alexander to his study, where he'd been surprised to find himself nervous. He hadn't exactly consulted with her before calling the priest, but despite the brief time in which they had known one another, he'd never felt more connected to anyone before in his life. He'd wager all his gold that she felt the same way. But still.

"What's going on?" Amanda had asked as he led her into the chamber where his men and the priest were standing. He'd squeezed her hand gently for luck before chancing a look at her.

"Amanda, this is Father Paul," he'd explained, figuring it best to get straight to the point. "He'll be performing the ceremony."

"What ceremony?" Amanda had asked, confusion clouding her face, and for a moment Alexander had feared he'd made a mistake, misread everything.

"Our ceremony," Alexander had replied, hoping she wouldn't balk.

Lucky for him, she hadn't objected. They were married. Their vows repeated in minutes, and Alexander had placed a silver band upon her finger eagerly. When she'd asked where it came from, he'd told her it has been made that morning, along with his own, which he'd handed to her to place on his own finger. Then everyone else had left the room and they'd stood there alone together.

"For a long time, Amanda, I've believed in very little, and have known happiness only with my daughter. But you're here for a reason, and I'll not let you go."

"I don't want to go anywhere, Alexander. Not anymore. Not ever."

Stephen put a hand on his shoulder, drawing him from the memory. They spent the next two hours going over their plans. Their evacuation plans.

◀◀   ▶▶

Amanda retired to the parlor. She knew Alexander would join her when his business with Stephen and his men was addressed. A new commission, perhaps? Orders from America? It wasn't enough that she had to be worried about being ripped away from him and Callie and sent back to her century out of nowhere, not that she knew that was going to happen, but she honestly didn't know that it *wasn't* going to happen, either. Alexander had warned her, begged actually, to stay far away from the tunnels and the cliffs and she'd agreed easily. She had no desire to tempt fate as it were. Though she and Alexander had been separated much of the three months they'd been together, she considered the times they were together as some of the best of her life. Sure, she missed home and the twenty-first century. Who wouldn't? She'd had what some would call a dream life. A gratifying career, with major accomplishments and accolades. Beautiful homes and really any luxury she could want. She missed her father, of course, but she could miss him here. Robert, no way she missed him. She was sorry he was dead but better him than her. So really that left only Samantha. Her one true friend. And yes, she missed her dearly. But she kept her close by sharing stories about her, and them, with Alexander and Stephen, and even Callie.

She absently fingered the keys of the piano while watching for a sign of Alexander from the hallway. He was a man of his word, if he said they would start and finish their conversation later, they would. She just worried for his safety. He was walking a fine line between America's Patriots and Britain's Loyalists, and every time she was gone, she racked her brain for everything she could remember from history classes long ago, trying to figure out what was going on—and what would happen soon—based on the year. She truly never felt fully at ease unless she could see him, touch him. And when he was home, God bless the man, he was the best husband and friend. She knew he worried about the same things; he'd told her he feared she'd be gone as suddenly as she'd appeared.

She walked to the window overlooking the back of the property, the rocky cliffs, and churning sea. When he wasn't home, she found herself here in the evenings, hand pressed to the glass, watching for his safe return. Then she heard his footsteps and turned as he stepped into the parlor. She held out her hands in a *come here* motion. He smiled. "Wait for it…" he teased, turning toward the sideboard. He poured a scotch and joined her by the windows. A place they often found themselves on such nights as these.

He kissed her soundly, his large hand cupping her head. Then turned her. As she felt him behind her, she relaxed against him. His arms circled her waist, his chin rested on her head. And as he did most nights, he eased her fears, sometimes just with the cadence of his voice. He began pointing at the stars in the sky then, telling her again how learning of their placement helped him navigate most of the seas. How by applying mathematical laws and those of physics he could chart his course. That lunar cycles had effects on the water's currents. He spoke of having a sense of lights from ashore, those that beckoned to harm, and those that guided him home.

She told him of how she studied dance and classical piano. That losing her mother at a young age had left such a deep void that she didn't know how to fill. That even though her father had thrown himself into his work and remarried, she knew he loved her more than anything. She told him of her friendship with Sam, how they'd met, supported each other as though they were sisters, and some of the antics they'd been involved in.

He told her of family duty. His arranged marriage. The joy of his daughter and the anguish of losing his son. That being wealthy and titled, achieving a coveted rank did not bring the joy people assumed.

They would always be sitting on the floor by the time they'd talked themselves out. Alex leaning against the window with Amanda between his legs, leaning against his chest. They'd finished the ever-present glass of scotch a while ago and it sat empty beside them.

Now he held his hand out for her. "Play something for me," he asked.

Amanda loved playing for him. Another thing she could do for hours—play and tell him all about music: classic and contemporary, composers and artists, songs and genres. She couldn't think of anything she'd rather do right now.

As Amanda walked to the piano, Alexander refilled his glass. She knew he felt better, or lighter as he would say, for having someone to share such things with. And she knew they were things they'd never shared with another. He crossed the room and joined her, taking a long pull of scotch as he leaned against the piano, running his finger along the rim of the glass. She reached for the glass, which he extended to her with a smile. If someone had told her she'd enjoy drinking scotch one day, she would have told them they were crazy. Knowing it was Alexander's drink made it taste amazing. It wasn't much later that they'd walked hand in hand upstairs and back to bed. Callie came in sometime in the middle of night and snuggled right between them. Amanda couldn't remember ever being so content.

CHAPTER
THIRTEEN

APRIL 24

NORTHERN CALIFORNIA

"Callie," Amanda called. "Come on, baby girl. Time for school."

"Coming, Mama."

Amanda waited at the bottom of the stairs, smiling as Callie raced down. She was going so fast that Amanda could grab only her backpack as she blew past, which stopped her daughter in her tracks. "What's this about?" Amanda asked, opening the front pouch of Callie's bulging backpack and pulling out two colorful rolls of tape. By the way the little girl wouldn't look her in the eyes, she had a feeling Callie was hiding something. A feeling that was only made stronger by the indignant "*Mama*" Callie threw her way.

The tape Amanda was holding was the kind athletes and dancers used to help them through injury and recovery.

Lately, between the stories she'd told Callie about her own injuries from ballet and how she'd used tape to help, and what Alex had told her about taping his hands for boxing, Callie had gotten the idea in her head that she needed it too. Amanda had to laugh. She hadn't wanted Callie to be too obsessive about it, but then again, was there really any harm in allowing her to use the tape? Guess it was too late either way.

"We've talked about this before, Callie," Amanda reminded her, trying to keep the smile out of her voice. "Dance practice only." Amanda held out the backpack for her daughter, then motioned with her head. "Move."

Callie crinkled her nose, stuck out her tongue, and ran to the courtyard. Amanda chuckled as she called over her shoulder, telling Rosa she'd be back, and followed Callie to the waiting Navigator. Stephen had already buckled her in and as she approached, Amanda heard him saying to Callie, "If you don't want to get caught, Cal, you have to keep your cool."

"Thanks a lot, Stephen," Amanda muttered, getting in next to Callie, but he must not have heard her, as he was already talking through his earbuds to the rest of the men in the four Navigators at the base of her drive. She'd only recently realized that those particular trucks weren't there for Alex but were for her and the kids. Two to travel alongside them, and two to stay behind. She laughed out loud then, thinking back to when she and Sam had gone out for lunch the previous week and Sam had remarked dryly, "Right, the traveling circus—got it," as the entourage had revved up to follow them. In the moment, Amanda had rolled her eyes and mouthed back *The brothers Montgomery*, with air quotes for emphasis. But there were worse things than being under their protection, and from where she was presently sitting, nothing better.

Today was no different. When Stephen pulled out of the gates, he flashed his brights and within seconds their truck was safely ensconced between two more from Calder Defense. Stephen adjusted the rearview mirror and gave her a smile. "You okay, Amanda?"

"Depends who's asking," she said with a wink.

Stephen returned her wink and a short time later, their trucks pulled into an overlook area off the highway. Amanda absently reached out to brush Callie's hair behind her ear as she glanced out her window at the side mirror, watching Alex's convoy join them. That was a surprise— a good one.

She'd missed him this morning. He'd been away on a business trip and only just returned, like maybe just now. In these last six weeks, ever since her first solo visit to his house across the lawn, they'd spent more time together, if that was even possible. Though time alone together wasn't granted often—time in that middle ground they found together—she couldn't have been more content. It was like enjoying the safest courtship ever. Like she knew where this was going so just getting caught up in the moment was okay for now. It was easy. No pressure. They'd kept the schedule they'd already fallen into, with Alex and the crew coming over early in the mornings. Breakfast on the terrace or on the few occasions it rained or was too windy they piled around the kitchen table. She'd even called Art a few weeks ago to tell him she had finally come around to accepting the invitation to attend the Night of the Stars charity event in May. Earlier, it had seemed like too much pressure, even if all she had to do was emcee the event. But now, feeling more grounded and knowing she'd have Alexander by her side, it didn't seem that overwhelming.

Little by little—taking Callie to school was just one example—Amanda was coming out of her hibernation. She'd actually gone to visit Alex at his offices the other day after dropping Callie off. She'd stood outside that building for the longest time, wondering why it seemed so odd to her that this was where he worked, or at least this was where some of his offices were located. She'd stared at the logo next to the letters that spelled out Calder Defense, a bit overcome, like blown away actually that this was his. And so proud of him, too. She knew this had been Art's baby, but still—the building *was* incredible. It was eighteen stories high, with a helipad on the roof, constructed halfway into one of the rocky northern hills, and overlooked the ocean.

That day, Stephen had pulled the Nav right up to Calder Defense's front entrance before leading her through what looked like thick bulletproof glass. They bypassed the security guards while Stephen made silent acknowledgments to at least fifteen others, all of them armed with weapons and technology.

Alex was waiting for them when the elevator doors opened on the top floor. He'd taken her hand right away, pulling her away from Stephen and into his office, where Alex closed the door and pressed her back against it. Then the man had kissed her senseless. Like rag doll senseless.

He'd cupped her face with his large hands, leaned down, and used his brilliant, British mouth so effectively that he should have been arrested. Only after she'd been left incapable of forming a coherent word let alone sentence, he'd greeted her with a "Hi, beautiful."

He'd looked ridiculously happy to see her—it had been a surprise visit—but then his expression had changed. He'd studied her face. "Amanda? Are you alright, sweetheart?"

"I'm fine. I just wanted to see where you went off to most days," she said, feeling her cheeks burn. "If it's a bad time, I can go."

"Never a bad time for you to stop by. Impromptu or not."

The man had an answer for everything. "Aren't you ever fazed?" she'd asked, meaning it.

Alex had smiled. "Not anymore," he'd told her as he brushed the side of her neck with his thumb. She closed her eyes and let out a low groan of contentment.

He'd sworn a signature "Bloody hell," then kissed her again. She'd canted her head just where he liked it, wrapped her arms around his neck, and kissed him back.

"Should I go?" she asked when they came up for air again.

"No." He shook his head. "I have a meeting in"—he'd looked at the face of his watch—"three minutes. Stay here?"

She nodded. "Yes, I'll stay." He'd led her to the sitting area on the opposite side of the room, sat her down, then started depositing items in her lap. First it was the remote to the large plasma TV, then he'd grabbed a laptop. Next an iPad. When he'd reached in his pocket and pulled out an antique compass she'd started laughing. This time she'd done the pulling; he didn't resist, which helped a lot, and he'd landed right next to her. "I'm not five, Alex. You don't have to give me toys to play with while you're gone." She reached out and brushed his hair back with her fingers. "I'll be right here when you get back."

"You make my head spin," he'd admitted with a lopsided grin. "Fresh coffee's on the credenza. If you need anything, *anything*, tell me," he'd said, slipping an earpiece into her ear. "This only transmits one way, so I'll be able to hear you, but you won't be bored with the details of our conference room meeting." Then he'd kissed her forehead and walked to his office door. He'd turned and looked at her before opening it. It was another one of those if-she'd-had-a-picture moments, but seriously, *if she'd had a picture* of the look he'd given her, like she was his everything, she would have kept it forever.

Lately, things had just fallen into place, begun to feel routine in a good way. Now in the evenings their large family-style dinners were even better. Music always playing in the background, laughter wafting throughout. And no matter what, it felt good. Seriously, she'd often just sit back, taking in Stephen and Samantha either whispering or bickering, Stan rolling his eyes at something Michael and Trevor were saying. The boys, as Alex called them, *were* adorable, and she knew Alex had a special place for them in his heart. They were always with him, after all—jeez, they lived with him. Rosa continued to outdo herself daily with each meal she prepared, but dinners especially. Helen was still with them, not that Amanda needed a baby nurse anymore. Zander and Callie were a bit attached, though, and Evan had suggested keeping her on for now until things became normal again. She'd almost laughed in his face when he'd said it. Normal? Ah, yeah, whatever *that* was. And then there was Alex, always at the head of the table, like he was born to be there, conducting his troops and jumping in at any given moment to help with the kids. Games, puzzles, and sometimes movies after dinner became the nightly norm. And Alex was always a part of bedtime with the kids.

For weeks, she had stopped making the mistake again of sending him home. For one, they were his children, and two, they really had settled into a comfortable space as a couple. If they didn't join the crew for billiards, they went for long walks on the beach. She loved climbing on his back on the way down, before walking or being chased in the sand as the moon lit up the night, and always, lying between his legs once they'd come back to look at the stars. They danced, too, everywhere, and sometimes they'd end up sitting on the floor in front of the picture windows at his house overlooking the sea. Something about those moments in particular filled her with an immense feeling of joy—so much that she'd recently asked him if they used to sit like that before. He'd responded as he always did: "Every chance we had, sweetheart."

And kissing? There wasn't a wall he hadn't pressed her against. An angle he hadn't held her head at. A brush, pull, or stroke of his lips on hers that she hadn't experienced. It seemed he had a thing for walls. And she couldn't say that she minded, because *she* had a thing for *him*. At Evan's advice, she'd started keeping a journal of her déjà vu moments. As of late that's really all she *had* been experiencing, and Amanda had a sneaking suspicion the kissing was at the center of that.

She watched now from the sideview mirror as Alex got out of his mobile command center, her heart skipping a beat as he stretched to his full height. The man was dressed to the nines today. When he opened her door and smiled, saying "Morning, beautiful," he laid his large hand across her thigh, the heat of it going right to her bones, then looked at Callie.

"Morning, angel," he said. "Mama and I are going to talk for a minute."

Suddenly, Amanda's stomach dropped and she wondered if something was wrong. The smile on her face started to feel plastered instead of natural. She let him help her down out of the truck, but when she started to lean back against it, preparing for their normal passionate greeting, he shook his head.

"No, sweetheart," he said before he moved her about a foot over, probably out of Callie's line of vision, and grinned a smile so broad and so natural that Amanda felt herself relax. Nothing was wrong, he'd just wanted a moment of privacy. Alex brushed her hair off her shoulders before those large hands swooped up and cupped the back of her head. "Bloody hell, I missed you." Callie yelled for the swear jar from inside the truck and they both chuckled.

"You should really work on that," she told him, rolling her eyes.

"I plan to." Then he leaned down and kissed her. Another earth-shattering assault that awakened every nerve ending in her body. Seriously, this man could kiss; his lips, mouth, and tongue had her head spinning. And when he pulled away, she just stared for the longest time, not even sure where she was. Alex grinned, no doubt pleased with himself. "I asked you a question," he reminded her.

Amanda grabbed his lapels. "Bloody hell, Montgomery," she told him breathlessly. "I can't remember the year before Zander was born, so if you think I can remember what you asked me five minutes ago...before, you...you—"

"Use your words, sweetheart," he teased with a grin.

She crinkled her nose at him, cocked her chin, and told him, "Use your mou—mmmp." Jeez, for a second, she went boneless and felt him lean in, like his entire body, which felt amazing, to keep her upright. Yep, rag doll. She did, however, hear Callie making "mwah, mwah" sounds from inside the truck, which meant they were being loud. Every time they kissed it was like the Bluetooth was connected and broadcasting it through the speakers. He gave her one last nibble, then whispered, "Bloody hell, sweetheart," when he finally broke their kiss.

"You missed breakfast this morning," she said, still reeling from the kiss and unable to think of anything more creative.

"I know. We only just landed, I'm sorry."

"Rosa made you eggs. Just the way you like them."

"Fried? In butter?"

"Yes. And yes."

"You really want me to have that coronary, don't you?"

While she knew he was teasing, her hand went over his heart. "Please, God, no," she said, a now almost old joke between them. The first time, Alex had gotten in her face, which he had a penchant for doing, and told her emphatically that he'd had almost a dozen since he'd met her, so what was one more? And now he continued to tease her, muttering under his breath that she was going to be the death of him. Amanda laughed, knowing it was a joke, but then she caught a glimpse of him flexing his hand, as if working out a kink. He'd been doing that a lot lately, unconsciously it seemed. And it worried her. Maybe he wasn't teasing after all.

He took her hand and kissed her open palm, his gorgeous eyes gleaming now. "Dinner tonight, then dancing with my girl?"

She nodded. "Uh-huh."

He grinned, still staring, waiting, for what she didn't know. "Callie's going to be late for school," he said finally.

Well, *that* got her attention. She hit his chest with a "shut the front door," and laughed out loud. "Jeez, Montgomery," she whispered, her cheeks feeling like they were on fire. "I forgot!" He laughed, gave her a quick kiss, and put her back in the truck. He went to the other side, opened the door, and gave Callie a hug and a kiss before telling her to have a good day at school.

"Dance practice?" he said, just before shutting the door for good.

Amanda smiled and nodded. "And after, Sam and I are going to pick out dresses for the Night of the Stars gala."

That made him beam. "Outstanding, sweetheart."

Yes, Amanda Abigail Marceau had taken her place in the real world once again, and it wasn't so frightening after all. Who knew? But then maybe having her superhero around had something to do with it.

◁◁ ▷▷

It was seven thirty by the time Alexander made it to Amanda's. Business was picking up, and not just because he'd been out of town, or for that matter, because he'd been getting acclimated to business period. Calder Defense was being retained by a slew of new clients. Now that Amanda was back on the scene and in public, their services had been made known, and suddenly they were on the "it" list. Hell, just today they'd picked up two new clients from Amanda and Sam's shopping excursion. Add to that the Night of the Stars charity event coming up and time was in short supply. He'd called earlier to let Amanda know he and the crew were running late and to start dinner without them.

Walking in through the front door, Alex was greeted by Callie running down the hall, in her pajamas with wet hair. She was hollering, "Mama, the admiral's here, we can eat!" as she jumped into his arms. It was only then her words sunk in. Amanda and Sam came out from the living room laughing at something, and his shock must have shown, because a moment later, Amanda was at his side, reaching out and rubbing his arm.

"You okay?" she asked. She was holding the baby, who by this time was sound asleep and should have been safely tucked into his crib for the night.

"You waited?" Bloody hell, it wasn't often he was stunned anymore, but his heart clenched, and not in the painful way. He just happened to be overcome with emotion.

"Of course we waited," she told him a second before motioning to Zander. "Give him a kiss and Helen can put him to bed." Jesus. She'd kept him with her so he could see him. She must have read his mind, as she said, "I tried to keep him up, but he's been out for the last thirty minutes." He pressed his lips to Zander's crown, thanking Helen when she held him out again so he could touch him one more time. "Come on," Amanda said. "I'll get you a drink, then we can head out to the terrace."

"Where's Stephen?" he asked. The boys were already halfway down the hall with Sam.

Before Amanda could answer, Sam called out, "In the kitchen with Stan." She turned then, adding, "I think Evan's still here too."

Alex nodded. Good. Everyone counted and accounted for.

"Sorry I missed your dance practice today, angel," he said, squeezing Callie a little tighter.

She rubbed his cheeks and said, "That's okay, Papa. Mama said you've been really busy." She shrugged and giggled. "And besides, we can take care of ourselfs." Callie started squirming then, so he set her down and watched as she skipped down the hallway after the others.

Amanda grabbed his arm, stumbling into him.

"Amanda?" he said, steadying her, concerned.

She shook off whatever it was with a "Déjà vu," and pulled him into the living room to pour a scotch.

"Wait," he said. Jesus, the everyday care of it, it was too much. He needed a moment. She'd stilled midpour—*funny girl*. He took a breath, then covered her hand to help her finish before pulling her back against him and closing his eyes. Bloody hell, he felt like he was in a dream tonight. Not that they hadn't had plenty of dinners together. Or nights for that matter. It was just the level of comfort they'd reached. Now. Again. No matter how different the surroundings were. Her warm welcome, keeping the baby close, Callie skipping down the hall, the rocks glass of scotch. In all honesty, he was a bit speechless, overwhelmed as it were. His heart was beating so fast, he made a concerted effort to slow his breath and concentrate on the fact that Amanda was whole and in his arms. They were together, *and* they were all safe. She turned then, rubbed her face against his shirt, and burrowed right in the crook of his neck. He loved when she did that. Music played softly on the overhead speakers and he slowly rocked them back and forth. Until he heard Callie coming back down the hall. "Company," he whispered, and kissed the top of her head.

"We always have company," she told him half-jokingly.

They were at the dinner table moments later, their conversation centering on the Night of the Stars charity event. The purpose behind the gala was to raise money for retired police and military personnel, wounded warriors and their families, as well as those who lost someone in service.

The black-tie affair itself honored different members and families each year. While he'd heard that it was usually one of the hottest tickets in town, and pricey to boot, this year had exceeded previous expectations and rapidly. It might have been due in part to the announcement of Amanda's appearance, but then Art told him they always had at least one major headliner in attendance, so maybe not. Alex chuckled to himself, still marveling over the fact that his wife, on top of being beautiful, kind, and wickedly funny, was what they called an "A-lister" here in the twenty-first century. Not that he doubted her talents, but there hadn't exactly been paparazzi hanging around their eighteenth-century estate, and the last few months Amanda had spent on private property, so he just hadn't been given much of a chance to see it—until recently.

Still two weeks out and they were at full capacity, with a head count close to five hundred. While the hotel where it was being held wasn't the largest venue in town, it was the nicest. Easily five- or six-star accommodations, and completely sold out. Luckily, Calder Defense had held a block of rooms and comped each of the families and service personnel being honored. It was the least Alex felt he could do for them, a small price for their sacrifice. He'd also held on to a suite in case Amanda needed to get away from the masses. It would be her first night out in a big crowd and she may need some space.

Their dinner table discussion moved to their upcoming trip to New York to celebrate Callie's birthday. It had been Callie's request to have her birthday there and Amanda said she was okay with it. They'd spoken with Evan and thought it may be the next best thing outside of a trip to Great Britain, which, in his mind, was still not an option. *Yet*. By the time the table had been cleared and they started on dessert, Callie was half asleep.

"Come on, angel," he said, reaching out. "Let's read a story and get to bed."

Amanda waved him on, telling him she'd be up shortly. Once through Callie's routine, he lay down next to her and read her one of her Amelia Bedelia books. Halfway through, she whispered, "Papa?"

"Angel," he whispered back.

"Are we really going to be together? For real?"

He knew what she meant. While he lived next door, and they spent a lot of their time together, they weren't all under one roof. He lifted her chin and nodded. "We are, Callesandra. I promise."

"But Mama doesn't remember still," she said, shaking her head, looking terribly worried.

He did his best to ease her fears. "Mama might never remember, Callie." A fact that he just might have to live with. It had been over three months, and from speaking with Evan about it repeatedly, they were still dealing with option two. Perhaps with a twist. Maybe her instinctively knowing him and a spattering of memories here and there was the most they could hope for. All that they may ever have. Amanda was having more occurrences of déjà vu. But no memories. At least not discernible in any case.

It wouldn't be the end of the world if she didn't remember the first four months they'd had with each other. He realized with a start that they'd spent almost more time together now than they had before. Intimacy aside. And, if that happened to be all he got, he'd live with it. They could start over from here, now.

"But I want her to," Callie said. "I miss talking to her about Janey...or Goodly...or even Mrs. Beasley. The real one, I mean."

Alexander understood how she felt. Goodly had been a constant in her life, and honestly, he missed Goodly himself. Callie had also developed a deep affection for Janey in the short time she'd been in their household, and Mrs. Beasley was Callie's favorite doll that she left behind. Amanda didn't know it now, but she'd had her replicated for Callie before leaving Great Britain last year, and though Callie loved her new doll fiercely, Alexander could tell that for her, it wasn't the same.

"So do I, angel. So do I," he whispered.

"Well, aren't you two all serious," Amanda remarked as she came in and plopped down next to them.

"Mama!" Callie climbed over Alexander to crawl into her lap. She put her little hands on her face. "Are we for surely going to New York for my birthday?"

"Oh, we for surely are, Callesandra." Amanda kissed her and hugged her. "I promise, sweetie." Alexander and Callie shared a grin, and Amanda asked, "Is there something I don't know?"

Alexander laughed and shook his head. "So not touching that one, Amanda." Then they tucked Callie in, checked on the baby, and headed back downstairs.

When they hit the foyer, Amanda looked up. "Movie? Or do you have to go?"

Jesus, how did she not know? He pulled her close and told her, "I don't have to go anywhere, Amanda. I just want to be with you." He kissed her forehead. "That's all I want, all I've ever wanted since we've been together. Let me tell the others we'll be in the library. Go pick out what you want to watch."

He found her on the sofa, *Bridget Jones's Diary* frozen on the big screen. Alexander picked up the remote, turned off the lights, and stretched out on the sectional behind her, pulling her flush against him. His body always reacted to having his wife so close in his arms, but he'd found himself in this place where he was content to just be with her, be near her. Kiss her yes, hell yes. But he'd sat on the edge of her remembering for weeks now, and he wanted her to remember them before going any further. It was an odd crisis of conscience, thinking that while making love to Amanda for him would be a consummation of finding each other in the "here and now" quite literally. But for Amanda, if she didn't remember, then what would that be for her? She'd be giving herself to the him of now, not then. Jesus, he was a selfish bastard, because as much as he was willing to have Amanda without her memory returning, he would much prefer to have her with her memory fully intact. In any case, he had no intention of telling her he'd "traveled" from the eighteenth century. Ever. Amanda would either remember and know the truth, or she would never know, period. He was giving it until their trip to New York. After which, moot point. Then she wiggled her bottom, messing with his resolve.

"Hey, start the movie," she said.

He did, rubbing Amanda's back the entire time they watched. Stephen came in long after Amanda fell asleep in his arms so they could go over tomorrow's schedule. That sorted, Alexander told him to send the boys home and to turn off the TV on his way out.

Alexander couldn't remember the last time he'd slept with his wife—not made love to her, just slept beside her. He threw the cushions behind him to the floor, giving them another foot of room and scooted back, taking Amanda with him. He closed his eyes, thinking that normally he would have been saying good-night about now, and how lucky he was instead to luxuriate in the moment. As if on cue, Amanda rolled over. No pretense tonight, as if knowing in her sleep what to do, she stretched her long, lean, beautiful body chest to chest and toe to toe with his. Jesus, he wrapped her up tight, deciding he wasn't going anywhere until she woke. The last thing he did was silence his cell and toss it to the floor. The boys were on their own tonight—all of them.

He woke up to the gentle stroke of fingers on his face. When he opened his eyes, he could see it was barely morning. Predawn light cast the room in soft shadows. Amanda's blue eyes were focused right on him. He hadn't slept so well in…hell, he honestly couldn't remember. Centuries, undoubtedly. She was looking at him so deeply, a million emotions raw for him to see.

"No one should be so handsome," she whispered, continuing to trace his forehead and temples. "Sometimes, Alex, it hurts." She grabbed his hand and placed it on her chest. "It hurts right here when I look at you."

"Jesus, sweethe—"

"Shh, let me finish," she said, her fingers on his lips. "When I woke up…tangled in you, I felt so content. All the things you always make me feel," she said, looking right at him, naming each one. "Whole…safe…cared for…wanted…beautiful… Everything you convey with a look or sometimes the simplest action."

He took her hand and kissed her open palm. "Let's start this over, Amanda," he told her, his voice still gruff. "Morning, beautiful."

She smiled. "Morning back," she whispered, before adding in a chiding tone, "We had all night, Montgomery."

He chuckled, knowing exactly what she meant and positioned her beside him. He kissed her neck, every part of her face, before ending it with a very poignant kiss to her lips. Her "Mmm" was answered with a grunt that rumbled deep within his chest.

"I want some more of that brilliant mouth," she whispered. "Kiss me again. Please."

He gladly complied. And it was brilliant. All of the two minutes they'd enjoyed until they heard Zander cooing through the monitor.

"Divide and conquer, sweetheart," he told her in between a few more nibbles. "Zander or coffee."

"I'll start the coffee. You get Zander."

"Deal."

He helped her up but couldn't stop from grabbing her a second later as she stretched. He hugged the hell out of her, just because he could. Rubbed his face in her neck and breathed in deep.

She whispered, "I love when you do that to me." Then she did the same and whispered again, "I love doing it to you more, though."

She grabbed the monitor and made her way to the kitchen as he headed for the stairs. And as he went to fetch his son, he had the distinct thought that in the grand scheme of things, where he and Amanda happened to be right now, in this "middle" they'd found together, he was actually quite content.

CHAPTER
FOURTEEN

At five o'clock on Saturday evening, the day of the gala, Amanda and Sam finally made it downstairs dressed and ready to go. It had taken two hours, four outfit changes, and one additional blowout. While she had the means to have a makeup artist and hairdresser on call, Amanda liked doing it herself. Well, she and Sam did, anyway. They'd perfected hair and makeup over the course of boarding, undergrad, and grad school. So, more times than not, they ditched the professionals and took care of it themselves. As they headed to say goodbye to Callie, and to grab Stephen, Amanda was struck for a moment that she couldn't remember if she had ever left Callie for the night. Not recently, of course, but before. She'd spent some time in the evenings with Alex, but that was always after Callie's bedtime, and she'd always woken up in her own bed.

"You're wondering if you left Callie for the night?" Sam repeated when she asked her, in true sarcastic Sam fashion. "Are you frigging kidding?" She made a ridiculous face, lips pulling in opposite directions. "You wouldn't let her out of your sight, much less think you were entitled to a"—she used air quotes—"girls' night out." She softened it then with, "Not that I blame you, Ammy, ever. We managed."

Amanda was ruminating on what Sam had said, trying to retrieve…well, anything, as they stepped into the kitchen. Stephen was sitting at the table playing cards with Callie, while Rosa finished getting dinner together.

"Fish or war?" Amanda asked.

Callie, deep in concentration, pursed her lips, and whispered, "Crazy Eights, Mama."

"Good choice," she said, bending to kiss the top of her head. Helen was feeding Zander, but handed him to her, bottle and all at her gesture. It was a smooth pass and the baby didn't miss a beat. "Sorry you have to wear a tux tonight," Amanda said, turning to Stephen. As she did, Amanda caught Sam flicking her eyes in his direction, too, and blushing. It looked like she was about to say something but changed her mind. *Interesting*, she thought with a small smile. It looked like her suspicions were right.

He looked up from his cards for the first time. "Christ, Amanda," he said, his accent a little thicker in playful aggravation as he took in her dress. Then his eyes caught Sam, and Amanda had the pleasure to get a glimpse, albeit only for a second, of what this man clearly felt for her friend too. *Wow.* How had she not seen this before? *Because you've been freakin' obsessed with analyzing Alex, DUH.* Okay, that much she knew. And now wasn't the time, but Amanda let herself wonder for a moment if something was going on between her best friend and Alex's brother.

Sam's dress was off-the-hook hot and Amanda winked at Sam, and then at Callie, who had placed the swear jar next to her uncle with a meaningful thump. Amanda rubbed her fingers and thumb together in the universal sign of "pay up" before setting the bottle down and patting Zander's back. After a quick kiss, she deposited the baby back in Helen's outstretched hands.

Stephen had already taken his wallet out, shrugged, and dropped a twenty in the glass container painted with beautiful lettering by none other than Callesandra Eleanor Montgomery herself. She'd never forg—

"Shut the front door!" Amanda exclaimed aloud, leaping out of her chair. Stephen started swearing again when he saw the slit that ran up the entirety of one side of her dress and tossed his whole wallet in the jar before reaching for his gun.

She and Sam chuckled. "Really?" Amanda asked, momentarily distracted from the memory that had just hit her like a ton of bricks.

"Yeah, *really*, Amanda. Between you and the princess," he said, jerking his head toward Sam, "I'll have my work cut out for me tonight." Having already taken his gun from the holster, he removed the clip, looking at it carefully before clicking it back into place. "When Alex gets a load of you in *that* I might as well just shoot any poor bastard who looks at you wrong."

"Listen," Amanda said, breaking in, "it's my first *real* night out in forever. And I have to say, I'm really looking forward to it. So no trouble, okay? And *that's* only going to happen if Sam doesn't have to do some fast-talking on your behalf."

Sam did a double take. "Why? Isn't Chris coming tonight? You can be represented by none other than Calder Defense's finest."

"Are you saying you wouldn't represent me?" Stephen asked.

Sam leaned over the table. "Listen, pretty boy, while I haven't practiced in a while, I pity the poor bastards who try to keep you down." *Wow*, for Sam, that was…revealing to say the least. And Callie jumped up again, moving the swear jar over to where her aunt was. Then Sam asked her, "Wait, what was 'shut the front door' about?"

Amanda shrugged like it wasn't a big deal anymore. "Oh, nothing, I just remembered when Callie painted that," she said, pointing to the swear jar. "We were sitting outside, and I was so big and pregnant with Zander, you had to provide leverage as I sat down next to her."

Sam started laughing too. "Oh my God, Am, remember how we got to the ground?" She came over and they relived the moment.

Amanda had to wipe her eyes from laughing so much. "And then when you tried to help me stand—well, we couldn't."

Sam started talking before Amanda finished. "And we were laughing so hard, we couldn't catch a breath, and Stan had to help you up a few minutes later."

"Wait a minute," Amanda said, looking at Sam. "There was something else too. Not just the painting of the jar, but Callie's name. I thought in my head, 'Callesandra Eleanor Montgomery,' like I *knew* it. Isn't that right, baby?" she asked, turning to Callie, who beamed, clapping her hands.

"Yay, Mama," she cried.

Amanda tried searching for more, but came up blank. At Sam's and Stephen's inquiring looks, she just shook her head, shrugged, and said, "That's all I got." On the bright side, it *was* the biggest moment that she'd had in a long time, and the nicest. This was no horrifying flashback or vivid snapshot that freaked her out. Just a pleasant memory. She motioned with her head then toward Stephen. "You really should fish your wallet out of that jar before we go."

Sam, who was closer to the jar, reached in, muttering, "Don't forget who has your back," and grabbed the wallet as Rosa and Helen came in to set the table for dinner, which was going to be small tonight, given that everyone else was going to the gala. Amanda hugged Callie goodbye, told Rosa she'd check in later, and skipped out of the room, actually feeling *excited* for the night.

An hour later, when Stephen pulled into the hotel parking lot where the event was being held, Alex was already standing outside among a cluster of hotel staff, Calder Defense employees, and partygoers. Between his mysterious appeal, business acumen, access to the stars, and his ridiculous good looks, the man was fast becoming a celebrity himself.

Sam grabbed her hand as she and Stephen both asked if she was okay. She shrugged, grinned, and said, "I can't explain it, but I feel great." She fingered the exquisite diamond chain that Alex had given her the other night. A night that had included a late-night walk on the beach. Not one to act nervous, his behavior had taken her by surprise. She had enough anxiety to deal with lately, so she'd just asked him flat out what was up. He'd turned to her and grabbed her shoulders to bring her in close. What could she say, the man liked her there. Then he'd grinned and said, "I know you don't care much for jewelry, Amanda, but I saw something the other day and I simply couldn't *not* get it for you." She was so surprised, mostly by his sheepish expression.

"Really?" she'd said.

"Yeah," he'd answered with a nod.

She'd hit his chest. "Then show me," she'd laughed and he'd fished the rather large box out of his front pocket, watching nervously as she'd opened it. Her jaw almost hit the sand when she saw the beautiful long thin delicate chain of diamonds. It shimmered stunningly in the moonlight. Not gauche or over the top, just simply the most incredible piece of jewelry she'd ever seen. "I love it," she'd told him, meaning it. "I'll wear it to the event this weekend."

Stephen and Sam started bickering then about which valet lane to get in, drawing her attention back to the present. "*Ser-i-ous-ly,*" she drawled out while rolling her eyes to stop them. They both smirked, obviously not that upset with each other. Then Stephen pulled up right next to the entrance, reached into the center console, grabbed a small leather pouch, and got out of the truck. He waved off the attendant, opening her door himself.

"Remember how this works?" he asked, handing her the earpiece Alex had gotten for her the other day. As he slipped it in place, she repeated what he'd told her before.

"You'll be able to hear me, even if I whisper."

"Smart girl." He waved off another attendant eager to move the SUV next to the others belonging to Calder Defense. There had to be twenty parked alongside the circular drive. Alex wasn't kidding when he'd said there'd been an uptick in business lately.

Sam started giving her the rundown of the who's who of the night's guests, snorting as one couple in particular walked by.

Amanda's head snapped to Sam. "Really? They're back together?"

"Seriously, Ammy." Sam shook her head. "I've missed the hell out of you."

Amanda crinkled her nose in response, feeling truly light and free. "It feels good to be back." She really had virtually been underground for quite a while now. And while she hadn't jumped back into writing or recording, much less performing, she had started to reach out to a select few from the industry. She and Alex hadn't announced their relationship, whatever it was, either, but they *had* been seen in and around town a few times recently. Twice, sans the circus, though she knew Alex had told his men where they'd be, so they had protection, they just weren't sharing a table. Gregor drove them, and they'd snuck into one of her favorite restaurants for a late-night supper after putting the kids to bed. It was kinda like a first date, at least one that was out and about. The maître d' had been thrilled to see her, the waitstaff too. That night, she'd had the most amazing time. He was so frigging smart she could talk to him all night long. And they did, well after closing. She was sure they'd been photographed on the way out, but Alex just shook his head at her, and said "Don't worry, beautiful." So she hadn't. Later, when she'd searched her name, she came across a few articles, things like: "A Modern-Day Fairy Tale: Alexander Montgomery Puts Amanda Marceau Back Together Again," and another, "Beauty and the Billionaire: Look Who's Coaxed Amanda Marceau Out of Hiding." The pictures weren't bad, either. She had to admit, they made a stunning couple.

And now here he was standing outside her door, taking up a considerable amount of space, and looking ridiculously handsome. "Hi, sweetheart."

"Hi." The smile was completely reflexive and one thousand percent unstoppable. He just had that effect on her.

He stepped closer. "I missed you. How's my girl?" Since no one knew which way this would go, as in how she would feel being in such a public forum, she knew everyone was a bit cautious.

She nibbled her bottom lip as she looked at him, thinking that there was nothing better than getting all dressed up for *that* guy, being a part of an amazing group of people and going out to enjoy stellar company, great food, a lovely atmosphere, not to mention an outstanding cause. She really couldn't remember—all kidding aside on the remember part—feeling so carefree. Like ever. And looking at Alex, something clicked, one of those pieces that hit her on such a deep level, she was almost overcome by the wave of emotion that accompanied it. She knew they were connected from the onset, knew she was comfortable with him, knew so many things as to why being with him felt right, but what she *felt* now, what she *knew* now, was that she loved this man. Deeply. She may not remember him, or them, but she knew without a doubt she loved him. She felt it in her bones. She shook off the overwhelming part of it and embraced the pure rush of adrenaline that came with the certainty that this was where she belonged, with him, here, now. And tonight was going to be a celebration of it all. "Alex," she said, "I'm frigging amazing."

He threw his head back and laughed, like a full-on booming fill-the-room-with-sunshine laugh. "Yeah, you are," he said, stroking her face. "You ready to light things up, beautiful?"

He reached for her hand to help her down. Then, upon seeing her dress, a litany of swear words lit the night, making all of her nerve endings zing to life.

"Thanks," Amanda said with a sly smile. Though she was wearing four-inch platform stilettos, her head was level with his chin, and she looked up to tell him, "You look incredibly handsome yourself, Alex Montgomery." She reached out and straightened his perfectly straight bow tie. She couldn't help it. She loved touching this man. While her arms were still extended his large hands circled her waist, holding her still as he stared down. She shivered in reaction, and when he bent his head to kiss her, she met him halfway, wrapping her arms around his neck. Flashes went off as photographers and paparazzi alike started taking shots. She didn't even care, she leaned in and let him take the kiss deeper. God bless the man, he did.

<< >>

Of all the scenarios Alexander envisioned for tonight, Amanda's *joie de vivre* was wholly unexpected and so infectious he had difficulty concentrating. Something had changed since he'd seen her this morning, and he couldn't say he minded. He wasn't sure they'd ever had an opportunity to be completely at ease and carefree. When she'd first come to him in his time, there had always been the underlying worry that her stay may not be permanent. And, well, case in point, thinking about what had ultimately happened. He heard swearing in his ear from the men stationed around the perimeter as more flashes lit the night. They were just trying to keep his and Amanda's life as private as possible. An impossibility for sure, but at least until they had things—like their life—figured out, it would be simpler to not have to worry about what was being bandied about in the press. While they could still sweep things from the internet as best they could, they really hadn't been of late. Amanda wasn't hiding anymore. Not that he presently didn't wish she was. She looked spectacular tonight. When she gave him a nod to let him know she was ready, he laid a hand on her bare back and led her inside. Bloody hell, there wasn't a man present who didn't turn as they passed. Benefactors, patrons, *and* employees. Her full-length dress was classy as hell and fit like a glove. The plunging halter in front was held by a measly tie behind her neck and was entirely backless, not to mention the slit up the side, which ran the length of a long, beautiful leg.

Once inside, they grabbed drinks from the bar and mingled with some of the guests. Amanda and Sam did their best to provide color commentary before making introductions. He knew some of the guests, having worked with or for them, but anytime Amanda wasn't sure, she was quick with an introduction. His wife excelled in the art of etiquette. A few times she looked surprised by his own display of social graces. Coming up in eighteenth-century Britain had its advantages.

Why he'd expected trouble he wasn't sure. Everyone was happy to see Amanda and only a few people asked questions that crossed the line, using exaggerated hushed tones and referring to the video. Nosey and obnoxious, yes, but in light of Amanda's present state of mind, seemingly harmless. They laughed the questions off more often than not that night. After an extended period of hors d'oeuvres, the dinner bell rang as was apparently custom at these events. Alexander scanned the room, conducting a visual check-in with the crew. Stephen was alongside Sam, who was laughing at something someone said, and he clearly couldn't take his eyes off of her. After a moment, he did look at Alex, giving a bashful nod when he caught his eye, confirming he was walking the line between business and pleasure. Alex turned to Gregor, who smirked, taking in the entirety of the room from where he stood against a back wall, sipping a drink. Yeah, Gregor loved this shit. Stan gave him a salute, and the boys were doing their best to look serious while checking out girls. Alex chuckled as Evan and Chris walked by them, giving each a knock upside the head.

"Hey," Amanda said, drawing his attention back. She placed her hands on his chest, fingering his lapels. Jesus, no pun intended, but Jesus Jones's "Right Here Right Now" was playing, and its lyrics about how there was no other place he wanted to be mirrored his sentiments exactly. And for the first time, he suddenly didn't care if Amanda remembered. Maybe everything that had happened, everything they'd been through was leading to this. *Right here, right now.*

People were still finding their seats when they reached the ballroom. Between himself, Art, and this year's cochairs, they had three tables. The crew was divided among them and each table welcomed an honoree of tonight's affairs, their family or guests as well. The rest of the room was filled with a few celebrities, mostly local but a few other headliners, too, besides Amanda. That left a mixture of the town's socialites, law enforcement, and retired military. Most of the latter either trained with or worked for Calder Defense in various capacities.

Being used to large dinners, Alex considered tonight's table of ten an intimate gathering. The conversation flowed easily as they moved through three courses before the main entrée was served. At one point, he was laughing at something Rick, the honoree sitting at their table, said. When he glanced at Amanda, she wore an odd look on her face, her smile faraway. "You okay?" he asked.

She leaned in and whispered, "When you laugh, it's like my whole world is right." She shrugged. "I don't know why, it just is."

Overcome, Alex bent to kiss her, then took a long pull of his drink before extending his glass to her.

"Like I drink scotch, Montgomery," she teased, rolling her eyes and fingering the necklace he'd given her the other night.

Bloody hell, he loved her so much it still hurt. She took the glass and twisted it in her hands before taking a small sip from where he had. Then the lights dimmed, and Amanda made her way to the front of the room to help with the night's festivities. A short video was shown, and three honorees spoke after Amanda presented them with their awards. They sat around the table afterward for coffee and dessert. The entertainment for the rest of the evening was a twenty-piece band, complete with male and female vocalists, *and* backup singers. They were very good, and very expensive. When they started in on a duet, guests began moving toward the dance floor.

Alexander watched as Stephen and Sam, sparks almost visibly flying between them, headed out toward the lobby. Then, Amanda excused herself to go to the ladies' room and when he stood to follow, she shook her head, and said. "I've got this. Go grab another drink or check in with the guys."

He nodded and gave Stan the signal, not that he needed to, since his wife was already being followed by most of the crew. Jesus, he hoped she didn't turn around.

He hadn't planned on the night going as well as it had. Before this evening, he'd set his mind on New York and Callie's birthday, nine days from now. He'd decided that once he'd had Amanda at what would be their east coast compound, memory or not, they would be together. Finally. Biblically. Now he was rethinking his best laid plans. Presently. It was fluid and changing moment by moment.

Everything had gone so smoothly throughout the night so far that when Amanda walked back into the ballroom and motioned with her head toward the dance floor, he found himself mouthing *fuck yes*. She grinned, eyes sparkling, and waited for him to join her.

"Come on, gorgeous," he said, lacing their fingers together when he reached her. He looked toward the band, made eye contact, and got a nod in return. Satisfied the plans he'd made with the bandleader earlier in the evening were clear, he led Amanda through a very crowded dance floor. He kept her safely positioned behind him as his large frame parted the moving couples, making sure Amanda didn't bump into anyone. When he found a suitable spot, he brought her around with a gentle pull of their joined hands, and with a perfect twirl she was flush against him. She got comfortable in the crook of his neck, but a moment later, just as the song was ending, she leaned back and gave him a critical, questioning look.

"Did you request something?" she asked. "Back there...?"

After a quick kiss to her soft lips, he smiled, pressing his forehead to hers. "Wait for it, sweetheart." And on his cue, it began.

"Oh, Alex," she whispered at the opening notes, "it's Paul McCartney." Yeah, it was. "The Long and Winding Road." It was one of the first songs she'd played for him back in Abersoch. They'd sat on the piano bench together as she fingered the keys and sang to him about that road that led to his door, and how she hoped it wouldn't disappear. She'd thought the lyrics poignant then, considering their circumstances. And now, Jesus, they were even more so in light of finding her. He pulled her close, feeling freer than he could ever remember. Ever. Sam and Stephen danced their way over, and he shared a look with his brother. Contentment, joy, validation, vindication. Bloody hell, they did it.

They stayed on the dance floor for a good hour. He'd long ago removed his jacket and tie, and he held Amanda up as she'd taken off her shoes. All the dancing they'd done in the parlor of their Abersoch estate, and his home here in Cali, came to life right here in high def at this gala on this dance floor. It had to be one of the most enjoyable nights he'd ever had. Period. All company included. All the history they carried with them and behind them.

They were catching their collective breaths when Art took the mic and started to thank everyone for such a successful night. "I know we hadn't planned this in advance, and Montgomery's next song request is going to have to wait," he said, laughter sprinkling throughout the room as everyone craned to look at him. *"But,"* Art continued, "in honor of my beautiful wife, Betty," he said as he lifted a glass in her direction, "and in celebration of our fiftieth wedding anniversary on Sunday, I'd like to ask a special favor of Jason Wild and Amanda Marceau."

Alexander turned to Amanda, raising his eyebrow questioningly when he heard her whispered "Oh, jeez." Blushing with embarrassment over the attention, she quickly filled him in on how five years ago she and Jason had also sung Art and Betty's favorite song at that year's gala. When he asked her which song, she'd only grinned her signature wait-for-it grin. Which meant he would know the song. The anticipation was killing him already. When Art said, "Jason, Ammy, will you do us the honors?" Jason, whom Alexander had met briefly earlier that evening, stepped forward with a sheepish smile and extended his hand to Amanda.

"You okay with this, sweetheart?" Alexander asked, before relinquishing her to Jason.

She nodded. "Yeah, I'm good," she said before following Jason to join Art in front of the crowd.

"So, a little history with the song," Art said. "I know it's considered an oldie in certain circles, but way back when, my wife and I would go out every Saturday night for dinner and dancing with our best friends, Lynne and Jack Marceau. And we always finished the night with this one."

With that, Alexander knew it was "Whenever I Call You 'Friend.'" Amanda had sang it for him often, and bloody hell, he couldn't wait to hear her sing her parents' favorite song, here, now.

"I have to tell you," Art went on, looking at Amanda, "there's not a day that goes by that we don't miss them. You were the light of your daddy's eye, Amanda Abigail, and so was your mother. He never got over losing her. Ever." Jesus, Art was choking on the words. Alexander teared up along with him and Amanda. Art wiped his eyes, and shook it off with a "Whew…so, Jason, you be Kenny and Ammy, you take on Stevie, and I'm going to dance with my gal."

Everyone clapped, and Amanda and Jason each grabbed a mic while Art led his wife to the center of the dance floor. Then, as the music began and back-up singers harmonized, his barefoot beauty swayed back and forth, smiled right at him, and joined Jason. He couldn't take his eyes off of her. Neither could the crew who'd all gathered around him, Stephen and Sam too. She was so good, and her direct eye contact with him as she sang that she'd come to understand that everywhere they were they were meant to be let Alexander know she was singing right to him. She and Jason received a standing ovation, after which they thanked everyone profusely. He'd had a waiter bring a Diet Coke for her and she drank half the glass.

"You were amazing," he said, pulling her into his arms.

"What's next, Montgomery?" she asked.

"Our whole lives, sweetheart," he said, though he knew she was referring to the song request. Amanda had told him during one of their dance sessions that the song he'd cued up for next was all the rage on the party circuit now, and considering the lyrics, they should add it to the list of "their" songs. The band was waiting, and together he and the crew each lifted a hand high in the air, in the universal display of one. And the band played "One Call Away" by Charlie Puth. Yeah, it was cheesy, but she melted right in front of him, loving it. Amanda wrapped her arms around his neck, letting him rock her back and forth as he whispered the lyrics to her, that he'd be there and save the day, that Superman had nothing on him because he was only a call away. And when the song was over, he couldn't wait another moment.

"Come with me?"

◁◁   ▷▷

Out of breath from dancing and singing with Jason, Amanda froze at Alex's pointed words, stunned and wondering if she'd heard him correctly. Her heart skipped a beat, then filled and all but flowed over. She clutched his shirt, got right in his face, and said, "Anywhere."

When he grabbed her hand and pulled her toward the doors, she almost squealed from the rush she felt inside. From the top of her head to the tip of her toes, her insides were churning more than on any teacup carnival ride. He made a hand signal to Stephen, and said to all listening, "Mama and papa bear—out. Hold down the forts. All of them." She could only imagine the cacophony from his earpiece by the grin on his face. They got stopped three times on the way out, and were both so anxious to get—well, she didn't know where they were getting, but when they had to make pleasantries, they practically bounced from foot to foot and squeezed each other's hands so tightly it became a game. Finally, the front door was in sight, but when she started toward it, he pulled her back flush against him and whispered in her ear, "We have a suite."

She turned and grabbed his shirt again. "Oh, my god. You're a genius."

Then he was pulling her again, and as if by magic the elevator doors opened. She was familiar with this hotel, so she knew that they were headed up in one of the private key-access-only elevators to a penthouse suite. Without taking his eyes from hers, Alexander lifted the fob to the control panel inside the elevator. As the doors closed behind him, his eyes pinned her to the wall, his nostrils flared, and this time she squealed for real. He came right at her, pressed his body fully against her, and kissed her so passionately, it was almost devastating in nature. She felt it, *him*, deeply. There was something so different about this kiss. Or maybe it was that they were both fully, like really fully engaged, and knew where this was going. They couldn't get close enough, *be* close enough, bodies rubbing, hands all over each other, and…and the most ridiculously loud sounds… Amanda broke away for just a second. "Is that us?" she asked.

"Yeah," he said, his voice thick in accent and desire. He demonstrated again, using his mouth in expert precision to extract those same loud noises from her, and answered each in kind. Loud smacking sounds came next, and they both snorted and laughed.

"That *is* ridiculous!" Amanda said.

"Tell me about it." He pressed his forehead to hers. "I've been waiting a long bloody time for this, Amanda."

"Please don't wait any longer," she whispered.

"I couldn't if I wanted to. And I don't. Want to."

He kissed her again, pulling her head back just where he wanted her, and went in so deep she felt it all the way to her center. She'd just wrapped her leg around his waist, thanks to the slit in her dress, and Alex's large, warm hand spread across her back, when the doors opened, and she froze in horror.

"Nooo," she cried out and Alex swore.

"Sorry, concierge floor," he muttered, but they didn't move. Instead he gave her another scorching look and kissed her senseless. When he stepped away to press the "close door" button, she started slipping to the floor like a rag doll, but he grabbed her just in time. "Three minutes tops, sweetheart," he said, anchoring her to his side. "Ready?"

Amanda half laughed, half groaned, and grabbed his shirt. "Bloody hell, Montgomery, why'd you have to push the button?"

He gave her a lopsided grin and pulled her close again, leaning back against the closed doors. She shivered as his teeth grazed the hollow of her shoulder, and then he was kissing her again, his hand wrapped around her leg. They missed the ping, so when the doors opened, they fell out onto their correct floor this time.

"Left side," Alexander said, his voice hoarse. "2602."

Amanda looked at the plaque and corrected him. "Right."

They kissed their way down the hallway. "Passed it," she said, giggling. He turned them and pressed her against the door while he fumbled with the key card. "Alex!"

"I'm trying!"

"Try harder!"

They laughed as the door swung open and they went in with it. He turned around looking for the way to the bedroom. "Bloody hell, we should have gotten a smaller room."

"I would have been happy with the elevator."

⟨⟨ ⟩⟩

Alexander growled and went back in. He got them to the bedroom *and* to the bed. Then Amanda started tugging at his jacket. He helped her help him out of it. Clothes started flying after that. Shoes, shirt, and slacks. And thanks to Amanda's backless dress, once it was off, she was already down to a thong.

"Bloody hell, Amanda. You are so beautiful," Alexander said, his voice a low growl. He traced his hands over her watching as she arched her back and her eyes went wide. He did it again, just to see her reaction, this time skimming the delicate lace covering her.

"Alex!" she cried.

"Shh." He was enjoying himself immensely, and traced her body again, using his palm to apply pressure as he rubbed his hand against her. She arched into him, and he gave her what she wanted. Bloody hell, he almost came when his fingers slid against her. Hot, wet, *his*. He gave a gentle push against her chest with his hand and she fell to the bed and the mountain of pillows. He followed her down and lay next to her, moving the tiny strip of cloth to the side and slid his fingers down her center again. He almost chuckled at her *bloody hell*, then pulled her in tight, pleasuring her until she arched against him. Jesus, he was so close to losing himself, he didn't know if he would make it until he was inside her. Frantic hands, hers *and* his, removed her thong. Then she motioned with her hands for him to come to her.

"Please," she whimpered.

He was trying to be gentle, but Amanda was tugging on his shoulders and pulling at him. He moved her just where he needed to and was finally able to thrust himself completely inside. Jesus. *Home.* He waited for her body to uncoil, looking at her the entire time. Then she grinned and nodded.

"More, Alex. Make love to me, please."

He did, and luckily it was still early. They made love lazily throughout the night, lightly dozing in between. They took two long showers together and after their last bout of lovemaking, Amanda cried mercy and asked him to soak with her in the clawfoot tub, which he did gladly, even trying his hand at modern-day multitasking by picking up the hotel phone while his wife lay against him to order champagne, Amanda's favorite.

She sighed with satisfaction and tapped his chest to get his attention, suggesting it might taste better with a club sandwich and house-made chips. She was correct.

As he lay in bed shortly after dawn, holding Amanda snugly at his side, he realized that nothing else mattered than what they had now. Where they were now. They were safe, and alive, and together, their children were healthy, happy, and well-adjusted considering. What did it matter, actually, if Amanda ever remembered those brief—though exhilarating—months together? Isn't it better to live in the moment, whenever the moment is—eighteenth century or twenty-first—and not dwell on what no longer is?

To hell with the past—all of it.

CHAPTER
FIFTEEN

MAY 17
NORTHERN CALIFORNIA

Amanda laughed, stepping under Stephen's arm as he held the door open to the bakery. It was just before closing, but Amanda knew that Lizzy, the bakery's owner, would stay open for her. She and Alexander were trying to wrap things up before leaving for New York, and so they'd decided to divide and conquer after dinner and Amanda was on birthday cake duty. Alexander had gone with the crew to the offsite compound they'd been frequenting lately. Art had built it years ago, and they all loved going there to play war games or whatever they did. Amanda knew the guys were going to miss the easy, or at least *easier* access to it while they summered on the east coast. Stephen, the saint, had made the supreme sacrifice to accompany her to the bakery, and given that it was his brother, Alex had even relinquished their tail for the night, though it had taken some cajoling. Seriously, they were just going to a bakery.

Lizzy had called shortly after lunch to say she was swamped and asked if Amanda could come on the later side. Lizzy said the last thing she wanted to do was rush the design of Callie's very specific birthday cake. Besides her baked goods being the *best*, Lizzy's freehand cake decorating was off the chart, and well worth the wait. Unfortunately, her store was way north, tucked away in the quaint little town of Baron's Cove. The drive always reminded Amanda of that On Star commercial where the woman swerves to avoid hitting a deer and ends up lost in a vast expanse of foliage. Though, on this drive, only one side of the road sported that lush oasis, the other was a rocky drop to the sea.

"I'm telling you, Amanda, he doesn't like chocolate." It was the third time Stephen had said it, and she still couldn't figure out how she'd missed that detail about him. She was a chocolate fiend, so it's not like it wasn't around.

"Are you *sure?*" she asked one more time. Stephen rolled his eyes, herding her toward the counter. She and Alex had decided—among a lot of other decisions they'd made lying in bed the morning after the gala—to celebrate Callie's birthday in California before they left for New York. It would be a tight schedule, but they could manage. That way Callie could invite friends from school over and have dinner with the circus. They'd decided to have the party on Saturday, right before leaving on Sunday, which was the day before Callie's actual birthdate.

The cake, it turned out, was well worth the wait *and* late evening trip. Lizzy had outdone herself; the detail was amazing and it couldn't have been easy. But kudos to her favorite cake-maker aside, what kid wanted an Amelia Bedelia cake? Amanda chuckled. *Her* kid. Not that the series wasn't adorable, endearing, and exceptional—it was—Amanda just couldn't figure out Callie's fascination with it. As she looked at the replication of Amelia on top of the cake, with her rosy cheeks and bonnet, Amanda supposed it was because Amelia looked just like Janey. Seriously, they could have called the series Janey Wainey or something of the sor—

Amanda froze. That was it.

The last piece of the puzzle locked into place, her memory crystallized, and what felt like small fragments of lifetimes fraught with every emotion was now exposed in full, a landmark panorama of remembering she'd tucked away for later viewing. *OHMYGOD*. A sound much like a gurgle escaped her lips, though it sounded far away, not from her, as the cake fell from her hands. Amanda's head whipped up on its own accord, and her eyes locked on Stephen, who dropped his phone in his rush to grab hold of her when her knees buckled.

"Amanda?" She knew Stephen was shouting, completely panicked, but his voice sounded like they were underwater. Amanda's vision swam as he continued. "Lizzy, call 911," he yelled over her shoulder, lowering Amanda to the ground gently, trying to avoid the sheet cake that lay between them, and some on them. He tightened his hold as she wobbled on her knees and started shaking uncontrollably, then she clutched his arms.

"OhmyGod, *Stephen*," she said in a sudden moment of clarity before her eyes blurred again.

"Christ, Amanda," he said, looking terrified. "Tell me what's wrong. Where do you hurt— Jesus, Lizzy, *how long!*"

Shaking her head, Amanda reached her hands up for his face as the dam broke. "*You're* here…*he's* here. Oh my God…you're both…*here*," she sobbed, unable to handle the impossibility of what she was now realizing was the complete and utter truth somehow.

"Bloody hell, Am." His eyes filled with tears too. "You remember."

She nodded, still too overwhelmed to speak as Stephen pulled her up and hugged her tight.

"Christ, I missed you," he said, his voice gruff with emotion. "Cancel that call," he told Lizzy, still keeping her close.

Amanda started convulsively nodding as she found steady footing, and then clutched at Stephen's jacket, jumping up and down, ignoring Lizzy's—rightfully—confused expression.

"Take me to him," she cried, tears still flowing, this time from happiness.

Like it was infectious, Stephen did the same, nodding and jumping before grabbing her hand to run from the store.

"Wait," Lizzy called after them, handing Stephen his phone. "Should I make another cake for tomorrow, Amanda?"

Amanda shook her head, smiling broadly, and said, "We're good, Lizzy." Then she laughed. "My husband doesn't like chocolate, anyway."

Lizzy looked even more confused, but then chuckled and said, "I'll make it vanilla and deliver it myself."

Stephen pulled Amanda outside as she waved to Lizzy and thanked her, feeling like the whole world had righted itself. Stephen started calling his brother as he opened the door to the truck, but Amanda covered his phone. "No," she said firmly. She wanted to tell him herself. Oh God, he'd found her, her eighteenth-century Royal Navy admiral—*her husband*—had found her. Just like she'd always known he would.

"How far are we?" she asked when Stephen pulled onto the highway.

He checked his navigation, looked in the rearview mirror, and told her, "I'm taking the shortest of three routes, and still the compound's about an hour and half southeast of here. Do you want me to have him meet us at the house instead?"

"No." She shook her head, barely able to contain the giddiness she felt. "Don't say anything." She wanted to take his glorious face in her hands and tell him that she remembered. Everything. Sighing in anticipation, she palmed the window, fingers splayed in that gesture that had been a part of her sorrow-filled days for so long. How many nights had she craved that tactile touch, as if staring out the window with her hands pressed firmly to the glass would bring him home? Or make him feel her love wherever he might be? Their headlights provided an occasional glimpse of the mountains as they sped by, the only thing illuminating the all but deserted highway at this hour.

Amanda kept thinking back to that morning after the gala. How they'd decided to wait until they'd arrived in New York to make their new togetherness permanent. At the time it had made sense and seemed like a good place for them to transition. He'd held her in his arms then, and told her the past didn't matter any longer. God, she'd had no idea then, the lengths that this man had gone in pursuit of her. The discipline he must have, the restraint amazed her, because after tonight, she wasn't letting him out of her sight. She wanted to know everything—*everything*—that had happened from the time she'd let go on that cliff to when he'd found her. What he'd done. *How* he'd done it. But all she kept thinking now was, *I'm coming, Alexander.*

Halfway through the drive Stephen told her the turn for the compound, where she'd never been before, was coming up. Other than that, they'd barely said a word. She sat, tense with anticipation as Stephen drove. And then he wasn't driving anymore.

Her stomach churned as the truck swerved and Stephen yelled out something that sounded like "Hold on, Amanda," but she couldn't quite hear him over the blood rushing through her ears. She screamed as they struck something, and her head banged against the window. The truck spun, and as Stephen fought for control, the front passenger-side tire hopped over the guard rail. With the speed they were going and weight of the Nav, the driver's-side tire went over next. Like a seesaw, the truck dangled on the steel embankment, metal eerily creaking on metal as it rocked back and forth. Amanda and Stephen shared a look, a snapshot no more than a millisecond before the truck pitched forward on the downward swing hitting something else before the ground beneath them fell away completely and the truck plunged to the earth below.

〈〈　〉〉

"Pour some scotch, boy," Alexander told Trevor with a grin.

He and his band of brothers, extended crew included, were at their compound. He loved it. God bless Art Fisher, who'd seen well into the future and built the state-of-the-art facility hidden deep in the mountains. It was constantly bristling with activity. Combat training, SAR training, weaponry, explosives, surveillance, bloody hell, add to that list ad infinitum. Looking around him, Alexander realized that his purchase of JDL months ago really had been the beginning of a new empire. Here. Now. There wasn't any other place he wanted to be. He and Amanda had a future. And it would be good. And it would be together.

Bloody hell—YES!

Having just finished a round of war games in the underground part of the facility, the crew had gathered around the large conference room table, still in full regalia of fatigues and face paint. Alexander laughed when they opted for waters and power bars instead of cigars and scotch. The lights flickered a moment, which caused him to look up briefly, but he didn't pay it much attention. They were talking of expansion now; Chris was explaining the particulars. Bloody hell, business was very different than—

The lights flickered again, then went off completely. Ten seconds later the generator kicked in. Trevor started hitting the keys harder on his computer.

"That won't help," Alexander laughed.

"I think we've lost the mainframe," Trevor said, his brows drawn together in puzzlement.

"Why I don't really care for computers," Alexander told Trevor, thinking nothing of it. "Power's down, computer's down. As Amanda would say, *Duh!*"

Trevor shook his head. "It's not the power, boss."

"Alexander."

Amanda's voice came through their earbuds and he froze, the smile falling from his face.

They all looked up from what they were doing— Alexander, Gregor, Stan, Trevor, Michael, Evan, Chris— and just stared at each other. It was the first time she'd used his given name since they'd taken her from the hospital. Since before. He'd only been Alex to her here in the twenty-first century. Up to now. *She remembers. Bloody hell, sweetheart. You remember.*

"Amanda," he said as everyone stared at him.

Her voice cracked. "Alexander." She started crying. "It's not good."

He stood so fast the chair fell. "Tell me, sweetheart." His chest tightened, his heart beating furiously. She didn't answer. "Amanda!" He ripped out his earpiece, fidgeting with the controls.

Trevor gave him a you're-an-idiot look and sighed. "Hers are only outgoing, remember? She can't hear you," he said, and Alexander cursed himself for not thinking that she might at some point need to hear him as well as speak to him.

"I don't know if you can hear me." Amanda's voice came through faintly. "I hope we're close enough." He paused and he listened as she took a deep breath. "I took Stephen's earpiece, so it goes both ways, I think." Trevor shrugged, mouthed *my bad*, and for a moment, Alexander had a flicker of hope. "But, uh…part of it looks damaged."

Hope gone. Alexander could barely control his emotions. *Why? Bloody hell.* What had happened that there was damage to speak of? "Trevor, can you—"

"Oh, *now* you like this shit?" Trevor said, holding up his computer.

Fuck, the boy was right.

"Alexander—God, I can't stop saying your name. I missed you so much." Her voice caught on a sob then. "I'm sorry I let go. I'm so sorry." She started crying again. "I was so scared. I thought they were going to kill us. Then when Callie slipped from the ledge, and I screamed… God, I was so relieved you'd found us…I never imagined what would happen next. And I wondered, too, like every frigging day, if I had just held on another five seconds maybe you could have saved us both." Her voice caught on a sob. "I missed you every second of every day we were apart."

Don't cry, sweetheart. He shook his head, stunned for moment. "Amanda?" he tried again. "Bloody hell, *tell me what's ha—*"

"We were in an accident," she said, and the rest stood at once. "Stephen and I. God, I hope you can hear me."

Eight pair of eyes on Trevor and Alexander willed the computer to start up, for the satellite tracker to respond, but Trevor shook his head.

"Satellite's not responding."

"We hit something, Alexander," Amanda said through the earbud. "Something big and metal."

That answered the satellite question. God, he wished he could speak to her. He just needed to know where she was and then he'd be there in an instant. *Bloody hell, tell me where you are, sweetheart.*

"We were coming to you, Alexander. I just wanted to surprise you. There must have been something in the road, I don't know, and then Stephen yelled." She started crying again. "We must have been awful people in a previous life to get stuck with karma like this."

Alexander's chest tightened. *Jesus.*

"Remember how you used to tell me you could figure out where you were simply by looking up at the stars?" Alexander nodded, though she couldn't see him. *Good girl.* "Well, if I look up, I can see…"

"I need my tools," Alexander said quietly, firmly. It was a command and his men responded in kind. "And a map—maps of the area—topographic and hemispheric." Gregor and Michael ran in separate directions, both of them moving with militaristic precision.

Tell me what you see, sweetheart. Alexander willed his thoughts to reach Amanda.

"Ursa…um…Major, yes, Major, I'm sure of it. Ursa Major is to our left. Boötes is, wait, I need to get oriented. If Ursa Major is to my left…" She trailed off and Alexander cleared the table with a sweep of his hand, as Michael strode into the room just in time, spreading the topographical maps on it. Gregor was back seconds later, sliding into him as he handed off the wooden box that held his instruments.

"I found Arcturus, Alexander," said Amanda, her voice breaking the tense silence among the men. "Oh God, the red star! If twelve o'clock is right above us, Arcturus is at three o'clock. I miss how we used to sit and look at the stars together. Do you remember, I would always say which one is that?"

He remembered it all. *Tell me what else, sweetheart.*

She screamed.

They all braced themselves. "What! Bloody hell, what!" He looked at Michael and motioned above his head with his hand—universal sign for chopper. While they had three at this location, he'd recently finally landed a stroke of luck with an SAR, a search-and-rescue ten-passenger helicopter, equipped with all the bells and whistles to use for training. It couldn't have arrived at a better time.

"I don't know how far down we are. I got to the front with Stephen." She cried again, and he could hear her whispering to his brother. "Be okay, please be okay, Stephen," she was saying. "He's been out since we…we—" She didn't finish.

Alexander rolled up the maps and grabbed his tools. "Go, go, go."

Emergency lighting cast the hall in an odd yellowish light. As deep in the mountain as they were, it was a good mile to the stairwell that would take them aboveground. At their pace, he estimated six minutes. The men who ran the operations of the facility, a few there for training, and the rest of his detail must have sensed something was up because they fell in line as they passed their bunkers. Minutes later in the stairwell, the strange hue was amplified by the grayish tinge of the walls. Up four floors. Piece of cake. No sounds other than the footfall of their steps and Amanda's beautiful voice.

She talked to him the entire time. Told him how she'd realized what had happened after she and Callie had fallen from the cliffs. How she'd held Callie tight and rocked her back and forth, her heart broken. Her hope that he would find them. Her joy when she realized they were having a baby. A boy. And then when she'd read the ledger, how the ground beneath her had swallowed her whole. Bloody hell, they were all grown men and she had them all in tears. He didn't know if he had another loss in him.

Then she started recounting their entire history together. Short that it was.

"Alexander, when we were still in Abersoch and you came home that night and said we had to go—now...oh my god." She inhaled deeply. "I ne-need a sec." Jesus she was breathless, and he wasn't sure if it was from talking so much or if she was injured. "I just remember standing in the hall as everyone started running in different directions, thinking, *Oh my god, we're leaving*. And after I'd spoken with Janey...oh, I miss her...and Goodly too. When I'd come back downstairs—you guys had moved so quickly, there had to be twenty huge chests already stacked by the front doors and more outside your study—I didn't know Callie was hiding under your desk. And when you pointed at that ship and said we're on it, I remember thinking, *Doesn't he know that I'd go anywhere in this world* or *another with him?* That's how much I loved you then, and how much I love you now, Alexander." She was quiet another moment before chuckling again. "God, I hope you can hear me and I'm not just some crazy rambling woman in a busted SUV."

Michael held the door when they reached the top. The chopper sounded in the distance as they headed for the gear shack and helipad just beyond. Then Amanda started singing their song to him. She hadn't done so since they were last together in Abersoch, before that night that the world crumbled at their feet. Halfway through, she screamed again, the sound accompanied by crumbling sounds and metal crashing, and his entire body tensed. They kept moving, but he could see the effect it had on the men in front of him, same as him. Tightening of the whole upper body. It was jarring, terrifying. And this from grown men trained to know better.

The gear shack was opened ahead of their arrival and everyone filed in to grab rappelling gear, weapons, explosives. Jesus, at this rate who really knew what they needed? It was an anything goes kind of mission. Gregor jumped into the helicopter first, and then thrust his hand out to haul everyone in. Hugh, their pilot, motioned through the noise to grab a headset and hold the fuck on. Trevor, their best navigator, grabbed the maps from Alexander as he climbed aboard and headed straight for Hugh. They were locked, loaded, and ready for takeoff by the time Hugh nodded at the coordinates Trevor showed him on the map.

"Go. Go. Go."

Lift off.

Her location wasn't brain surgery, not when he knew she'd been on the way to the compound. There was only one satellite that could have been taken out, at the northwest entrance. But where they'd landed in the truck was another story. The mountain range carried for miles— hollows, valleys, and depressions of varying degrees all around. Depending on the topography, however, he knew Amanda wouldn't have had a view of certain constellations. And armed with that knowledge, he at least had a firm impression of their location—just not how far down they would be. Or what they would find when they got there. Maybe Amanda was right and they had to keep replaying this nightmare until they got it right.

They started securing their harnesses, as Evan… Jesus, Evan was getting his tools ready.

"We're nearly there," Alexander called behind him to his crew, clocking a familiar copse of trees.

"I can hear you, Alexander," Amanda said breathlessly.

"I've got a visual!" Michael cried at the same time.

"I climbed in front next to Stephen," Amanda repeated. "The window's gone, but I think there's enough room to get him out first." Bloody hell, he could see them now. Not Amanda. But the truck on its side, driver's-side up, dangling precariously on the edge of an outcropping, supported by two ancient evergreens from below.

Alexander shook his head accessing the crash site— no, he told himself, landing site. There wasn't room, or time. He looked at Gregor. They'd both drawn the same conclusion and said "Grab and go" simultaneously. They reconnoitered with the crew, and the two SAR members who had to come along as protocol. Plan in place, Alexander and Gregor informed the SARs this was their job, but then Michael pushed between them and said, "I'll go with you, Alex."

Jesus, he'd amassed a loyal retinue. He was about to tell Michael how this was going to go down, when Gregor stepped in and said it for him. "I love you, kid, but this is my job."

"Let's do this," Alexander said to Gregor, giving an acknowledging nod to Michael. And then they cast off, rappelling down. When they were close enough, Alexander could see Stephen was cut and bleeding, a huge gash on the side of his face. Amanda had her arms wrapped around him.

"Amanda," he called over the noise. "You have to let him go so Gregor can lift him."

She started crying. "I don't want to do this again."

"It's okay, sweetheart, we'll get it right this time," he said, not sure if he believed his own words. "On the count of the three, okay? And when Gregor takes him, you and I are going right after. Understand?"

"Affirmative."

"On three, not before, not after, Amanda."

"Got it," she said through gritted teeth. By the sound of it, her tears had all but dried. Her voice was calm and even. She was tough, his wife.

"One…two…three."

Amanda let go as Gregor slowly lifted Stephen. Slow was the name of the game. One, they didn't want to disturb the truck's balance, and two, they had to clear his legs. And so, as his feet left the vehicle, Amanda's hands reached out the window and Alexander grabbed them both, lifting her easily. Jesus, she wrapped her legs around his waist and buried her face in his neck. He couldn't see through his tears as he looked up to signal that they were good to go. The guys above got the message, though, and lifted them to the hovering aircraft.

They landed on the floor of the chopper; Evan was next to them already working on Stephen. Amanda was still wrapped around him as the guys hoisted them up together.

"I need to look at you, Amanda. Check you for injuries," Alexander said, his voice thick with emotion. She pulled back then, and at the sight of her face covered with blood, he felt his entire body suddenly seize from a sharp pain. His vision blurred slightly and, Jesus, it was like watching the scene in the helicopter from afar and in slow motion. Then he was falling. Amanda screamed as he went down, and Evan started barking orders as he pivoted from working on Stephen and ripped Alexander's shirt open. The last thing he remembered was Stephen taking his hand and whispering his name. He only hoped they were both on the side of the living.

◁◁   ▷▷

Alexander woke up to a filled hospital room. The circus was definitely in town, and the ringmaster's wife lay beside him in his bed. Stephen lay in a separate bed next to him, looking over and giving him a thumbs-up. He felt his chest to see if they'd cut him open, and Amanda's hand covered his as she snuggled closer, if that was at all possible. While he felt a bit woozy, nothing he could sense in his body gave way to surgery or a procedure of some sort. Then Amanda straddled him, grinning from ear to ear. She was a bit scratched up, but besides the tape covering a small half-inch cut on her right temple, she looked sound and whole. The blood must have been Stephen's.

"You didn't have a coronary," she told him cheerily. Jesus, you'd think they'd won the lottery based on her declaration.

"Bloody hell, sweetheart." His eyes teared just looking at her.

She leaned down and kissed him, whispering, "I love you too." He all but crushed her, pulling her in.

Evan was standing at his bedside. "Anxiety attack, Alex."

"Excuse me?"

"You had an anxiety attack."

"Are you for real?" Jesus, he sounded like Amanda.

"Considering what you've been through this past year, it's honestly no wonder. If you had told me the symptoms you'd been having, we could have bypassed—no pun—this entire fiasco," Evan said, clucking his tongue. "I did, however, give you something to help you relax. You obviously caved under pressure."

Alexander could tell Evan was enjoying himself immensely, and the crew, too, as chuckles sounded throughout the room. And all the while, Amanda sat there beaming, practically on his chest.

Then she threw her head back, punching the air, shouting, "Yes, yes, yes!" She looked down at him again, her blue eyes sparkling, and said, "Are you *ever* going to say you love me, Montgomery?"

She screeched as he flipped her beneath him. "I jumped off of a cliff two hundred and forty-five years ago for you, Amanda Abigail Montgomery. So, do I love you? Fuck yeah, I love you. I'd jump again tomorrow if I had to."

"Wow, good answer." Then he kissed her. He forgot the circus was still in his room as they all cheered. Loudly. He told them to get the hell out.

EPILOGUE

Alexander popped his head out of the study, grinning as squeals sounded from down the hall. Callie was on the run from the kitchen, Amanda hot on her trail. He and the crew had been kicked out about an hour ago when the girls commandeered it to get ready. The crew had grumbled half-heartedly about the turn, but considering the feast being prepared on the back grounds, they'd taken it in stride.

The Montgomerys—Jesus, it felt good to say that, or would soon—had finally settled in New York for the summer and only a week later than scheduled.

That pain he used to feel in his chest, he chuckled, it *was* anxiety. It was only now that he'd been free of it that he realized just how persistent that pain had been, and how much he'd just gotten used to it. While he was grateful it wasn't his heart, he couldn't believe something of the sort had taken him down. Literally. Evan told him to get over it. That millions of people suffered from anxiety, and considering the last year and then some, he'd had every reason to exhibit the symptoms he had. Landing in the hospital was a wake-up call. They needed to slow down and enjoy every moment they had. He wasn't going to stop working or anything. And neither was Amanda. They both loved it too much. She was back at it already, writing songs and playing her beautiful music.

And then there was their east coast compound, which was nothing short of spectacular. Think Anthony Hopkins's estate in *Meet Joe Black*. Right now, event planners were tweaking their finishing touches on the terrace and lawn. Yeah, today he was going to marry his girl. Again. The last helicopter had landed two hours ago, which meant the circus was back in town. In addition to the crew, there were a few special guests. Art and his wife, Betty, Jason Wild, whom he'd struck up a friendship with since the gala, and of course, Lizzy. How could they not include her when it was her Amelia Bedelia cake that had snapped Amanda's memory back in place? Alexander laughed to himself thinking again about how fickle fate and chance really were. A cake of all things. *A cake.*

As Callie sped by, he snaked an arm out and bent to grab her. She giggled, clutching Mrs. Beasley closer and fixing the wreath of flowers on her head. He stood up, his daughter in his arms, and she rubbed his whiskers, which were just a bit longer now. Amanda liked his five o'clock shadow so much, he'd indulged her with something more akin to a midnight shadow. When she'd first seen it, she'd mouthed *hot*. He'd kept it. Obviously.

Amanda stopped short at the sight of him, halfway down the corridor, already dressed in a white knee-length sheath dress, stunning and classy, bare feet aside. He motioned with his free hand for her to come here. She did. Bloody hell, she was about to be his, legally, in the twenty-first century. He couldn't wait.

"Hi, gorgeous," he said, his voice low. Her cheeks were flush, eyes bright as hell. Jesus, she lit his every last fiber.

"Just a few minutes more," she said, taking Callie back.

And at five o'clock on that very day, he walked up the stone steps of the terrace and extended his hand to her.

"Come with me, Amanda?" he asked.

"Anywhere, Alexander."